THICKET

ask me why

USA TODAY BESTSELLING AUTHOR

HARLOE RAE

Cover Artist: Limade Designs

Interior design and formatting: Champagne Book Design, www.champagnebookdesign.com

novels by
HARLOE RAE

Reclusive Standalones

Redefining Us

Forget You Not

#BitterSweetHeat Standalones

GENT

MISS

LASS

Total Standalones

Watch Me Follow

Ask Me Why

This book is dedicated to Renee Mccleary.
It's the little things that matter most, and count for more
than given credit. You're truly amazing.

And to alpha a-holes. No further explanation necessary.

ask me why

One deep breath. Two slow blinks. Three hollow beats.
I'm still here.
After three years, that reminder isn't as necessary. But everyone has their bad days. This is definitely one of them. Until an adorable little boy dashes into my store. His zest for life makes me smile in a way that's been long lost. Then I meet his father.
Well, confront is more like it.

Brance Stone is volatile.
Offensive.
Harsh.
And can't be bothered to care.
Not that I want him to. I get frostbite just looking into Brance's glacial stare. But there's something undeniable about him.

My misery suddenly craves company. The suffocating numbness lifts whenever Brance is near. That alone should have me running in the opposite direction. Try as I might, there's no avoiding him. If only I could understand why. As if he'd let me.

I don't ask. He doesn't tell. A silent, bitter truce settles between us.
That was our first mistake.
It's certainly not the last.

playlist

"At My Weakest" – James Arthur

"Weak" – Halloran & Kate

"How Long Will I Love You" – Ellie Goulding

"Queens Don't" – RaeLynn

"You & I" – John Legend

"Stand By You" – Rachel Platten

"Wild Love" – James Bay

"Rainbows" – Kacey Musgraves

"Always" – Isak Danielson

"Till the Sun Comes Up" – Gavin James

Listen now on Spotify—http://bit.ly/PlaylistAMW

"The moment you stop believing is the instant
everything loses meaning."
—Braelyn Miller

prologue

BRAELYN

CRASH

A GUST OF FIERCE WIND NEARLY KNOCKS ME SIDEWAYS, BUT I barely feel it. My skirt billows wildly behind me while I follow the dirt path. I try to avoid rocks and debris, but burning moisture clouds my vision. I swipe furiously at the tears that never seem to quit.

Why would they?

My body is in an utter state of misery, seeping from every pore and molecule. I'm being cracked in half by a jagged edge. Anything good is currently draining out of me. Soon there will be nothing left. But that suits me fine. I don't want to be here without him.

The grief is all consuming, unforgiving and unrelenting. Devon's death was a nuclear bomb. Everything has crumbled into rubble and dust. We had so many plans together, all tightly woven and tied to one another. The impossibilities scatter through the tall grass in front of me. I'll never be whole again, just a jumble of unrecognizable pieces. There's no me without him. But here I stand. Alone.

I twirl the ring on my finger. The significance of what could have been seems to fade without his presence. But I can't bear to take it off. Not yet, maybe not ever. Somehow that makes all of this more permanent. I need to keep pretending for the sliver of sanity remaining.

There's a bitter breeze coming off the lake. My hair whips around and several strands stick to my wet cheeks. I'm so cold. This chill is bone-deep, soaking into my marrow. The hole in my chest expands and I'll never be warm again. Just like Devon, buried six feet under. They said I was lucky to survive—this type of accident is almost always fatal. The fact I'm still standing is some sort of miracle.

Why does it feel like I died with him?

I shiver when the memories crash into me. I don't have enough energy or willpower to stop the torment from taking control. Needles prickle along my scalp, sliding down to cover my entire body. The nightmare taunts me on repeat, and I can't escape. I'm back in our mangled car, suspended upside down. Devon is staring at me, unblinking and completely still. His eyes are frozen wide open. The deep brown color had always been vibrant and intoxicating. Now there's no sign of life, only dull emptiness remains. I scream and yell until my throat is on fire. But no one ever hears me.

The vision vanishes with a strangled gasp. I curl my fingers until the bite of pain stings my palms. Numbness blankets me, a protective shield against the onslaught of agony. The sensation of nothingness has already replaced my heart, taken my soul. Might as well have the rest of me.

Is this my new normal?

I move toward the cliff's edge, peering down into the calm water. The serenity waiting below is tempting me. How easy would it be to jump? Put an end to this suffering?

It would only take a few measly steps. I stare at my feet and beg them to take the leap. This might be the end. I can't live like this.

A low howl carries over the wind, and I look toward the sound. There's a rainbow arching through the cloudy sky. My vision blurs and I swallow roughly.

"Devon, come back to me." The impossible words tremble off my lips. He's gone forever, but that doesn't stop the desperation from sprouting roots. I squint and can almost picture his smile blending into the backdrop. My knees wobble. I almost collapse under the weight of it all.

How can I move on? The future seems so bleak.

With a shuddering breath I barely manage to take, my sluggish brain begins to process. It's not my time to go. I blink slowly and shuffle away from the ledge. A hollow beat echoes through my chest. I exhale harshly, infusing my battered systems with some form of strength. For him, I'll push forward. I'll live for both of us.

This battle is just beginning, and tomorrow is a new day.

chapter one

BRAELYN

TAFFY

THE MUG TREMBLES IN MY GRASP AS I SET IT ON THE TABLE. I stretch out my fingers, but the tremor remains. Ice fills my veins. I quickly glance around the crowded coffee house, finding nothing out of sorts. There's a long line by the register and most of the seats are already occupied. But groups of people don't bother me.

Why can't I shake this? I rub at my numb arms, the constant chill clinging harder than usual. After three years, the dull ache in my chest is deeper than ever. I hardly notice the hollow sensation anymore. But the cruel memories strike often enough that I'll never forget. Not that I ever could.

Those less than friendly reminders are always lurking, lodged in a hidden part I can't reach. The visions from hours ago still hover in the forefront of my conscience. Whispers echo in my ears. I can't take a decent breath. My eyes feel puffy and dry. I rub at them to alleviate the sting. It doesn't help. At least the awful churning in my stomach quit.

A thick sigh eases out of me. I inhale slowly. The strong aroma of dark roast and early mornings fill my lungs. That calms my racing pulse slightly. I let my lashes flutter closed, blocking out the hustle and bustle around me. I've learned to deal, somewhat.

"Hey, you okay?"

I lift my gaze and meet Sadie's worried stare. "Yeah, I'm fine."

She reaches for my hand. "You don't have to pretend, honey. Not with me."

My heart pounds a steady rhythm as I find comfort in her genuine expression. I scratch my temple and dig for an explanation. Too bad the caffeine hasn't kicked in.

"I know, and thanks. It's just the same old shit. I don't need to drop more weight in your lap." I attempt a smile, but my lips aren't cooperating.

Sadie's frown deepens. "Do you need help at the store today? I can cover for you."

I wave off her concern. "No, no. I'll snap out of it. I just… didn't sleep well." And that's putting it very lightly. These lingering effects of trauma are nasty. The flashbacks are fewer and further between. But when they hit? Total annihilation. Those moments leave me shattered.

"There's more to it, Brae. I can see the pain on your face."

I smooth my features, the urge to hide fierce. "The struggle has been rougher than usual lately. I had a bad episode, nightmare included. That's all."

"Want to talk about it?"

I shrug and look away.

She leans closer. "Was this one about the accident? Or him?"

My eyes burn. "You can say his name. Not sure it'll get worse. I saw Devon, like last time."

"It's not your fault for living, Brae. He'd want you to be happy. It's not a crime to carry on." Sadie's tone is meant to be soothing, but it chafes my skin like sandpaper.

I take a gulp of coffee to clear the grit from my throat. "Yes, I know. My therapist pounded that message into my brain loud and clear for two years."

"So, why don't you believe it?"

"Some days are far worse than others, okay? The loneliness gets to me. Then I think about him, and what we lost. A downward spiral shortly follows."

"The anniversary is coming up, right?"

I chew on the inside of my cheek. "Next month."

She reaches for my hand again. "Maybe you should schedule an emergency session with Doctor Thair."

I curl my shoulders in tighter. "I can handle it on my own. This was just a bad episode. She'll tell me everything I already know to do. I've got a pile of coping strategies."

"You're sure?" Her eyes are pleading with me.

I avert my focus to a crack in the ceiling. "Positive. Being at work helps keep my mind occupied. I'll be good as new by tonight." The lie rolls easily off my tongue. Sadie is my closest friend, but she doesn't need to waste more breath on me. Lord knows I've taken enough from her.

Her grin is sad. "Okay, I'll back off."

"Thank you," I murmur.

She taps her phone screen. "Are we ready to go? If you don't want help, I should get my ass to the office."

I quickly slurp down the rest of my drink and stand. "Anything interesting planned this week?" Hearing about her projects gives me something else to think about.

"We're finalizing the layouts for a chic boutique downtown. It'll be the place to shop once we're done." Sadie bumps her shoulder into mine as we step outside. The sun is already high and heating the air. It's going to be another hot one.

"Can't wait to see it. Will they sell swimsuits?"

"Only the skimpiest." She wiggles her brows. "We can lounge by the lake without getting tan lines."

I snort and roll my eyes. "Oh, that's hilarious. Might as well go to France and visit a nude beach."

She grabs my arm. "Do you want to?"

Her obvious excitement gives me pause.

"Uh, maybe?" I kick at some pebbles on the sidewalk.

"That's better than an immediate no. We're young and should act like it."

"Speak for yourself. I feel ancient."

Sadie shakes her head. "But you're not."

We stop in front of Thicket, my little shop, and share a quick embrace.

"Love you, friend. I appreciate you meeting me," I whisper.

She pulls away and squeezes my upper arms. "I'm always here for you, Brae. No matter what."

I nod slowly. "I owe you a trip to Europe just for that."

She bounces on her toes. "Yes! Please, please? A vacation would do us both a lot of good."

"I'll think about it."

"And I'll call you later. Let me know if you need anything."

I give her a light shove. "You're gonna be late."

She blows me a kiss and starts walking backward. "Love you, lady. You've got this shit."

"I'm a strong, independent woman," I recite.

"Exactly," she calls and points at me.

I manage to laugh and turn toward the door, unlocking it quickly. After disabling the alarm, I flip the lights on and watch my pride come to life. I pour everything into this space. If it wasn't for Thicket, I'd be a lost cause. Owning this store gives me a reason to wake up and keep moving.

Other than Sadie, I don't have much pushing me along. My family is all out of state, too far away to be bothered. Not that I blame them. My parents have their own problems to deal with. They don't need to take on more. And it's better for me if they stay away. My siblings are busy finding adventure at every turn. I'm doing my best to accomplish a small semblance of that.

With a slow spin, I take a long look around. Collections of odds and ends cover any available surface. This piece of property is all mine. Well, my name is clearly printed on the lease. But that's a minor detail. In my mind, this space is bought and paid for. Maybe it will be one day. A girl can dream.

That stops me short. Devon was the one who encouraged me to fulfill my fantasies. With him gone, most of those hopes were dashed. Except this one. Thicket is what's left for me.

The morning bleeds into afternoon as it always does. A steady stream of customers keeps me busy without pause so the haunting memories fade into the background. I'm about to start unpacking a new shipment of mugs when a twinge in my chest stops me.

When I blink, a blur of movement outside the window catches my eye. All I see is a patch of red dashing by in a hurry. I furrow my brow and concentrate on the task at hand. After a quick beat, the welcome chime sounds and a little boy darts inside. I'm guessing he's around four or five, hints of baby fat showing off his youth. His light eyes are blown wide open as he scans the shop from wall to wall. Something grabs his attention and he skips forward. I follow his stare, trying to figure out what he's focusing on.

He dashes down the far aisle in a flurry I can barely track. His tiny feet pound on the floor as he searches the shelves. He zips this way and that, a super-charged pinball darting around the confining alley. His delight is infectious and impossible to ignore. I feel my spirits lifting, just like that.

As I continue watching him hunt, his excitement bounces in every direction. I gladly absorb it all, the layer of ice under my skin thawing ever so slightly. He's bubbling with pure happiness and carefree bliss. I lift my lips in the most genuine smile I can muster. He makes it easier. This kid radiates everything that's good in the world.

Eventually he circles back and screeches to a halt in front of me, slightly out of breath. "Where is it?"

I move from behind the counter. "What're you looking for?"

"Candy! I saw a lollypop on your sign." His chubby cheeks are dented with glee and I feel my smile stretching in return. A mop of brown hair flops over his forehead and he sweeps it away with stubby fingers.

Gosh, he's adorable.

This cutie pie is stealing all my attention so I don't notice the woman standing by the entrance. Until she clears her throat, very loudly.

Our gazes whip in her direction.

"Oliver James, what did we just discuss?" Her mouth is set in a firm line, showing off deep wrinkles.

Oliver's dimples melt away, and he stares at the ground. "I'm not supposed to run off."

"And what did you do?"

"But—"

She holds up a palm. "No buts."

I watch their exchange, the need to intervene compelling me to speak up. "At least he ended up somewhere safe. It's quite all right if he does laps for hours. I don't mind."

The older woman studies me with a wary squint. "You might not, but his father will."

"And that makes you his…" I let my words trail off, hoping she'll fill in the blank.

"Nanny, yes. Although I prefer honorary grandmother. Lord knows the poor child doesn't have any biological ones to rely on. But that's a tale for a different day. I'm Mary, and that little rascal"—she points to the boy beside me—"is Oliver."

"But you can call me Ollie." He grins up at me, the joy reappearing in his expression.

"Nice to meet you both. My name is Braelyn, and you're in Thicket." I motion around the space with a limp flourish.

Mary takes a cursory glance around. "It's charming. There's much to see."

I dip my chin under her watchful eye. "Thank you. I appreciate that."

"Have you been here long?"

"About two years."

Mary nods. "We've never ventured along this street before. But I'm sure Ollie will never forget now that we've found this place."

I feel a tug on my shirt and look down. Ollie's smile hasn't dimmed since being rejuvenated. I find myself grinning back.

"Will you show me where the candy is now?" he asks.

I point behind me, to the row of tubs under the window. "Do you like taffy?"

Ollie's expression morphs into sheer wonder. "The super-chewy stuff?"

"Yes, I have a bunch of different flavors."

He dashes toward the bins. "What's your favorite?"

"The rainbow swirl," I whisper.

Ollie lowers his face closer to the sugary treats. "What do they taste like?"

I swallow the lump in my throat. "Happiness."

His button nose wrinkles. "That's a weird flavor."

I pluck one from the bunch and pass it over. "Try it and see."

He unwraps the colorful roll and pops it into his mouth.

Ollie chews loudly, his eyes sparkling bright. "Urm me gesh, whish ish so gerd."

I laugh at his jargon. "You like it?"

"So good," he mumbles.

I tug a paper sack out of the slot and scoop in a hefty amount. This should keep him occupied for at least ten minutes. I grin at that, picturing him gladly munching away. I want to bottle a sip of his energy and drink it later when the blues return.

I glance at him, finding him watching my every move. "This loot is for you. On the house."

Ollie's lips twist in a ridiculous way. "What's that mean?"

"I'm giving it to you," I explain. "For free."

Mary strides over. "You don't have to do that. We can pay."

I wave her off. "It's my pleasure. This little tyke has brightened my day."

"I have?" Ollie squeaks.

"Absolutely," I confirm.

He makes grabby-hands at the bag. I hold it up and out of reach. "I don't want to spoil your dinner."

Ollie pouts, his lower lip trembling slightly. Wow, he's good. My resistance is no match for this kid.

I pass the candy to Mary, giving her control. She mouths a silent thank you and beckons to Ollie. "We should get going. Your dad will be home soon."

At the mention of his father, he begins hopping in place. "Oh, I hope he brings me a surprise."

Mary raises a brow at him. "Isn't this enough?" She shakes the taffy all about.

Ollie seems to ponder that. "I guess." His gaze swings to me. "Can I come back, Miss Braelyn?"

The urgency in his tone takes me by surprise. "Of course, Ollie. You're always welcome here."

"Maybe tomorrow?"

There's no denying him. "I'd really like that."

His grin is huge and honest. "Me too. I can't wait."

As I watch them walk out the door, the storm clouds threaten to roll in. An unexpected wave crashes over me, but I'm not drowning in it today. No, I'm soaring above the violent sea.

Without realizing it, this taffy-loving kiddo gave me a reason to smile.

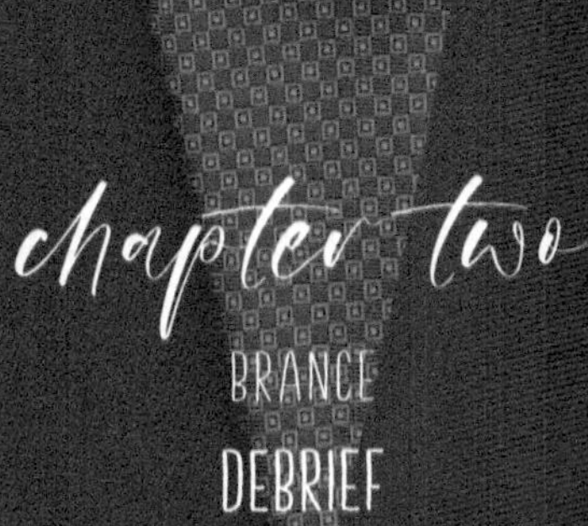

chapter two

BRANCE

DEBRIEF

A LOUD KNOCK INTERRUPTS MY INTENSE FOCUS ON THE deposition laid out in front of me. Dammit, I was finally making a dent on this shitty file. I lift my eyes and find my assistant fidgeting just outside the doorway. When she remains silent, my irritation spikes another notch.

"Yes?" My voice is a harsh lash across the distance between us.

She's wringing her hands so tight that the knuckles are white. "Uh, um—"

"Spit it out, Kathy. We don't have all day."

She sighs, and the weight on her shoulders deflates. What a fucking mouse. "Missus Kleinston is here for her appointment."

I glare at my watch. "She's over an hour late."

"Should I send her away?" Kathy's face loses more color, as if the thought alone is terrifying. I imagine the conflict she was battling on whether or not to alert me almost caused her an ulcer. But she doesn't complain and does a decent enough job. Good help can be hard to find.

I glance at the stack of papers in front of me, a fight of my own beginning to brew. But at the rate Missus Kleinston is paying me, I can't afford to lose her business. I swallow down the knee-jerk response and check my temper.

"Give me five minutes. Then bring her in," I mutter.

"Yes, sir." Kathy scurries off with fire licking her heels.

I pick up my phone and stab at the number pad, dialing Mary's cell. She answers after one ring.

"Hello, Brance. On the way?" Her chirp is crisp as usual.

I blow out a heavy breath. "Unfortunately, no. Would you mind watching Ollie for a bit longer? A client just showed up, and I've been waiting to meet with her."

"That's no trouble. He's quite entertained at the moment."

"With what?" I squeeze my eyes shut and picture his smile. My son is the only reason I haven't turned to solid rock by this point. His bright presence keeps me grounded, a reminder there's more to this shallow existence. He's proof that I can do something right. Well, other than win a shitload of cases.

"We found a new shop in Bebliff. They have a generous assortment of candy. Ollie especially loves the taffy," Mary explains.

"Does he now?" I almost laugh. That boy could eat his weight in sugar and go back for seconds.

"Oh yes. And the owner is a delight. I think he's quite taken with her. She's very lovely." Mary hums her approval.

"Just great," I grumble. A crush is the last thing Ollie needs. I scrub my forehead and groan. My son's standards are stupid low when it comes to women. He will deem any-one with a pulse fit to fill the role of mommy dearest. All I need is another gold digger sinking in her claws where they don't belong. His desperation for approval is sadly maddening. I hope that bitch who birthed him is real fucking proud of the mess she made.

Mary huffs down the line. "Don't be a grouch. Not every woman is like your mother. Or *her*." The emphasis she places on that last word makes my skin crawl.

"Not sure what either of them have to do with this." It's eerie as fuck how well she reads me, even over the phone.

"You're assuming the worst of the girl we met today. All I had to do was mention that Ollie liked her."

"Didn't say anything of the sort," I mutter.

"You don't have to. I know how you feel about this subject."

My exhale is loud. "I find no worth granting them a chance to prove me right. It's safer to assume they're all out for the same thing."

"And why is that, Brance? You'll never be happy this way."

I bite back my scoff. "Do you hear me complaining?"

"I worry about you, dear." Her tone is placating and grates on my nerves.

"Don't. That's not what I'm paying you for. Do your job and make sure Ollie is taken care of."

Mary *tsks*. "Such a shame. You're not helping anyone with this attitude."

"And why would I? Also, I'm done with this conversation."

"Your son wants to speak with you," she states casually.

I stare at the ceiling, a smile already forming. "Okay, put him on."

"Daddy!" The sharp squeal is directly tied to the amount of sugar he's consumed.

I chuckle and rub my ear. "Hey, buddy."

"Guess what?"

"Um, Mary got a speeding ticket?"

He scoffs. "No! That's silly. Miss Mary's a super slow driver."

"Darn skippy," I hear her call from the background.

"Okay, Ollie. I give up. Tell me." I close my eyes and get lost in his voice.

"I found the bestest store of all time. She has toys and games and candy! Like the taffy kind that's super-duper chewy. It's stuck in my teeth!" He giggles, and my heart squeezes. His happiness is all that matters to me.

"I'm glad you're having fun, buddy."

"Uh-huh, yep. And Miss Braelyn is so nice. She's pretty too. I can't wait for you to meet her."

I blink wide and clutch the pen in my hand. "I'm not sure that's going to happen, Ollie."

"But why?" His whine stabs at my chest. "I told her we'd be back tomorrow."

"Without asking me first?" Am I such a softie that he already expects I'll give in? Maybe I need to harden up a bit. But just thinking about being harsh with him leaves a sour taste on my tongue.

Ollie pops his lips. "Didn't think you'd really care, Daddy. You always let me choose what we do on Friday nights."

"What if I have to work late?" I argue.

"Do you?" The wobble in his tone strikes me deep.

"No."

"Good. Then, that's our plan."

I raise my brows at his certainty. "Just like that?"

"We'll have so much fun. I promise."

The need to counterattack buzzes inside of me. My gut tightens on instinct. "I'm not so sure about that, Ollie. Maybe we should visit the park instead."

"M'kay, Mary wants the phone. And I have more taffy to eat. See you soon, Daddy."

"Bye, buddy."

Mary is laughing when she comes back on the line. "He's got you tied tight around his little finger. That boy is gonna rule the roost soon enough."

"He already does," I grumble.

"Ah, let him. He deserves to bask in some extra attention."

"Yeah, yeah."

"What's it going to hurt, Brance?"

I scrub over my forehead. "I don't want him getting attached to a silly shop, or the owner for that matter."

"It's a new discovery. That's all. Next week he'll move onto something else."

"We'll see about that. Listen, my client is waiting. Tell Ollie I'll be there soon."

"Sure, okay. I'll have him home in an hour or so." I can feel her hesitance.

"I appreciate it, Mary. I'll do my best to get outta here soon."

"Don't concern yourself over a thing. We'll be just dandy. I've got this situation handled."

I grunt. "Yeah, I bet you do."

"Tootles," she sings.

I roll my eyes and hang up the receiver. My gut twists that I'm not the one enjoying these seemingly mundane experiences with my son. This fucking job is too demanding. But now isn't the time to analyze my workload.

As if on cue, another knock echoes across the room. My client sashays through the door in a cloud of sickly sweet perfume and death-defying heels. I stand as Missus Kleinston reaches my desk.

I motion to the empty chair. "Please take a seat."

She delicately folds herself into the leather scoop back. Her light blonde hair is pulled into a severe bun that's perfectly coiffed. Blood red gloss coats her overly pouty lips, making them stand out far more than normal. Her too-smooth forehead shines in the overhead lights, and I almost chuckle at the irony. This woman clearly wants to hide her age, but the work she's had done is glaringly obvious. Missus Kleinston reeks of entitlement and manipulation and broken dreams. Fucking typical.

"Thank you very much for meeting me today," she coos.

I make a show of checking my watch. "And only ninety minutes late."

My meaning doesn't hit the mark. Missus Kleinston leans forward, giving me a grotesque view of her fake tits. "I've heard you're the best. I'm more than ready to separate from that cheating asshole I've been calling husband. Can you believe he assumes I'll only get half of everything? What a joke."

I flare my nostrils and beg for patience. "Ma'am—"

"Lianna," she corrects.

"With all due respect, my time is very valuable. I don't appreciate tardiness."

A bony hand flutters to her chest. "My sincerest apologies. Lunch with the planning committee ran late. I told the driver to hurry."

I all but roll my eyes at her pitiful excuse. "No need to explain. Please don't let it happen again. Being respectful of schedules is something I take seriously. You chose me because I'm the best. I know what it takes in this business."

"And I want to win."

"Of course. That's the ultimate goal."

"Good." Her smile is predatory. "How about we go out to dinner, my treat. I'd love the opportunity to make this little delay up to you."

I wave her off. "That's not necessary. And besides, I'm late enough getting home."

"To your wife?" Lianna's face seems to pinch. It's hard to tell.

I snort loudly. "Hell no. My son."

"Pity," she mumbles. "Children are so demanding. Talk about high maintenance. I'm so glad we decided against having them." Her forehead stays unmoving even though her statement calls for some emotion. Now that I look closer, she doesn't have a single wrinkle. Her skin looks plastic.

"Definitely a good choice," I mumble.

Lianna's brown eyes laser into me. "What's that supposed to mean? Are you insinuating I'm not the motherly type?"

"I'd never suggest such a thing." Although I highly doubt she has a maternal molecule in her body. "Kids tend to have a difficult time with divorce. They add a messy layer and make the fighting more brutal."

She steeples her fingers and nods knowingly. "Ah, good point. Although taking away his privileges would've been a nice touch."

I grind my molars at her conniving suggestion. Children should never be pawns. And a father has every right to see his kids. I take a deep breath and manage to refrain from lashing out.

"Thankfully, it didn't come to that," I say slowly.

"Indeed," she agrees. "I don't want more trouble coming my way. He deserves to be the target for it all. I need to sully his reputation. Let all our friends know what a dog he is. In our circle, that's the worst punishment."

I avert my eyes to the window so Lianna doesn't catch the disdain reflecting there. She's referring to the high society, country club bullshit I've purposely stayed away from.

"And there are no transgressions on your part?"

Her gasp is over the top. "Mister Stone—"

I hold up a palm. "Brance, please."

Lianna delicately clears her throat. "I assure you all

wrongdoing was solely on his behalf, Brance. I'm a faithful wife. Straying from my marriage never occurred to me. But my husband? He's been screwing hussies all over town. The tennis instructor, for goodness sake. She can't be older than twenty-two. Can you believe that?"

Her sob story doesn't lift an ounce of pity from me. I scrounge up a halfhearted frown for her benefit. "Sounds positively wretched, Lianna. How did you cope?"

Her lashes flutter shut on an exaggerated sigh. "That's a good question. I thought we were happy." She sniffs and dives into a dramatic retelling of their marriage.

Keeping her talking is key, peeling off the layers to see what's hiding underneath. Surprises during litigation are not my idea of fun. So, I nod along. I scribble a few notes. But the truth is I've done this song and dance more times than I can count. After being in this practice for over three years, I've realized divorce cases are all the same. Once I had a few under my belt, the rest began bleeding together. Not that I'm complaining. This woman sitting in front of me will be padding my pockets nicely, and there's no use turning away easy money.

After I've filled a few pages in my legal pad, Lianna's tale comes to an end.

She elegantly crosses one leg over the other. "So, what happens now?"

I tap my pen on the desk. "We build your case and prepare for negotiations."

"There's no way I'm backing down. I refuse to settle."

"That's good to hear. I rarely take no for an answer."

Lianna pounds a bony fist against her palm. "I want to bring that man to his knees."

I smirk at her. "That's what they all say."

chapter three

BRAELYN

SUGAR

THE AIR CONDITIONER HUMS TO LIFE, PUMPING OUT A COOL blast and making the store's temperature bearable. My skin is balmy, making goosebumps rise when the chill wraps around me. It's a rare occurrence that I don't have to chase away the cold. That's probably due to the fact I've been going nonstop since open. Unloading orders and stocking shelves keeps me moving.

Today has been a good one.

There's no darkness clouding the edges of my vision. Terror isn't holding me hostage. The nightmare from yesterday has lost intensity. I even feel a little light on my feet while stacking the extra inventory in the storage room. There's a pep in my step as I walk to the front. I lean against the counter and take a moment to breathe.

The craze that typically clogs Maple Street is slowing down. I watch the occasional car leisurely pass by. Traffic is sparse, signaling the evening hour. The sun is already hiding behind the buildings. An expansive glow of orange and purple and yellow peeks out in every direction. Soon it will be dark, the shopping buzz fading, while partygoers begin to stretch their legs.

Friday nights used to be exciting, a celebration after a long work week. There was always something to look forward to. Now this is just another unremarkable point in a long line, slowly creeping and dragging. What do I have planned? A whole lot of nothing.

The Dapper is calling my name, loud and clear. I'm a die-hard regular at the diner next door. Most of the time they know my order before I do. My stomach rumbles and gurgles while I think about dinner. I'm in the mood for a juicy burger and extra salty fries. Usually I'm a light eater, but my body is craving more sustenance. Burning those extra calories has left me famished.

I check the clock again. Thirty minutes until close. I can survive that long. If only a customer or two would come in and take my mind off food.

As if hearing my silent plea, the door swings open. The bell calls out, and a familiar little figure zooms inside. I peer around the display case that's obstructing my view. Ollie sends me a beaming smile and my hunger pains are instantly forgotten.

Oh, this kid is going to break so many hearts when he's older.

"Hi, Miss Braelyn." Ollie strides up to me like we're the best of pals. Maybe we already are.

My depleted energy seems to spring back. I give him a wave. "Hey, Ollie. Glad to see you again."

"Sorry I'm late."

I shake my head. "Nonsense. You're right on time. Is Mary with you?"

His forehead creases. "Uh, no. She went home. We

would've been here sooner, but my dad was working." Ollie hitches a small thumb over his shoulder.

That's when the door opens with a bang. A tall man stomps in with the power of a hurricane. Is the ground shaking? If it is, I barely notice.

Holy. Hotness.

Who ordered the sex in a suit?

The guy's laser focus is on the boy beside me so he doesn't notice my slack jaw. He's tall, but not overly bulky. His thick hair is styled in a messy sort of way, and I want to smooth the unruly flyaways. A five-o'clock shadow dusts his jaw, the first signs of stubble barely visible. The contrast between his light eyes and dark features is hypnotic. An impeccable suit covers his broad frame, cut to fit his wide shoulders and trim waist perfectly. He could easily sell this look. Hell, after one glance I'm ready to buy it off him.

He's fucking lickable.

"Ollie, I told you to wait. Selective listening isn't cute anymore. Why do you insist on running ahead of me?" The stranger's boom ricochets around us.

I blink, and the haze evaporates. What the actual eff was that? I look down at the child in question and wait for him to answer. He's squirming all about. Ollie barely gives his father a second glance, too busy studying the assortment of candy on display. But no worries. I'm giving this man more attention than he needs anyway. I can hardly take my peepers off him.

Ollie lingers for another beat, then quickly dashes to the taffy bins. I see him move from one to the next in my peripheral vision.

"Need a camera?"

I startle at the harsh growl. "Huh?"

"Then you can take a picture." His frosty blue eyes narrow on me, and I'm frozen in place.

"Excuse me?" Why is my voice so breathy?

"It'll last longer." He raises a dark brow.

Clarity seeps into my stupor, and the urge to tuck tail streaks through me. But I don't. I raise my chin and openly appraise him. "I like your suit."

"It's custom fit."

"Looks that way."

He crosses his arms and stands straighter. "You're not my type, taffy girl."

I fight the urge to scratch my temple, being stumped again. "Okay?"

"Stare all you want. It'll get you nowhere." He points between us. "Never gonna happen."

For a moment, all I can do is gape at him. I feel my face go up in flames. Is he for freaking real?

"I w-wasn't… no, I didn't mean," I sputter. "I'm not hitting on you."

His smirk is devilish. "Save it for the judge, sugar. I get it."

Before I can defend myself, Ollie zips toward us and smiles at me. "Do you like my dad?"

Everything inside of me skids to a stop. I pop my mouth open, but nothing comes out. My throat is a tight fist, and swallowing is a challenge. How the hell do I respond to that?

I tug at the collar of my shirt. "Uh, well, we haven't really met. I don't even know his name."

Ollie's gaze bounces between us. "He didn't tell you?"

"Nope." There's no hesitation. Throwing this cocky dick under the bus is an easy decision.

The ass glares at me. "We didn't get that far."

Ollie shakes a finger at his dad. "That's not polite. You're supposed to do introductions first. That's what you taught me."

He remains silent, thoroughly scolded by a child. Ollie

huffs loudly. I lift a hand to cover my growing smile. Something tells me this imposing man wouldn't appreciate my humor.

"Brance Stone," he finally offers. A weaker woman might wither under that icy stare. Too bad for him, I'm all out of shits to give.

"It's a pleasure to meet you. I'm Braelyn Miller." I plaster on an extra wide grin for good measure.

A muscle jumps in his jaw. "Likewise."

I turn my attention to the one who deserves it. "You have very nice manners, little guy."

"Thank you!" Pure sunshine beams off Ollie. He gives my mood an instant boost, unlike the grumbling grouch looming in front of me.

"Daddy?" Ollie tugs on Brance's sleeve. "Can I go play?"

"Sure," he answers without taking his eyes off me.

Ollie doesn't recognize the suffocating tension in the room and runs off toward the toy aisle.

Brance calmly loosens the knot of his tie. He oozes confidence and swagger. I can tell this man is used to calling the shots. But this is my store.

"So, *Braelyn*," he spits my name like a curse, "what sort of game are you playing?"

I twist my lips. "Um, not sure what you mean?"

"There's no point trying to fuck with me. I know your type."

I don't bother asking why he has a massive chip on his shoulder. This guy is clearly pissed at the world, or me specifically. Even if I scrounge up a useful question, the chances of him answering honestly seem slim.

Might as well have a bit of fun.

"A small business owner trying to make a living?" I tack on a cheesy smile, just for kicks.

He makes a show of appraising my store with thinly veiled disgust. "What the fuck kind of name is Thicket?"

I keep my expression flat, refusing to give him a

reaction. "It's a place to get lost in. An escape from reality. Somewhere to be free."

Brance clucks his tongue. "And you sell what exactly?"

"A little of everything. Odds, ends, and everything in between."

"Sounds stupid."

In this moment, I'm yanked from my grey bleakness. The numbness that's been cloaking me for years falls to the floor. A fire burns in my belly and I glare at him. I take pride in being even tempered, but everyone has their limits. This guy is making me lose my cool. Quite literally.

"Care to rephrase that?" It takes every ounce of strength to force away the tremor from my voice.

"No," Brance says simply.

He's ridiculing my dream. My job. My livelihood. My blood, sweat, and tears. All with a nasty smirk on his handsome face. Warning bells clang loudly in my brain, but I don't need them. Brance is the type of man I know damn well to stay far away from.

"No one's forcing you to stay."

He nods in the direction Ollie went. "Kid wanted candy. He's been blabbing about this place nonstop. Your luring tactics are successful."

I point to the door. "You're free to leave."

"Kicking out a paying customer?"

"Ollie can stay. He knows how to treat people with respect, which is plenty more than I can say about his father. You can wait outside." I massage my throbbing temples.

"I'd rather not."

A scream brews in my chest, but I gulp it down. This man is pushing every button I have. I suck in a cleansing breath through flared nostrils. It barely takes the edge off.

"Do you have a problem with me?" I lift my arms, letting them fall to my sides.

"What gives you that idea?"

I gesture toward him. "Every condescending thing that's come out of your mouth."

"It's best practice to be honest. I'm just speaking the truth."

"And ripping me apart is a necessary evil?"

Brance's eyes flash, filling with destruction, but the emotion is gone in an instant. A shallow flatness replaces it. I recognize the hollow gleam as my own. But that's where our similarities end.

This man hides everything behind a fierce mask of indifference. He's a shell wrapped in extremely handsome packaging. My pain is stark and on display for all to see. Sorrow leaks out of me on a constant basis. I prefer keeping to myself and avoiding confrontation. His presence takes up the entire store, and not in a good way. He's dragging in a black cloud that almost makes me shudder. But I won't let him cut me down. I take care of that on my own.

Our glaring match continues. He's commanding and domineering, but I'm not shying away. What the hell is eating this guy? I'm too terrified of the answer to ask. Turning the tables feels like a safer choice. At least for now.

I lean against the counter, trying to appear relaxed and confident. "Has anyone ever called you rude?"

Brance snorts. "Constantly."

"And that doesn't bother you?"

"Don't worry about hurting my feelings, sugar. I couldn't care less what others think of me. My zero tolerance for most people certainly helps with that."

I waver for a second but allow curiosity to reign. "And who, dare I ask, makes the top of your list?"

He rocks on the soles of his leather loafers. "In general? Bad drivers, liars, smokers, manipulative shop owners, spoiled women…"

I'm barely listening after he says the first one. His voice slaps my cheek, a lash I wasn't expecting. I almost raise my hand to rub at the phantom sting. Static buzzes in my ears, and I lose focus.

I always complained about Devon's driving. He was on the reckless side, speeding and taking risks. I used to beg him to slow down. He never did.

The sound of metal crudely bending screeches into my mind. Mangled visions smash into the walls of my weak mental state, demanding entry. I squeeze my eyes shut against the onslaught.

Fuck, not now. I can't let this happen in front of him.

But the memories don't relent. Flashbacks pound into me, screaming and yelling. It's too loud. There's so much blood.

"What the hell is wrong with you?" His brash tone crashes through the rising panic. I slam to the present with a jolt.

Sharp pain shoots up my torso and I almost double over. I feel my chest rising and falling, far too fast. Fire licks at my face, and I flinch. Black spots speckle my vision. Dammit, I'm going to pass out. I stumble backwards in my haste to put more distance between us.

With shaky fingers, I yank at my hair. "I-I've got s-something to do. Show yourself out."

The need to escape slithers through me. My skin prickles from the foul sensation. I turn away without another word.

"Where the hell are you going?" Brance booms from behind me. "I'm still talking to you."

I don't respond—I can't. My body is physically wrung out. I'm practically sprinting toward the back corner. Locking myself away from everything is top priority. There I'll suffer and agonize in peace—alone. Nothing else matters at this point, and it probably never will.

I slam the storage room door and sag against the unforgiving surface. My eyes are hot, tears already forming. The cinch around my ribs makes it hard to breathe. Shit, I'm a disaster. My shallow panting echoes across the dark space and doom settles around me.

Will I ever recover?

chapter four

BRANCE

STROLL

THE MID-MORNING SUN STREAKS THROUGH THE LEAFY BRANCHES overhead. Shadows splotch the sidewalk, mixing with a few scattered puddles. Ollie is bouncing in his sneakers beside me. His little hand is firmly clasped in mine while we amble along the wooded path. He tugs on my arm, silently begging me to speed up. When that doesn't work, he stomps his foot and halts abruptly.

"Daddy," Ollie whines.

I chuckle and smile down at him. "Is there something wrong?"

His bottom lip sticks out in an award-winning pout. "All the good swings are gonna be taken. We need to hurry."

My shoulders shake as I laugh harder. I seal my lips to avoid spilling some harsh truths. What I wouldn't give to be a child again, my biggest worry being picked first for kickball. But I'm not so lucky. Adulting can kiss my ass.

"We're almost there, buddy. It's still early. There's plenty of stuff you can play on."

"But I love the red swing best. What if someone's using it?"

I comb through his messy hair. "Then you'll wait until they're done. The green seat is just as good."

Ollie shakes his head wildly. "Is not."

I take a deep breath, fully aware this conversation will not end in my favor. "Okay, okay. You're right. I promise you'll get plenty of turns on the red swing."

"And then we'll go to Miss Braelyn's store for candy?"

Her name is enough to make my muscles twitch. "We're nowhere near that place."

"But it's not far away. We got there super fast last night." His tone raises an octave. Ollie's breezy explanation isn't swaying me in the slightest.

I squint at him. "Your concept of time is a tad skewed."

A furrow forms between his brows. "Huh?"

"Never mind."

"Does that mean we're going to Thicket?"

"No."

His nose wrinkles. "Why not?"

"Just because."

"You're not giving a good reason."

When did my son become so well versed in the art of communication? The tether holding my patience together stretches taut. "I have to choose just one? That's pushing it. The options are endless," I mutter.

"Why, Daddy? It's really fun there! She has toys and games and pretty pictures."

There're so many things I could say in this moment, none of them good. I settle for a simple excuse. "We were just there yesterday."

"So?" His round eyes bore into me, searching for answers I won't give.

I try the easy way again. "There's no reason to go back this soon."

"I'll just run in and grab some taffy super quick."

I cross my arms. "That woman will distract you with her"—I swallow a curse—"chatter."

"Miss Braelyn? I like when she talks to me." His smile is wide and bright.

"Of course you do," I scoff. My son is so naive. He'll learn soon enough how conniving the female race is.

"Is that a yes?"

"Definitely not."

"But—"

"No," I snap.

Ollie looks down, blinking fast. My stomach bottoms out, and I want to kick myself in the nuts. Fuck, I'm an asshole.

I rub his shoulder. "Hey, hey. I'm sorry for yelling, buddy."

His lashes are damp when he looks at me. "Why don't you like Miss Braelyn?"

My son has always been perceptive. I've never minded more than in this moment. "Not sure what you mean," I deflect.

"You used the angry voice with her, like you just did with me." His somber tone is a straight shot to my black heart.

Dammit, this kid rips me to shreds. I glance up at the clear sky and contemplate how to dig myself out of this mess. My gears are rusty and grinding, providing zero help. I dare a peek at him. His stricken expression ruins me all over again.

I bend forward and ruffle his shaggy hair. "I didn't mean to, Ollie. I'll try harder to hold my temper." The vow solidifies in my chest, quickly turning ironclad.

Blue eyes the same shade as mine stare up at me. "With me or Miss Braelyn?"

I almost sneer at his suggestion. Why is he still thinking of that woman? "Just you, buddy. You're the only one that matters."

In an attempt to move on, I steer him in the direction of our original destination. But Ollie doesn't budge.

"Daddy?"

I tamp down the bellow ripping at my throat. "Yes, Ollie?"

"Why do you hate Miss Braelyn?"

I grind my molars as we circle back to this topic. Again. After blowing out a string of silent expletives, I manage to force out, "I don't."

"Yes, you do."

"What's the point of asking if you're certain?"

Little fists park on his hips. "Because I want to know why."

"It doesn't matter how I feel."

"Does so."

If there was a brick wall nearby, I'd bash my head against it. There's no wonder where he gets this stubborn streak from. "And why's that?"

"I want you to marry her. My teacher says two people get married when they're in love. How do I get you to love Miss Braelyn?"

That notion alone is inconceivable. "Never gonna happen, Ollie. And I've heard enough about her for one day. Let's get going." I point to the path, my fingers scissoring in the signal for walking.

His slim shoulders slump, but he follows my command. Thank Christ for small miracles. We trudge off toward the park, a murky cloud looming over us. Birds whistle overhead, the tune an attempt to soothe. All I hear is static. Ollie's mood doesn't improve when the playground comes into view. His steps are slow as he shuffles to the sandbox and sits on the edge.

I drag a hand through my hair. There's a neon sign hanging above me that lists all the ways I'm failing him. I stomp over to a large oak and park my hip against the trunk. This parenting gig never gets easier. But I'll never quit giving that child all of me.

His insistence on finding me a wife has intensified tenfold in the last few months. A part of me, albeit very small, feels guilty as fuck that he doesn't have a mother. I'll admit it stings that he doesn't consider me sufficient enough to fill both roles. But that's selfish on my part. Too bad for him, my outlook on the opposite sex will never change. If Ollie knew why I'm so hellbent against relationships, it'd give him nightmares. And that damn shop owner is another level entirely.

At first glance, Braelyn appeared meek and mild. Her backbone came by surprise and surfaced out of thin air. She met my jabs with strikes of her own, firing off clever comebacks dipped in snark. Her anger got me hard. I fed off that shit. Arguing is what I do for a living, and I'm damn fucking good at it. Finding a worthy opponent is hitting the jackpot. I almost fooled myself into thinking she might be a decent sparring partner. But our battle came to a premature halt.

Try as I might, Braelyn hasn't wandered far from my thoughts. She hijacked my predictable routine and replaced it with mayhem. Her soulful gaze saw too much, peeled away layers I never reveal. What the fuck was it about her?

I suppose she's stunning in an understated way. An abstract sculpture that needs closer inspection to comprehend its true beauty. She didn't wear any makeup or seem to put forth much effort into her appearance. Not that she needed to. Her blonde hair is long and wavy, the slight curls a golden waterfall. With long lashes that frame mossy eyes, I was sucked in. Her high cheekbones and arched brows are perfectly symmetrical. I bet she'd look beautiful with a natural flush coloring her skin. I'd like nothing more than to offer up a quick fuck. She'd guarantee a wild night with that sassy mouth and quick temper. I'd gladly find another use for those pouty lips. And that sharp tongue would wrap around my shaft quite nicely.

My blood rushes south, and I swerve away from the temptation. I adjust my position against the tree I'm still leaning against. The shade might conceal the arousal pounding into me. I inhale slowly, the scent of freshly cut grass reminds me of my location. This is the last place I should be getting turned on. But my mind and body are at war.

I glance around for offended park goers wearing looks of disgust but find none. The expansive fenced-in area is relatively quiet for a Saturday morning. I seek out Ollie, trying to deter my dirty imagination. He's scooping up sand and filtering it through his fingers. His lack of motion doesn't provide much of a distraction. Visions of her swoop in with the cool breeze.

Braelyn's face is a flawlessly molded sculpture, but the entire package is better. Even under her loose clothing, I caught the subtle hint of curves. But she's thin as a rail, almost too skinny. But not in a way that's intentional. If I had to guess, she skips meals without realizing it. Distracted by all the shit cluttering her shop's shelves. I could toss her willowy ass over my shoulder without effort. How'd she react to that? I shake my head, expelling the idea immediately.

Women usually lose their shit over me. Braelyn couldn't have been more repulsed. My attitude toward her might be responsible for that. Was I harsh? Perhaps. Did I treat her unfairly? Undecided. Do I regret my reaction? That's a hard no. That woman reeks of trouble. She's a charity case, and I'm not into that type of philanthropy.

But yet, there's something… intriguing about Braelyn. I want to know her story, pick apart her case, which is a dangerous feeling. I'm still trying to figure out what happened midway through our conversation. Maybe that's what interests me the most about her. There's a puzzle to solve.

If I was a spiritual man, I'd believe she saw a ghost. I don't know much about panic attacks—my experiences in that area are pathetic—but the evidence was pretty damning. The alluring confidence fled her features, replaced by what I'd describe as sheer terror. A haunting glimmer shuttered her eyes, followed closely with rapid breaths bordering on hyperventilation. Even to an ignorant asshole, it's clear she's hauling serious baggage. All the more reason to stay the hell away. I carry more than enough weight of my own.

The easiest solution is finding Ollie a new candy supplier. I'm liable to drive the feisty shop owner into a burning rage if we swing by there again. No doubt that'd be entertaining to watch. But I have to take Ollie's presence into consideration. For the moment, I cast Braelyn to the far recesses of my mind. She can wait there, or preferably disappear altogether. I need to focus on my priorities.

The sun is full and high, suggesting noon has arrived. Ollie is still sulking, his beloved red swing lacking the usual appeal. I watch him mope around the playground until acid boils in my gut. My son deserves better than this from me.

"Hey, Ollie," I call to him.

He turns and moves toward me, his pace more appropriate for a snail. "Yeah?"

"Should we go?"

His sneakers kick up stray wood chips. "Sure."

"Did you have fun?" I study him closely, waiting for his typical exuberance to make an appearance. All I get is a quick shrug.

"I guess." Ollie watches two kids dash to the swings. His heavy sigh holds the weight of a thousand pounds. When those big blue eyes meet mine, I almost crash to my knees.

"Hey, don't be sad. I love you, buddy." I lift his chin, hoping for at least a small grin.

"Love you, Daddy." His voice is too flat.

I need to step up my game. I clear my throat. "So, I was thinking we could stop for ice cream. How's that sound?"

A switch flips, and his face lights up. "Really? Before lunch?"

I exhale, shoving the boulder off my chest. "Yeah, why not? I've gotta make things up to you. It'll be a special treat."

"Yes, please! I want two scoops."

A chuckle rattles through me. "Don't forget the sprinkles."

Ollie claps and runs circles around me. His happiness soaks into me, and I laugh harder. Mary is right. My son has me wrapped around his pinkie. I wouldn't have it any other way.

"Let's hurry so we beat the rush." I reach for his hand and swing our arms.

"You're the best, Daddy." The megawatt smile is a cherry on top.

My wrongdoings are forgiven. For now.

chapter five

BRAELYN

SIP

T HE COUCH THREATENS TO SWALLOW ME WHOLE WHEN I haphazardly plop down. I snuggle deeper into the velvety cushions, giving my permission. Not sure a nap has ever sounded better. A whistle of wind gains momentum, turning tree branches into punishing whips against the window. Shadows streak across the ceiling, and I track the wavy movements. The swirls are hypnotic, lulling me into a state of utter relaxation. Drifting under takes zero effort. I let my eyelids fall, warm tingles spreading through me.

A harsh nudge against my foot drags me to the surface.

"Really? You're sleeping? This is supposed to be girl's night."

I blink up at Sadie, a glow from the lamp surrounding her.

"Just resting."

She passes me a stemless glass. "This'll help."

I take a tentative sip. "Pinot?"

"Of course."

"I knew we were friends for a reason."

Sadie laughs. "More than happy to relieve your stress by any means necessary."

I give her a small smile. "Thanks, Dee." I swallow more crisp fruity goodness, my insides already getting warmer. She's right—getting a slight buzz never hurts. The chaos from this week begins to calm, and I can breathe easier.

"Better?" She takes another sip of her own.

A hum vibrates my throat. "Much."

"Dinner will be ready soon. Tell me about your week. We didn't get a chance to chat much."

"Well, the shop was busy, which was good."

Sadie kicks her feet up onto the coffee table. "Any, uh, dreams?"

I give her a narrow side-eye. "You don't have to tiptoe around me. No, I didn't have any episodes. Not since last Friday."

"When the hot guy was there?"

Wine dribbles off my lips. "W-what?" I sputter.

"Come on, Brae. Did you already forget the skinny details you dished out? Did Mister Tall, Broody, and Sexy swing by for round two? There's no use denying me at this point."

I glare at the decorations meticulously lined up on the mantel. "No, he hasn't been back. Just Ollie and Mary." My grin returns thinking about that little cutie pie. He's quickly becoming my favorite customer.

Sadie snaps her fingers. "Well, that's a bummer. I was hoping to hear more saucy spice."

I shake my head. "He's all yours, friend."

"Uh-huh. Yeah, right." She doesn't say more, letting the subject drop. I couldn't be more thankful.

A comfortable silence surrounds us again. The quiet doesn't bother me like it does at my place. Being home alone isn't my preference for that very reason. There are too many memories and ghosts waiting to strike. Sadie has offered to let me move in here on numerous occasions, but I'd be imposing. Sharing a space with me would drag her down. She doesn't need to be worrying about me at all hours.

I swirl the wine in my glass, watching the pale yellow liquid slosh against the sides. A daze blurs the edges of my vision. I don't fight the pull, letting my mind wander. I allow my heavy lids to slide shut again. A certain arrogant asshole materializes, wearing a smug smirk on his perfectly angular face. Brance crooks a finger and beckons me closer. My imagination is a slave to his demand. I'm very aware that my cheeks are on fire like the rest of me. The room is suddenly scorching. Steam whooshes around me, and I'm positive all systems are misfiring from overheating.

"What's on your mind, Brae?"

I crack an eye open, easing out of my self-induced lust-fest. "Uh, nothing much."

Sadie snorts. "Whatever. Spill."

"Just work stuff," I hedge.

"Since when does Thicket make you blush?"

Jeez, could I be more obvious? I scratch my temple, inhale more wine, and dig for an explanation.

"That good, huh?" She giggles into the mouth of her glass.

I focus on the elegant crown molding of her ceiling, avoiding her stare. Droplets splash at my forehead. I swipe the moisture away. "What was that for?"

Sadie points at me. "You're being lame."

I mock-gasp. "Me? I didn't do anything."

"Exactly!" She tosses her hands up. "Just spit it out already and let me live vicariously."

Realization suddenly hits me. I'm the one with something interesting to discuss for a change. When was the last time that happened? I can't remember that far back. I rub my nose and glance at Sadie, who motions for me speak.

"Okay, fine," I groan. "I might have caught myself thinking about him a time or two."

She wiggles her brows. "Thinking or fantasizing?"

I hide my burning face in a pillow. "Please. I don't need more embarrassment."

She yanks my makeshift shield away. "You deserve this, Brae. There's nothing to be ashamed of."

"Sadie, I don't understand what's going on with me."

"Hormones, honey." She taps my arm.

I stick my tongue out at her. "Meh, I'm immune to all that pitter-patter nonsense."

Sadie rolls her eyes. "Clearly not. You're reaching the peak of sexuality and need a release. Wake up and smell the man-meat, girlfriend. You're stuck in limbo, not dead. I bet that guy is fine as hell. I don't blame you for coming outta hibernation for him."

"I'm not a bear," I mutter.

"Mating is natural instinct."

I slap my knee. "Oh my gosh, are we seriously having this conversation?"

A bouncy shrug. "You brought it up."

She has me there, dammit. I should have kept my big trap shut.

"Because you practically begged me to," I counter.

"You're welcome."

"What would I do without you?"

She winks. "The real question is, whatcha gonna do about him?"

"Absolutely nothing." I make sure my flat tone leaves zero space for compromise.

Sadie doesn't look convinced.

"What if he visits again? Maybe tomorrow," she coos.

I widen my eyes. "Lord, I hope not."

Verbally sparring with Brance was one thing. Having a mental breakdown in front of him was something else entirely. I can only assume that extreme reaction was due to my heightened emotions. I was roasting mad, opening the gate for panic to squeeze past my awareness. I'd let my guard down and paid dearly for it. Well, to my pride. Brance is the type to never let me live that down. If I see that jackass again, it'll be a massacre.

Each time Ollie dashed into Thicket this week, I'd crossed my fingers and toes that Brance wouldn't be accompanying him. So far, my luck is holding out. But I'm not dropping my shields for a second. My plan is to remain vigilant and on high alert.

Sadie's heavy sigh breaks the silence. "Okay, fine. Hottie dad hasn't been by and you couldn't care less." Cue exaggerated eye roll. "What about the boy?"

My smile is automatic. "I've seen Ollie three or four times this week. My candy sales have never been better."

"With the nanny?"

I nod. "Or grandma, whatever title she prefers. I haven't quite figured out their dynamic."

Her forehead wrinkles. "Where's his mother?"

"No clue."

"You haven't asked?"

I gape at her. "That's not my business."

Sadie waves off my words. "That's a perfectly logical question. They're regulars so you've been chatting. You're bound to be curious."

"That seems too personal."

"Guess you'll never find out," she mumbles.

"I don't know, Dee. I get the feeling his mom isn't in the picture."

She rests her chin on a closed fist. "Oh?"

I bounce my shoulders up and down. "Ollie never talks about her. Mary's made a few snide comments about women letting him down. Makes me assume."

"Ah, sure. But don't make an ass outta yourself."

"Thanks for the advice."

Sadie's brown eyes sparkle. "Maybe he wants you to take the place of mommy dearest."

I cough out a gasp. "Highly doubtful."

"He visits your store almost every day."

"So? He loves sugar."

"He can get that anywhere."

I gnaw on my lip, the implications rolling over me. Getting attached will only lead to disappointment and pain. I'd hate to cause Ollie distress of any sort. My throat is too tight, making swallowing a chore.

I suck on the inside of my cheek. "Kids are creatures of habit, right? Ollie is building a bit of a routine, but it's only temporary. He'll move on to the next exciting prize soon."

"That sounds made up," Sadie drones.

"And how would you know?"

She twirls a lock of dark hair. "Touché. Do you ever want kids, Brae?"

I toss my head back and laugh. "Are you high? I can barely take care of myself."

"Oh, stop." Sadie shoves me lightly. "You're recovering well. Most would crumble and fall under your circumstances."

"Three years later and I'm barely hanging on." I blow out a long breath.

"Not true. I've been by your side and can attest to the opposite. You're strong and brave and an inspiration."

My eyes get hot as I look away. "You're giving me too much credit."

"And you don't give yourself enough." Sadie wraps an arm around me.

Warmth builds in my chest and spreads through me. "Thanks for everything, Dee."

"You're my bestie. This is what we do."

I lean further into her. "Well, I really appreciate your support."

Roast chicken and baked potatoes fill the air. My stomach growls, and I slap a palm over the noise.

Sadie glances at the clock. "Shouldn't be much longer. Sorry for the wait."

I flick her arm. "Yeah, Dee. Hurry it up. You're slacking tonight. I mean, you've only welcomed me at the door, cooked a meal that smells divine, and served perfectly chilled wine. For real?"

She snorts. "Brat. I'm trying to be a good host."

"You don't have to try. It comes natural."

"If only I could find a man to compliment me the way you do."

"Ugh, they complicate everything."

"Good point! Who needs them anyway?" She nods to my empty glass. "More wine?"

"Sure, why not. We're celebrating."

"And what might that be exactly?" Sadie grabs the bottle and pours in a healthy dose.

I tap my lips. "Being nightmare free for a week."

"Oh, that's a great reason. Don't forget the sexy man responsible. Complicated or not."

"Why in the world would we toast to that surly bastard?"

"Hate or love, he's bringing your fire back. You haven't been this... *alive* in years."

I pretend to ponder that for a moment, but the truth already breathes inside of me. Since Brance crashed into Thicket a week ago, the numbness has lifted. Pieces of me from before the accident and trauma have been slipping into place. It feels good, really great if I'm being totally honest.

"He's a thorn in my side," I mutter.

Sadie nudges me. "A little pinch never hurt anyone. He's a worthy distraction. I'm glad he's keeping your mind occupied elsewhere."

"That makes one of us." I'm such a liar.

"Thinking of him is just a taste of normal, completely innocent. Getting the juices flowing again."

I screw up my face. "I can assure you all my parts are still in fine condition."

Sadie giggles. "Humor me."

"Fine, he's a crumb."

She frowns, and I roll my eyes. "Okay, a nibble."

She gnashes her teeth. "A bite?"

"Maybe a sip."

"Oooh, yeah. That's hot. Drink him down." Sadie clicks her glass against mine.

I hold up an open palm. "Wait, what? No. No, no, no. I thought we were messing around."

"Meh, maybe. But promise me something?" She slouches deeper into the couch.

I squint at her, weighing the possibilities. "That depends."

"Give someone a chance to prove you wrong. You deserve to find love again."

The sweet Pinot turns sour in my stomach. That's never going to happen. But to appease her, I force a smile. "I'll try."

"That's a good start. This feels like a change in the right direction. I want you to be happy, Brae. Speaking of, have your folks called lately?"

"Nope. Not that I'm surprised."

"Don't they care about your recovery?"

"Clearly not." I rub at the ache in my throat.

"Have you ever considered going to visit them? Turn the tables on their silent treatment. I could go with you."

I'm shaking my head before she has the first sentence out. The thought of abandoning Thicket, even for a weekend, gives me chills. That shop is my baby, the closest I'll come to having a real one. Some might call me a workaholic. I prefer the term dedicated. I'd never be able to relax thinking about my shop dark and empty and cold. "I'm not interested. I can't just up and leave. I have responsibilities."

"But don't you miss them?"

"Why would I? My family isn't the sentimental type to get sad about. I haven't fit into their equation since leaving for college. And they live far away. Not that you'll hear me complain about that."

"You act like they're in Alaska."

"Might as well be," I grumble. Sadie's pinched expression stabs at me. I release a long exhale. "Fine, I'll think about it."

But I won't. Truth be told, my family has not been very supportive of my decisions. My parents never approved of Devon. After he died, they took that as an opportunity to try dragging me back to our small town in the middle of nowhere Iowa. I didn't go. The rift spreads wider with each missed call and forgotten holiday. They know where to find me, but the odds of that happening aren't in my favor. The sting of their rejection has long since faded.

"Paris will never happen, huh?"

I furrow my brow. "I didn't say that."

"You don't have to."

I peer over at her. "It's hard, okay? I'm comfortable in my little bubble. But visiting Europe is on my bucket list."

Sadie knots her fingers together. "I'm being a pushy bitch. Sorry, Brae. I got a little excited to see you smiling again."

"Don't apologize. I'm lucky to have you urging me on. If it wasn't for you, I'd probably never leave my house. You're a really good friend, Dee."

Her bottom lip sticks out. "For real?"

"Yes, dork. Don't be mopey. That's my job."

She wags a finger at me. "Not anymore. That ship has sailed."

"Don't get ahead of yourself. I'm by no means cured."

The timer dings and Sadie pops out of her seat. "Finally! Dinner's done. And so is all this talk of brutish men and neglectful family members and forceful best friends and emotional relapses. Let's watch a chick flick and finish the wine and regret our choices in the morning."

I giggle, the sound rich and full. "You're a nut. But that's the best plan I've heard in a long time."

Sadie shimmies her hips and dances into the kitchen. "And one more reason to celebrate."

chapter six

BRANCE

SUED

I OPEN THE REAR PASSENGER DOOR AND BEND TO FACE MY SON. "Ollie?"

He's practically vibrating in his seat. "Yes?"

"What's the rule?" I'd repeated the phrase enough in hopes he'd never forget. Wishful thinking, I know. But now is the true test. I lift my brows but remain silent otherwise.

"Stay by your side and don't run ahead," he recites in a diligent tone.

"And why is that important?" Keeping my expression neutral is a challenge when he's smiling so wide.

Ollie's lips twist. "Um, so I don't get run over?"

I chuckle. "Yes, that's true. I want to keep you safe from everything."

He nods. "Right, got it."

"Do you?"

He begins pulling at the straps over his chest. "Uh-huh, yup."

"I mean it, Ollie. You have to hold my hand," I remind him.

He reaches for mine and links our fingers together. "All done."

With some masterful maneuvering, I unbuckle him without letting go. Ollie springs forward and hops out of the car. Once his feet hit the pavement, we're off at breakneck speed.

My arm is straight out in front of me. "Ollie, slow down."

His neck swivels around. "I'm just walking."

"I can barely see your shoes." I swear the scent of burning rubbing is stinging my nostrils.

He looks at his sneakers without slowing down. "They're still tied."

"That isn't the issue," I laugh. Clearly my words went in one ear and out the other. Surprise, surprise.

"Daddy, Daddy, look! There it is."

Ollie cranks up his pace, almost dislocating my shoulder in the process. I attempt to reel him in with a light tug. That only causes him to double his efforts. I almost stumble from the momentum. Talk about a backfire. I appreciate him finally listening about sticking with me, but this is straight painful. He's freakishly strong for such a little tyke. Must be all that candy he's been consuming.

An acidic tang fills my mouth when I see the massive lollipop directly in our path. That fucking sign is a beacon for children. Good marketing? Sure. Doesn't mean I have to be happy about the tactic. I bet Ollie could find his way blindfolded, but that neon monstrosity certainly helps. Prying him away is becoming more challenging by the day. Mary informed me, while wearing a Cheshire grin, that they'd visited Thicket almost daily this week. Seems my son hasn't gotten over his latest obsession yet. Unlike his nanny, I was not encouraging this newfound infatuation.

My resistance didn't stop Ollie's determination. The

moment I'd get home from work, the begging and fussing would begin. Thankfully, I was able to distract him with other preferable activities. We went to his favorite restaurant that has an arcade attached. I loaded up his game card and let him go wild. The following night I suggested a new cartoon that hit theaters, along with promises of popcorn and gummy bears. I took him to the pool with waterslides and a lazy river. Yesterday we brushed up on our bike-riding skills. I've been collapsing into bed each night utterly exhausted. Worth it? Absolutely.

Today is a different story. I wasn't able to deter Ollie with the park or ice cream or even pony rides at a petting zoo. When his pleading started first thing this morning, I couldn't say no again. The last thing I wanted was a repeat of last Saturday. Even if that means spending an hour in this atrocious sickly-sweet sugar pit. I can play nice with the shop owner. At least somewhat. Maybe I'll hover by the door out of sight. I snort. Since when do I duck and cover? That isn't my style in the slightest.

Man the fuck up, I scold. *She's just a chick.*

But that chick is sinking her claws into Ollie. Braelyn would be a pitiful fool to even consider trying that shit with me. My bite makes grown men cower in the courtroom. If this woman has any sense, she'll back off.

We reach the building and Ollie snuggles into my side. "Thanks for bringing me, Daddy."

I suck in a sharp breath when my chest squeezes. The only soft spot left inside of me expands. This kid melts my stone-cold heart with a few simple words.

"Anything for you, kiddo." And I mean that with every breath left in my lungs. I'd never put myself in this position for anyone else. I open the door and shuffle him inside. That annoying chime rings out, announcing our presence.

A cheerful voice greets us. "Welcome to... oh, hey!

Great to see you, Ollie." Braelyn's perfectly straight teeth shine bright when she smiles at him. My body tightens for an entirely different reason. Fuck, why couldn't she be a troll? Maybe my real problem is the unnecessarily long dry spell I've been under. I need to get laid.

Ollie shakes out of my hold and dashes toward her. "Hi, Miss Braelyn!"

"Hey, pal." She passes over a colorful piece of taffy. "Got a new flavor this morning."

The demand that she asks my permission burns on my tongue. I swallow it down, sure that Mary allows him to have free reign. Ollie's little fingers make quick work of the wrapper. He pops it into his mouth and starts chomping away. There's no point savoring it when he has a slew of other treats coming his way.

"Mm-hmm, it's yummy. Bubblegum and uh, um, something else," Ollie mumbles around the candy.

"Strawberry," Braelyn supplies.

My son bobs his head. "Yeah, it tastes really good."

She ruffles his shaggy hair. "Glad you like it."

I silently observe their routine, already established and growing deeper roots with each passing moment. If I left, would they even notice? I won't give her the satisfaction of testing the theory. Instead I choose to keep my distance and let them do their thing.

Rays of sunlight stream through the window and cast a rainbow reflection across the floor. My gaze is drawn to the simple pattern, the irony not lost on me. This place is anything but ordinary. I'm not even sure where to look first. There's shit crowding every available surface. I glance at the crammed shelves and funky paintings. There're stacks of books surrounding a rocking chair and a collection of lamps in the corner. The room smells like fresh flowers and sugary perfume.

It's clear that most of her effort goes into the candy section. The confections are artfully displayed in a rainbow array of colors displayed along the wall. Every piece has a place, making the presentation very eye catching. No fucking surprise there. She might as well hang another sign or five. But I'll give her a little credit. Based off Ollie's stash, her supply is rather impressive.

After another quick visual sweep, I tune back into their conversation.

"I was beginning to think you'd forgotten about me," Braelyn says.

"No way! Never, ever. My dad just drives really slow."

I gape at them. "Weren't you here yesterday, Ollie?"

He glances at me over his shoulder. "Well, yeah." His deadpan tone raises my guard. When did he get so clever?

"It was a joke," Braelyn interrupts.

I widen my stance, preparing for battle. "Oh, really? I had no idea."

Ollie glances between us. "You remember my dad? He was here with me once."

While his attention is diverted, she glares at me. "Oh, yes. I sure do."

"He took me all sorts of places this week. That's why we were so busy," Ollie explains.

Her mossy eyes search mine, a storm brewing in those green pools. "Is that so?"

"Uh-huh. Daddy took me swimming and out for ice cream. We even went to the movies."

"Lucky duck. I haven't been to the theater in ages."

He makes a squeaking sound. "What? No way. Wanna come with us next time?"

Braelyn's slender throat bobs. I'm fascinated by the movement. I get a rise thinking about the conflicting emotions raging inside of her. How will she answer? There's no way in hell she'd agree. The air grows dense, enough to choke on, as her silence stretches.

Finally, she opens her mouth. "I'll have to check my calendar, buddy. It's hard to get away from the store."

He bounces on his toes. "Okay, great. Talk to my dad about it. Can I go play now?"

Braelyn beams at him. "Of course, kiddo. You know where the toys are."

That's all he needs to hear before darting down the designated aisle. I watch him disappear in a flash of red and denim. When I look at Braelyn, the thundering in my pulse roars. She'd been all smiles for him, but now all evidence of happiness melts away. When she turns to me, a scowl mars her features. My gut twists painfully, and that stops me short. Am I seriously jealous of my son? That'd be a hell no. I roll my shoulders and strengthen my resolve.

"Fancy seeing you here." Braelyn crosses her arms, shoving a pair of luscious tits up for my viewing pleasure. I almost applaud the shirt's low neckline, but thank the summer heat instead. No point giving her ass any credit for wearing less clothing.

I try to keep my focus on her face. "Is it?"

"No, not at all. I could smell your hostility from a block away."

Well, this is escalating quickly. "What's your fucking deal?"

Braelyn's mouth forms a flat line. "Care to be more specific? You seem to have a myriad of issues with me."

Her smooth features distort. I wait for her to explode or have another panic attack. She just continues glaring at me.

I clear my throat. "In general, what's wrong with you?"

The apple of her cheek twitches. "Real tactful, asshole."

"Meh, I'm not in the habit of mincing words."

"Clearly." Her tone is desert dry.

"So?" I tap my loafer on the tile floor.

"Not that it's any of your business, but I was involved in a car wreck. The accident left some lingering effects." Her blank expression hides the rest, and I choose to ignore her lack of detail. For now.

"Were you driving?"

"No."

"All right."

Braelyn rests her weight on one leg. "What's your story?"

I point at myself. "You're looking at it."

"Good to know the sharing was one sided."

"I never promised to return the favor." My smirk makes a reappearance. "At least not in that way."

The flush racing up her neck gets my blood pumping hotter. She ruins it with a sneer. "As if that'd ever happen."

That's the damn truth. The chances are higher that I'll run for president, but she doesn't know that. I grant myself permission to take a lazy perusal of her body. Goosebumps break out across her arms. Watching her squirm is fucking fascinating. "We'll see."

"We really won't."

Once again, she easily casts me aside. I don't care enough to ask her why. But the brushoff is still aggravating as fuck. I narrow my gaze on hers. "You're so certain."

"And, for whatever reason, you're extremely determined."

"Considering my profession, I'll take that as a compliment."

She studies me for a few moments. "What is it you do for a living?"

"I'm a lawyer."

She snorts. "That was my one and only guess."

I glance down at my plain tee and jeans, raising a brow. "Am I that obvious?"

Braelyn twirls a finger in the air, building up steam.

"You're very…" she trails off for a moment before settling on, "cunning and conniving. I imagine you mowing down witnesses in the courtroom."

I cross my arms. "Talk about a fucking stereotype."

"If the shoe fits." She shrugs, not backing down in the slightest.

Two can play at this game. I open my wallet and take out a glossy card. "If you're ever in the market for a divorce attorney, give me a call."

She scans the name—Bysek & Associates—and flicks my offering away. "Hard pass. I'm never getting married, therefore I won't need a divorce."

I scoff. "Looks like we agree on something."

"I find that hard to believe," she mutters under her breath.

"You're quite the spitfire."

Her husky laugh cups my balls and applies just the right amount of pressure. "Never in my life have I been called anything close to that."

"Well, there's always a first for everything." Am I fucking flirting with this chick? After a quick deliberation, I figure why the hell not. I take another opportunity to openly check her out, making my leering known. Other than the deep neckline, her shirt is nothing special. Her flowy skirt touches the ground and hides anything of value. Lucky for me, I have a vivid imagination.

Is it fucked up that I'm picturing her mouth stuffed full of my—

I slam a concrete wall down on that twisted path. Yup, most definitely screwed up. I keep my ogling above the waist, as an extra precaution. Braelyn isn't wearing any makeup other than some glossy shit on her lips. Her blonde hair is twisted in a loose braid. I want to unravel the golden waves and watch them spill over my hands.

What the actual hell is happening to me? Usually my dick gets hard for high heels and short skirts and seductive curves on display. This woman is the opposite of the chicks I usually fuck. Apparently the desperation is messing with my standards. Or my cock is confused from the arousing banter. Either way, I need to get laid. I'll take whatever at this point, except her.

"Problem?" The question drags my eyes up to hers.

I work my jaw back and forth. "Not at all."

"I can't begin to comprehend why you're looking at me like that."

"Then why bother asking?"

She wrinkles her pert nose. "Let's get one thing straight, I'm not your type. Desperate and needy clashes with this outfit."

I bark out a sharp laugh. "Don't flatter yourself, sugar. I prefer my women classy and refined and down to fuck wherever."

"Is that a realistic combination?"

"Haven't you heard of a lady on the streets and a freak in the sheets?"

Braelyn gawks at me. "You're worse than I thought."

I lick my bottom lip, slow and deliberate. "Know what you need? A good, long fuck."

She makes a choking sound. "Are you kidding?"

"Not at all. The endorphin release will set you straight."

"Oh, that's really interesting." She makes the sound of a buzzer. "Turns out it's actually not. That'll be a hard pass from me. Thanks anyway."

I knock on the counter beside me, the sound cracking through our tension. "Oh, I wasn't volunteering. Just a suggestion to keep in mind. Might make you less… bitchy."

Her eyes narrow into green slits. "You're such a pig."

I hike up a shoulder. "Oh, yeah? You stink like grief and sorrow."

Her face crumples, and I almost regret my words. But she's more prepared this time around.

"You're rotten to the core. I have no idea how you managed to conceive such a sweet child." Her voice is dripping with venom, and I hope she bites. My muscles flex and I can barely hold off. From what, I'm not certain. Her chest rises and falls rapidly, my eyes greedily tracking the movements. I need to get the fuck out of here before actual damage is done.

"Ollie," I bellow. "We're leaving."

"About damn time," Braelyn mumbles.

I point at her. "If it wasn't for him, you'd never see me again."

"If only I could be so lucky." She spits the words.

I spin on my heel and stomp away from her fortress. I'll gladly wait for Ollie outside.

Her giggle grates across my frying nerves. "I hope your big head fits through the door."

I give her the finger without a backwards glance.

chapter seven

BRAELYN

SOB

A N EERIE CHILL CREEPS UP MY SPINE WHEN THE WIND HOWLS. A misty fog blocks the path and impairs my sight, but I know the way. The sound of twigs snapping close by sends me into a tailspin. When I whip around, nothing is there. Damn, I'm losing my shit. I comb through my hair and take a deep breath. As if cemeteries aren't spooky enough on their own.

I hustle down the precisely measured row. Desperation is chasing me, the need to erase this distance gaining urgency. Thankfully the plot is easy to find. The familiar carved letters calm my erratic pulse. This is all that remains. Moisture immediately clouds my vision.

Devon's tall headstone is stark against the dusk backdrop. I make quick work of clearing away the leaves and weeds covering the surface. It's been several months since I've dug up the strength to visit. Guilt sinks into my bones, and I collapse in the dewy grass.

My back thumps against the unforgiving stone. I wrap an arm around my knees, seeking comfort in the empty embrace. The cold seeps in. I welcome the numbness. That puts us on even ground. I take a cautious look around me. The graveyard appears abandoned, without a soul in sight. At least from what I can see through the haze. A ball of lava clogs my throat. I rub at the lump, but it only grows. Dammit.

"Hey, Dev," I begin. "Sorry I haven't been by lately."

A flash of lightning streaks through the clouds. Well, that's fitting. Might as well add possible electrocution to my list.

"It doesn't get any easier to visit. Maybe it's even harder. Ripping at my stitches, you know? But I'll never stop, not entirely. I couldn't do that to you."

I rake my fingers through the overgrown sod covering his grave. The lush turf is flat and settled, deep roots growing stronger with each passing day. Devon has been buried long enough that there's no evidence everything was once torn apart.

"It's been almost three years. Crazy, huh? I'm losing faith that things will return to some semblance of normalcy. Doctor Thair said I don't need regular sessions anymore. She recommends maintenance appointments for when I'm feeling down. Not bad, right? Almost like I'm cured. Maybe the anniversary of your death has me sinking lower than usual." My laugh is brittle. "But I'll never be that carefree girl again. How could I, Dev?"

My questions are rhetorical, completely one-sided, but this makes me believe we're actually having a conversation. I prefer thinking of it that way, rather than me sitting here rambling to myself. I feel a bit better thinking that Devon is listening.

"Sadie is doing well. She's been so supportive. I feel guilty for how much she's still helping me. Not sure how I'd manage the challenges without her. That makes me sound pathetic. Or maybe everything does. Not like it matters. But guess what? I'm still chugging along."

I avert my gaze, ignoring the smoky doom I imagine swirling nearby. "Ready for the random story?" I smile in spite of the thistles prickling me. "So, I had a dream last night. It wasn't horrible. I mean, there wasn't any screaming or blood or death. But maybe this was worse. I was sleeping in this massive bed. It was so freaking soft, like a cloud. Remember those commercials? It was definitely memory foam. You should've let me buy one. The softness was so legit." I knock on my forehead, erasing the nonsense. "Anyway, I wasn't alone."

My lungs fill with lead. This was a bad idea. I'm not in the right frame of mind. But leaving isn't an option. Not when I'm already talking.

I yank at a patch of wilting wild flowers and toss them away. A small hole takes their place, mocking me. I dig at the upturned dirt until my nails are caked. Cleaning up this mess gives me something to do. I shift on the hard surface, and needles prickle down my legs.

"Okay, let me rewind. There's this new customer at Thicket. Two of them actually, father and son. Ollie couldn't be any cuter. He's five and loves candy. I want to believe he loves the store too. He's so bright, you know? Gives me a reason to smile. Unfortunately, his dad is the total opposite."

Thinking of Brance sets my skin on fire. Specks of ice attempt to stick, but melt in a shallow puddle. The metallic taste of copper fills my mouth. I startle, releasing my bottom lip from the guillotine of my teeth.

"Brance is so horrible, Dev. But maybe that's why I can't stop thinking about him. It's been years since I've felt anything except hollow nothingness. Why this guy? He doesn't deserve to steal my attention." My breaths are harsh pants, puffing in and out too fast. "Is it weird that I'm discussing this with you?"

I wait a few beats, almost expecting an answer. "He calls me sugar. What a joke. But that's not the worst of it. Yesterday Brance used my grieving as an insult. Can you believe the nerve of that man? He doesn't know about you or why I took off in a panic last week. I could be chronically ill, and he'd laugh at me. He's just rude on purpose. The arrogant type that has the best answer for everything. Oh, and he's a lawyer. Go figure."

The bricks on my shoulders crumble into dust. It feels damn good to let this all out. I'm really on a roll. "His boy is sweet as honey, and that should make him happy. But no, he's an awful person. So, of course, I find myself wondering why he's such an intolerable jerk."

I roll my eyes and huff out loud. "You're probably laughing at me. I still can't mind my own business. Always searching for reasons I'm better off not knowing." I kiss my palm and place it on the cool stone. "Why didn't you let me drive, Dev? I can't let it go. You should have listened to me. Things could have been different. Instead, you're gone." The last word tumbles out on a sob. "Was it worth it?"

Because I'm weak, or maybe lonely beyond reason, I wait for a response. Only silence greets me. My fractured heart splits further. I clutch my chest and try gathering the pieces. I'll need the captured fragments one day.

The downhill slide is fast and steep. A brutal kick to the ribs and all hope draining out of me follow close behind. In a blink, I find it hard to breathe without my body screaming. This is different than panic. The isolation and loneliness become overwhelming, crashing against me with unforgiving ferocity.

There's no use fighting.

The wind vanishes from my sails, and I sag into a pitiful

stoop. Smooth granite stops me from falling flat. There's some hidden message waiting below the surface, but I can't gather the energy to find it. I squeeze my hand into a fist and try to imagine the weight of his on top of mine. All I find is gaps and space. So much damn blankness. The longer he's gone, the more I forget. The sound of his voice is barely recognizable. Our love was virile and strong, or so I thought. These days it's hard to remember the happy moments. Loss is cruel that way. My mind plays tricks on me, warping cherished memories into a mysterious clump.

Tears trickle down my cheeks, and I swipe them away. Why am I so weak? It's always one step forward and five stumbles back. Something has to give. I can only hope that's not me.

My therapist's calm tone tries to break through the storm wreaking havoc inside of me. I'm strong enough. Today is better than yesterday. Nothing will break me again. The healing process is a wicked beast. Since I was there in the wreck, my progress is harder to achieve. The impact feels fresh, this crater inside of me impossibly wide and deep. But in reality, the hole is shrinking. Even when I pick at the scab and pain rushes in, the intensity has lessened. More recently, the wound doesn't hurt as much. I'm aware of the reasons, but I refuse to acknowledge him as one of them.

A roar of thunder shatters the quiet misery I'm drowning in. The warmth recedes from the air, allowing a frigid blast to sweep in. If someone comes along, will they want to save me? Would I want them to?

I wheeze, the quicksand pulling me under. It was a mistake coming here. The sky opens and freezing droplets pelt me from head to toe. The rope tying me to reality is fraying. I decide to let go for a minute, or maybe hours. In this space, time doesn't really matter. I close my eyes and let the darkness take me.

I STEP INTO THE LAIR AND TAKE A MOMENT FOR MY EYES TO ADJUST. The lighting is dim, glowing in certain spots to set a relaxed atmosphere. The main attraction is the glossy oak bar that takes up most of the space. I spot Jordan perched on a stool waiting for me.

"Glad the ball and chain let you outta the house," he greets. Jordan claps my shoulder when I sit beside him.

I shrug his hand off. "Fucking hilarious. My son isn't a shackle."

My friend chuckles. "I was referring to Mary."

That gets a genuine laugh from me in return. "I'll tell her you said hello."

The bartender stops by, and I order my usual draft. I'll save the bourbon for after dark.

Jordan smiles at me. "In all honesty, I'm glad you could make it. It's been too long since we've had a night to ourselves."

I give him a slow nod. "Sorry, man. It's getting harder to be away from Ollie."

"No apologies. We aren't young bucks in law school anymore, which is super fucking unfortunate."

A shrill screech whips up my spine and I shudder. "Not sure I want to relive those days."

"Ah, you're right. But our first year wasn't bad. Before Veronica ruined everything."

Her name is nails on a chalkboard. I almost cover my ears. "Let's not talk about her. I just wanna chill."

A reflective silence surrounds us. Before I can get stuck in a ditch with those memories, my beer arrives. I take a few healthy gulps to wipe the slate clean.

While settling in, I do a quick glance around. The bar is relatively quiet for a Saturday, which is fine by me. This establishment isn't appealing for the rowdy crowd looking to party. That's why I like it. Lair is a place to unwind without the pressure of more. I don't need women constantly breathing down my neck, begging for drinks or a quick dicking in the bathroom.

Don't get me wrong, I love to fuck. I'm the furthest from an abstinent saint. Having a woman purr in my ear to take her harder gets me off. But more often than not, that hassle is greater than the reward. Especially lately. Or maybe it's because I'm getting older and wiser. I've come to appreciate a quiet, laidback evening. That's all I need today.

Jordan clinks his glass against mine. "Here's to making partner."

I shift my weight on the padded seat. "I haven't gotten it yet. The promotion has been dangling in front of me for months. I've been busting my ass and still no word."

"That job is yours. There's no doubt. Don sees the work you're doing. He values you on the team."

"No, he certainly doesn't."

Jordan shrugs. "That's because you're a Grade A threat. You're younger, more attractive, and smarter."

I snort into my beer. "It's a little early to be hitting on me, man."

"I'm just stating facts. If you wanna take a ride on my cock, I'll need more drinks first."

"Your services won't be necessary. I'm not that desperate," I chuckle.

He clutches the place above his heart. "You wound me, man."

"I think you need to get laid more than me."

Jordan waves me off. "I'm all good. But don't let me keep you from fishing."

He clearly didn't get my earlier message. Women are the last thing on my mind, except one. I almost bang my head against the bar over that one. Instead, I finish off my brew and order another.

"How about her?" Jordan juts his chin toward a buxom brunette. "She's sexy as fuck."

And she is. This chick is everything I'd typically eat for dessert. She's dressed to fuck in a skin-tight dress, the color a deep shade of red. Her dark hair falls in loose curls that almost reach her ass. Ruby gloss coats her lips. This woman is a pop of color against the bar's muted hues. I'm sure she planned that on purpose.

She glances around while sipping her martini. Maybe she's waiting for someone, or hoping to find company. Either way, she's drinking alone. Easy prey. This vixen would deliver, no doubt. But I'm not in the mood to wake up with claw marks crisscrossing my back.

I lick my lips, finding the lingering taste of hops and malt. There's no flavor of desire waiting. My dick stays down, not even a slight twitch. As of late, my preferences come in a different package. Much to my displeasure. The war between body and brain continues.

"Sure, she's hot, but I'm not feeling her." I turn to Jordan and find him slack-jawed. "What? I'll never complain about beautiful scenery."

He narrows his eyes. "Someone else on your menu?"

"Nah, not at all. I'm just focusing on my priorities for now. Ollie comes first, getting partner is a close second. Mostly so I can provide the best for him."

Jordan's features soften. "Such a good dad. My pops could've learned some valuable lessons from you."

"Are you yanking my chain?"

"I wouldn't bullshit about that."

"All right, thanks. I appreciate it, man."

I pull my eyes away, scanning a row of framed black and white candid images hanging along the brick wall. I study the face of one woman, captured in laughter, and she morphs into Braelyn. What the fuck? I groan and scrub over my eyes.

Jordan leans closer. "What's your issue, Stone?"

"Oh, nothing. Just dealing with a few brutal cases."

"The best cure is getting balls deep in a woman. Heaven in heels over there isn't getting your cock hard, but there's plenty of other options. Need me to be your wingman?"

Not this again. "Stellar advice coming from the guy who doesn't follow suit. I'll pass."

Jordan leans an elbow on the bar. "No need to slay the messenger. What's wrong with sweeping a woman away to Paris and confessing my devotion?"

I make a gagging sound. "Everything is wrong with that statement. Way too complicated and messy. You sound like a bad hallmark movie."

"I'm more of a hopeful romantic."

"You're a fucking sap," I mutter.

"Don't get your pubes in a twist. One of us has to keep the faith alive."

"Guess that's the difference between working with business mergers compared to failed marriages."

He sits up straight. "You chose that path."

"With zero regrets."

"I know Veronica destroyed your—"

"Don't start on her again. She's ancient history. The only good she gave was Ollie, and that witch couldn't care less. She never even held him. What kind of person doesn't want to cradle their baby?" The beer is loosening my tongue, but this man already knows all the hell Ollie's mother put me through. Shit, he was there for most of it. He probably sees straight into my black soul.

"Yeah, that sucks hairy nutsacks. But if she had any interest, you'd be tied to her forever. That would've been a fucking disaster." A tremor passes through him. "Thank the Lord for small miracles."

"I'd consider that more of a jackpot. And I get the prize all to myself."

Jordan rings an imaginary bell. "Winner, winner."

I shift my weight. "Let's be real, I was screwed up before Veronica twisted the knife."

"She was a final blow." He whistles, and mimics a bomb detonating and exploding.

I nod at his gesture. "Exactly."

"But you can get back up. Fight for love, man."

My scoff is a hollow echo. "I'm not drinking wine, Jordy. Cheese isn't necessary."

"You're too cynical."

"And you're a sucker."

He doesn't deny it. "We'll see who ends up on top."

"I'll leave marriage and happily ever after to you."

Jordan smirks. "You're so kind. But for real, you're suddenly not interested in getting your dick wet. Should I be concerned?"

"Nah, I'm taking a little hiatus. I'll be back in fine form once Don finally makes a decision."

He jabs my arm. "You've got this in the bag. Half the firm will walk out if he chooses anyone else. That'd be a stupid move. Doesn't matter how intimidated he is."

"You're my biggest cheerleader."

"I prefer coach, thanks. And since you brought him up, how's the pops doing?"

I scratch at the stubble on my jaw. "Retired. Playing golf on the daily. Has three girlfriends. Living the dream."

"Sounds rough. He's my hero."

"Yeah, I'm glad he's soaking in the luxury. That man deserves a medal for dealing with my mom all those years. Fucking unbelievable we all survived." My stomach quakes, but I bury that shit. Like always. "I'm going to take Ollie down to visit. Bet my dad will love it."

He bobs his head, watching me for a moment. "How's the new kid-sitter?"

My neck almost cracks from the abrupt change in subject. Not that I'm surprised. I made the mistake of mentioning Braelyn after a board meeting last week. Knowing Jordan, he'll never let this go. I cross my arms and stare him down. "Real funny, asshole."

"Touchy, touchy. Did she deny your advances?"

I grind my molars. "As if I gave her the option. I wouldn't touch her wearing a HazMat suit."

"Oh, shit. She's really getting to you."

I automatically tense, my armor clicking into place. "Of course she is. Ollie talks about her incessantly. It's been two weeks since I've had the displeasure of seeing Braelyn, but he still frequents her store at every opportunity. Mary gives in, of course, and obliges him. She feels it's harmless."

Jordan lifts his brow. "And what do you think?"

"My opinion is the exact opposite. That woman is trouble."

"That's what you say about every chick."

"She's worse. I try not to think about how much she bothers me. My skin fucking burns whenever she's around."

"Are you sure that's not the clap?"

"Fuck you."

"Yeah, I suppose you'd need to have sex in order to catch a STD. Your balls are gonna shrivel up, man."

"You're a real comedian today," I grumble.

"One of us has to lighten things up. You're casting shadows over all of us. Let's fix this problem." Jordan taps my empty glass. "Then we'll solve some other shit." He waves the bartender over and gets us another round.

I'm edgy and can't put my finger on why. It's almost as if someone's watching me, and not fake Braelyn cackling over my shoulder. I swing my gaze this way and that. Nothing appears to stand out. The alcohol is making me paranoid.

The bar's din is low, intimate conversations in hushed tones. Lovers discussing their plans for later are huddling in the booths against the walls. A snag pinches my chest, as it occasionally does. The beating organ in my chest longs for a connection. I stopped listening to that soulful rhythm long ago.

She's not even here, but I feel her presence. How fucked up is that? Maybe I should give the brunette a go, just to bang Braelyn out of my thoughts. I cringe, the implication is curdling milk on my tongue. I'm screwed without actually fucking.

Jordan slams a beer down in front of me. "Earth to Brance. Knock off this melodramatic act. It's bumming me out."

I flick him off. "Sorry, dude."

"Apologize to yourself. Twenty-five-year-old Brance would be ashamed."

"He was an idiot."

"But loads of fun."

I shove him. "So, I'm a grumpy loser who's sucking the joy outta the room?"

"You forgot overly emotional. Bordering on fragile, if I'm being honest."

"Since when don't you like discussing feelings," I mutter and take a swig of beer.

"With hot chicks who need encouragement. Your ego doesn't need stroking. You just need to pull outta this funk."

"I'm fine," I say for what feels like the thousandth time.

Jordan snorts. "If only I believed you."

"Doesn't make a difference to me."

"So temperamental. If you don't wanna discuss work or women, tell me about Ollie."

"What about him? He's great as always. The happiest child known to humankind. I've registered him for kindergarten. Grilled cheese is no longer a favorite food. Paw Patrol is still cool. He's preoccupied with a certain someone lately."

His smile is all-knowing. "Seems like a trend with the Stone men."

"I don't get attached."

"I'm well aware. But it's not always a choice."

The padded stool wobbles beneath me. "Even if I was interested, which is a big fucking no, I'm a package deal. Women are shallow. They'd see Ollie as a bargaining chip."

Jordan knocks on the gleaming bar top. "Wow, you're jaded as fuck."

"You're just realizing this?"

"No, fucker. Just wasn't aware how deep the damage ran. It's gonna take a special someone to change your tune."

I chug a few swallows of beer. "She doesn't exist."

"How are you so certain?"

"Every woman that's been part of my life has left a toxic

footprint. Each one more potent than the last. I've learned my lesson. I hear the good word loud and clear. I'm not interested in repeating mistakes."

Jordan raises his glass. "I hope this one proves you wrong."

chapter nine

BRAELYN

TRUST

I FINISH BOXING THE MUG AND SET IT ASIDE. NEXT UP IS A GLASS-blown flower—rainbow colors, of course—and I scan the barcode. I make quick work of wrapping the delicate bloom in several protective layers. When I'm satisfied, it gets added to the growing pile of purchased items.

The woman in front of me is beaming. "I still can't believe this little slice of happiness has been hiding from me. I love it here."

I return her smile. "Thank you so much. I'm glad you stopped by."

"And I'll definitely be back."

I finish bagging the rest of her things, toss in some extra taffy, and pass them all over. "Repeat customers are always welcome."

"I wanted to buy everything. My AMEX will be getting a workout." She wags the plastic in front of her face.

"I'll be gentle," I joke.

She grins. "Don't worry, I can handle it. I'm a very willing participant."

We share a laugh, the soft noise stoking heat into my limbs.

"I'm happy to hear it. And you have great taste. I love your choices." I nod toward the bulging tote at her side.

She hefts the straps onto her shoulder. "It was impossible to decide. I could browse for hours. I'm a huge fan of your variety. What am I searching for? Oh, who can say. But I'll find it here."

"I try to offer things that anyone can enjoy. There's a little something for everybody."

"Thicket is a beautiful name. A place to get lost in. That's exactly how I feel." Her whimsical tone is music to my ears.

Her praise cracks my chest open and the sunshine pours in. I exhale, chasing the last bit of darkness away. "Thank you," I repeat. I know my lower lip is wobbling.

"It's my pleasure. You've done a perfect job with this store." She grabs a few of my business cards from the holder and tucks it into her purse.

I stroke the mosaic tiles that border the counter. "This shop is my baby."

She mirrors my movements, tracing the colorful pattern. "It really shows. I can't wait to tell all my friends. And with that little café next door? This street is killer. One bonus after the other."

I blink the heat from my eyes, not wanting to weep in front of a perfectly sweet stranger. "That truly means so much to me."

She pats my hand. "Be proud. You've created a magical retreat for the creative soul. Kudos!"

"Well, you've truly made my day. Probably my month." And I'm not exaggerating. If there wasn't a counter between us, I might hug her. Maybe I'll do it anyway.

She gives me a finger wave over her shoulder. "Until next time."

"Have a great day," I call to her retreating form. When she walks out, I'm still feeling ten feet tall. This afternoon is certainly taking a turn for the better. I mentally check my daily-due list of tasks. I turn away with a smile, set on getting some organizing done in the storage room. Before I make it three steps, the welcome bell rings.

My favorite customer bolts through the door at a speed any Olympic track star would envy. I cross my fingers over one another while waiting for his chaperone to arrive. Mary has been the one accompanying him these last few weeks, which I've been grateful for. But my guard remains firmly locked and loaded.

"Hi, Braelyn," Ollie greets. The kid is barely winded.

I give him a high-five. "Hey, buddy. How're you?"

"Great! And guess what? My dad—"

"Oliver James!"

My lungs threaten to collapse when that harsh tone cracks into the air. Any hope of avoiding another altercation vanishes with those four syllables. Ollie makes a show of locking his lips and throwing away the key. He bounces on his blue sneakers, tugging on my shirt. I lean closer.

"My daddy has something to ask you. But I'm gonna go play with toys, m'kay?" His voice is barely a whisper.

"Uh, sure?"

But he's already racing away, my response falling on deaf ears. No matter. Everything else fades into a colorful blur when Brance's looming presence blocks the entrance. When he stalks closer, my brain power melts into a puddle of useless goo. Good Lord, this isn't fair.

Brance is wearing another crisp suit, and I want to hate him for it. Those sleek fitting threads are some sort of kryptonite to my resistance. There's no doubt about the custom fit. If I wasn't positive before, this number does the trick. To add intensity to the fantasy, a blue tie pops against the gray fabric. Is that silk? Goosebumps prickle my skin at the promise of its feathery rasp. I jerk my mind out of the gutter.

"You've got a thing for suits, huh?" Brance offers a half smile, one hundred percent condescending.

I wince, knowing my face is red enough to stop traffic. He prowls into my personal space. I catch a heady whiff of his scent and almost moan. Crisp outdoors and spicy musk assault my senses. The combination is lethal.

Hello, pheromones. Please have mercy and take pity. I'm growing weak.

With a middle finger, he slides his sunglasses down. Those piercing blue eyes stab into me, and I fight to keep my expression neutral. He doesn't need to know I'm a quivering bowl of gelatin on the inside.

"Buy a camera yet?"

I ignore his barb. "Ollie told me you have a question."

"My son is very taken with you." Brance's gravelly voice is bitter.

I let my hackles rise. "And that's a bad thing?"

He shrugs. "Not necessarily. Just makes things more… complicated."

"How? Him being here often isn't hurting anyone." Not that I'm aware of at least.

"Attachments are messy," Brance retorts.

"Ollie is a child. He should be surrounded by love."

"And he is, constantly. Don't worry about how I distribute affection."

I don't bother disguising my scoff. "Yeah, you're Mister Warm Fuzzies."

"That kid gets the best of me. There's nothing left to spare. I'd apologize, but I'm not sorry." His chiseled jaw tics, giving away his true feelings.

I smile at that. "At least you're spending it wisely. That's how it should be."

"Great parenting advice. Find that in a pamphlet at the doctor's office?"

The words bite, but only surface deep. "I might've read a baby book or two. I always wanted children."

"Past tense?"

I nod slowly. "That ship has sailed."

Brance studies my face. "Why?"

"Not important."

He narrows his gaze. "Can't find a man to knock you up?"

His nasty insinuation makes my eyes sting. Just when I thought we'd passed the worst of it. I suck in a deep breath and dredge up more strength.

I point to the exit, the gesture becoming a reflex when this man is involved. "You can leave now. I'll get Ollie checked out."

Brance doesn't move an inch. "You're so sensitive."

"Thanks for noticing," I deadpan.

He tucks a hand into his pocket. "Enough bullshitting."

I let my jaw drop. "Because I'm the one stalling?"

"Whatever you want to call this. It's kind of our thing. I needed to warm you up first."

I rub my temples. "I can't begin to imagine what you mean."

"Braelyn." The word sounds forced, as if just saying my name grates on his nerves.

I look up at him. "Yeah?"

He dips his chin, breaking eye contact. "There's something I need."

"This ought to be good," I snort.

Brance's stare flies up to mine. His is roaring with flames, and I instantly feel the burn. I shiver despite my attempts to control the reaction.

"I have a favor to ask," he grinds out.

"Ask or demand?"

"Why do you have to make everything a challenge?"

"That's rich coming from you."

His eyes roll toward the ceiling. "Know what? Forget it."

When he begins to turn away, I place a hand on his wrist and stop him. "What do you need, Brance?"

He's silent for a moment, focusing on my fingers wrapped around him. I let my arm drop.

Brance straightens and adjusts his tie. He clacks his teeth together. Finally, he spits it out. "Can you watch Ollie tonight?"

I blanch, definitely not expecting that. Am I tripping? "W-what?"

"It would just be for a few hours."

"You want to leave him here with me? Alone?" The possibility of this happening is so inconceivable that it's jamming my circuits.

He bobs his head. "This was Ollie's idea. Mary insists I trust you."

At least I have their votes. But that's not what really matters. "And what do you think?"

"I don't have a choice."

I want to argue that he does. But the defeat etched into his brow stops me. We stare each other down, his blue eyes boring into mine. I'm still trying to wind my brain around this unexpected twist. Who's going to crack?

Brance scratches at the fresh stubble dotting his neck. "I wouldn't ask if I wasn't desperate."

I hold up a palm. "No need to lay on the charm. I get it."

"Mary isn't available. I have no other feasible options."

I jostle my hand, as if that will stop him. "Okay, I understand. You don't have to give a list of reasons why I'm your last resort."

His Adam's apple bounces with a heavy swallow. "I won't be long. Just a meeting, but it's in the city."

I wave him off. Clearly this guy needs to be heard, over and again. "That's fine. Don't worry."

Brance rocks on his heels. "He really wants to stay with you."

"That's very sweet. We'll have a great time. I can take him to Dapper for ice cream."

"Whatever blows your skirt up. Just don't ruin him."

Ah, there's the confident Brance I've grown to despise. I cross my arms and glare at him.

He scowls. "What's eating you now?"

"You could try curbing the attitude. I'm not the enemy."

"The jury's still out on that one."

"Yet you trust me to watch Ollie," I remind.

Brance's steel veneer cracks when he looks over at his son across the room. "You can thank him for that. He's a great judge of character. That kid wouldn't keep coming back if you were mean to him."

I gasp and clutch my neck. "I could never be anything but kind to that adorable boy."

He gestures toward me. "See? That right there is how I know he's in safe hands."

"Ollie will be very well taken care of." The steel in my voice clangs around us.

Brance gives a sharp nod. "All right. Glad that's settled."

"Anything else I need to do?"

"That about covers it." He opens his wallet and tugs out a familiar-looking business card. This time I accept it. "My cell is on here. Call if you need anything."

I hold out my palm. "Give me your phone. I'll enter my number, just in case."

He does, and I type the digits in. When the deed is done, I pass it back. Brance stares at the screen.

"Programming it to your memory?"

He glances up at me, a sneer curling his lip. "I bet you'd love that. But no, sugar. I'll be deleting it once this evening is over."

"Good," I retort. "Wouldn't want to be confused with one of your women."

He barks out a laugh. "There's no chance of that happening."

I chew on my lip, deserving that dig. I shouldn't be egging him on. "Okay, get going. Don't want to leave your client or whoever waiting." I shoo him off with a flick.

Brance sidesteps me. "Hey, Ollie? I'm leaving."

The little boy dashes toward his father and leaps into his open arms. My ovaries threaten to explode when Brance cradles him for a moment, hugging him close. I'm blinking fast, about to turn away and give them privacy. More for my sake.

"Miss Braelyn?" Ollie's soft question halts my retreat.

I cough to cover my sniffling. "Yes, sweetie?"

His hands are knotted in front of him. "You said yes? I can stay with you?"

"Of course. I'm excited to hang out, just the two of us."

He squeals and begins bouncing around in circles. "Me too!"

Brance chuckles and pats Ollie's head. "Don't get too wild. You'll scare Braelyn off."

Ollie whips around to face me. "Is that true?"

"Never! We can have a dance party once your dad leaves." I bop up and down, testing out my moves. Ollie laughs. Brance frowns. I'm calling it a win.

Brance glances at his watch. "Okay, I've gotta go." He kneels and grips Ollie's shoulders. The love flowing between them is so obvious. My chest squeezes so tight it could snap a rib.

"Love you, buddy." He kisses Ollie's forehead.

Oh, the butterflies are getting a workout tonight.

"Love you the mostest, Daddy. See you soon," Ollie replies.

"Behave for Braelyn," he orders. They exchange a look, saying so much without uttering another word.

Brance stands, nodding at me. "Thanks for this. I really appreciate it, even though it doesn't seem that way."

I shrug. "I got you. Go be lawyerly."

That earns me a laugh. "Will do." He takes one last look at his son and turns for the door. A calm silence follows, the dense atmosphere instantly easing up. I release a long exhale, thankful to have survived with minimal damage.

Ollie slips his hand into mine. "What're we gonna do?"

I tap my chin. "How about I close Thicket early and we go somewhere special?"

His eyes sparkle. "Yes! Let's do that."

"Do you like ice cream?" I tease.

Ollie begins vibrating in place. "It's my favorite!"

"Then I have a super surprise for you."

chapter ten

BRAELYN

SPRINKLES

IT DOESN'T TAKE MORE THAN TWENTY MINUTES TO SHUT THICKET down for the day. Ollie is patient as can be, following me between aisles to tidy up and straighten the shelves. I never thought having a partner in cleanup crime could be so entertaining. He talks nonstop about anything that pops into his brain. The retelling of his favorite cartoon episodes is my favorite. On top of that, he's a great little worker. I'm already considering future dates where he can hang around and lend a helpful hand. I'm sure he'd accept candy as payment.

I walk to the front with Ollie hot on my heels. His quick and uneven footsteps make the sweetest sound. I'm practically skipping, my mood higher than it's been in a long time. Having his company adds a shimmery twinkle to my vision and makes everything vibrant.

The realization stops me short. I shouldn't get attached. Brance already made that clear. But as I glance at Ollie over my shoulder, I already know it's too late.

With a roll of my neck, I shove those worries away. There's no room for troubles in this space. I grab my purse from under the register, switch off the open sign, and move to set the alarm.

"How do you remember all this stuff?" Ollie stops beside me, watching my fingers on the keypad.

I smile down at him. "It's a routine. I follow it every day except for Sunday."

"Because you're closed," he grumbles.

"Ah, yes. You found that out last weekend, huh?"

Ollie's frown is impressive. "I had to get regular candy instead."

"I'm sorry, buddy. From now on, I'll give you more on Saturday to last until Monday."

That turns his lips right-side up. "That's a good deal."

I stick out my hand. "We can even shake on it."

He giggles, fitting his smaller palm into mine. "A taffy promise."

"Those are the best. Now, let's take this party next door." I guide him outside and lock up.

"I'm so excited," Ollie squeaks.

"Me too. This is where I get lunch most days. Everyone is very nice. They'll love you." I doubt my assurance is needed. Ollie has the confidence of a Hollywood A-lister.

We're on the sidewalk for all of one minute before I'm steering him into Dapper Diner. "Here we are," I sing-song.

Ollie is quiet next to me, absorbing the bustling restaurant spread out before us. Pictures of customers, old and new, decorate every available inch of wall space. The checkered floor leads to an open floor plan dotted with tables and booths. There's a crowd already gathering, over half of the red vinyl seats occupied. Servers navigate the maze to drop off drinks and heaping plates. The dinner rush is in full swing. I inhale the aroma of being welcomed home. Today it smells like the pulled pork Wednesday special.

A long and narrow countertop separates the dining area from the kitchen. I point to the row of short stools with a front-row view of the talented cooks. "Those are the best seats in the house. You get to watch all the action."

Ollie is nodding before I finish. "I wanna sit there."

I let him choose a spot smack-dab in the middle. He hops up with ease and settles in like a regular. I follow suit, pleased as punch with this decision. Babysitting was a chore when my sister was little. Is that what this is? Doesn't feel like it. If anything, kid-sitting is more appropriate.

Ollie studies every square inch with wide eyes and new-found curiosity. I take a lazy look around while waiting for someone to check on us.

"I'm glad your dad had a meeting."

Ollie wrinkles his nose. "Why? They're boring."

I nudge him with my elbow. "Because I got to bring you here."

"I told my daddy that he had to let you take care of me. I wasn't going to talk to him for a whole hour if he didn't." His broad grin says it all. Appears father and son have a similar stubborn streak.

"Well, I'm very glad he listened to you."

Maude—a very familiar face—saunters up to us and leans an elbow on the counter. "Hey, Braelyn. Who's this handsome guy?"

Ollie blinks at the older woman. "You look like Mary."

Maude fluffs her graying curls. "She must be lovely."

His dimples are Oscar-worthy. "Uh-huh, she really is."

She gives his cheek a light pinch. "You're sweet as sugar, cutie pie. What's your name?"

He sticks out his little hand. "I'm Oliver, but you can call me Ollie."

"Oh, my! Such a gentleman. I'm Maude. Welcome to Dapper Diner." She gestures around the buzzing space.

"It's very nice to meet you, Miss Maude."

A wrinkled hand flutters to her chest. "Well, color me stunned. The feeling is very mutual. You're something special, kiddo. Your parents must be very proud."

Ollie sits up straight, his smile wilting ever so slightly. "It's just my dad. But he tells me I'm very well behaved."

Maude laughs. "Well, he's right. You're brighter than the sun. Don't lose that spunk, Ollie."

He's beaming at her again, the expression more than fitting. She passes him a kid's menu and a cup full of crayons. Maude gives me a raised eyebrow, gesturing to a glossy stack of menus, and I shake my head. She winks at me.

"I'll be back in a few," she says and walks off.

Ollie's forehead is adorably crinkled when I glance over at him. He studies the paper in front of him. "I can't read very well yet. Miss Heather, my preschool teacher, says I'm super smart and ready for kindergarten. But I can't sound out all the words."

"I'll order for you so it'll be a surprise. Do you trust me?"

His nod is enthusiastic. "Yep, so much."

Warmth spreads through my chest. "I hope you never lose that."

The creases on Ollie's brow make a reappearance. "I don't get it."

I laugh. "Never mind, kiddo. Just stay happy."

"That's easy!"

"It definitely can be," I whisper.

"Why do you look sad sometimes?"

I falter at that, searching for an explanation. "What do you mean?"

He leans closer. "I've seen you frown a lot. Your eyes look wet sometimes. That means you were crying. What's wrong, Miss Braelyn?"

This boy catches far more than most adults. I attempt a smile, but my lips tremble. "I lost someone very close to me years ago. Sometimes, when I think about him, I get a little blue."

Ollie's eyes are wide. "Did he die?"

My nod is slow. "He did. We were in an accident."

"But you're okay."

"Yes, I survived." Somewhat, at least.

He picks up a blue crayon, twirling it between his fingers. "My mom has never been around. She left right after I was born."

I rub his back. "I'm really sorry to hear that, Ollie."

His slim shoulders lift. "It's like I lost her. But I never really had her. I'm not even sure what she looks like. My dad doesn't have any pictures."

Jeez, no wonder we have a connection.

I'm in the center of a minefield without a map. I bounce my knee and consider what direction to take. "Do you, uh, ever wonder about her?"

His mouth pulls up on one side. "Meh, not really. Only when my friends have their moms around. And they're all super nice to me so it's okay. My daddy told me she's very busy helping others."

A fissure cracks my sternum and makes a bit more space for him. "I bet she's very sad with her choice. You're a great kid, Ollie. And you're loved by many."

He draws a perfect heart on his menu. "Yeah, I'm lucky. My dad tells me we don't need her. His heart beats twice as hard for me to cover for her part."

There's a hitch in my breath. I fall a little in love with Brance Stone in that moment. Heaven help me.

Ollie doesn't notice my strangled rasps. "He's a really good dad. Even though he works a lot, we spend a lot of time together. He always tries really hard to make me laugh."

"That's very nice of him." I'm glad there's a soft side to Brance.

"Are you married?"

Ollie's question catches me off guard. "What?"

On instinct, my gaze drops to my hand. Some phantom sensation has me looking specifically at my ring finger. But it's bare, of course. That clear fact is a stake straight to my shattered heart.

He tries again. "Do you have a husband?"

I clear my throat. "No, Ollie. I don't."

"My dad is pretty great, you know." His legs swing with abandon. I miss feeling that carefree ease.

"Oh yeah?" My response is the definition of evasive.

Maude saves my ass by swooping in at that exact moment. She's getting a big tip.

"All set?" She has a pen poised and ready.

"We'll have two of my usual," I tell her.

"Oooh, that's fun. I'll have those right up." She reaches behind her and produces two icy cups of water. "Hopefully this will hold you over until then."

I take a long drink to soothe the desert in my mouth.

"Do you like my dad, Miss Braelyn?"

This isn't the first time he's asked me. I'm positive it won't be the last. I pull in a deep breath, dredging up a watered-down version of the truth. "Uh, sure. He seems very sweet to you. And he's very tall."

Ollie's head bobs wildly. "He is. I'm gonna grow up big like him. Won't that be awesome?"

"I bet you'll be even taller and bigger and stronger."

He lifts his arm and flexes the muscle. I give his small bicep a squeeze, whistling for optimal impact. "Oh, wow. You're well on the way. Your dad better watch out."

"Really?" His face scrunches up with a growl. "I wanna be a policeman."

"Then that's what you'll grow up to become."

"But how about my dad?"

I tilt my head. "What about him, sweetie?"

"Do you love him?"

I choke on my sip of water. Just when I thought we'd swerved around this topic. "Oh, um… no. I don't know him very well. I think we're just friends. Maybe?" Yeah, because that's convincing. My flimsy cardboard voice isn't fooling anyone. I sound like a liar, and a bad one at that.

Ollie is quick as a whip and doesn't miss a beat. "I think you two should get married."

Holy shitballs, what tangled dimension did I drop into? It will be a fifty below zero in Hades before that's even a conceivable option. I attempt to gather my scattered wits.

"Uh, well," I start. "I'm not sure that's a great idea, Ollie."

"Why not?"

"It's kinda complicated."

"How?"

"I'm not sure how to explain it," I hedge.

"But why?"

"Because it's adult stuff."

"My dad and Mary talk about this all the time."

I doubt that very much. "Well, then you should ask them."

He rests his chin on an open palm, in it for the long haul. "I want you to tell me. Why won't you marry my dad?"

How bad will Brance hate me if I tell Ollie the truth? Can it get much worse? The hard truth sinks in my stomach. Denial is a much safer route, but I'm running out of steam.

Lord, if you're listening, please cut me a break.

An angel dressed as Maude sets two overflowing bowls in front of us. Whipped cream and sprinkles have never looked so good. Ollie's eyes are blown wide when he catches sight of the massive sundae just within reach.

"All this is for me?" His tone is packed with all the wonder in this world.

"Yup." I add extra emphasis on the last letter.

"There's even two cherries on top," he mumbles.

"It wouldn't be the ultimate deluxe without those."

"This is the best place ever. I mean, other than Thicket. And I guess my house. I like school, too. But Dapper Diner rules!" He pumps the air.

"Told you so."

His little fingers curl around the bowl, dragging it closer. "Won't this spoil my dinner?"

"I won't tell if you don't."

He zips his lips, those blue eyes never straying far from the tower of ice cream. "I'm super good at keeping secrets."

"Just this once. This will stay just between us," I whisper.

"But what if I want to come back?"

"Then I'll bring you." I hold up a hand. "Girl Scout's honor." I was never in a troop, but it still counts.

"Promise?"

"Absolutely," I vow.

Hello, safe ground. I've missed you.

I clink my spoon against his. "Enjoy, kiddo."

THE WORDS BEGIN BLENDING ON THE PAGE, AND I SET THE packet down. I rub my eyes, reaching for the mug in front of me. Cold coffee greets my tongue, and I choke it down. I glance at the clock, my shoulders drooping. I've already been at this for five hours.

I'm about to buzz Kathy for a fresh cup when my door swings open. As I raise my glower toward the sound, I'm met with the smug smile of my best friend.

"Good morning," he chirps.

I don't bother masking my scoff. "It's almost noon."

Jordan drops into the leather chair across from me, groaning with gusto. "But it's not yet. You can still get a do-nut in the lounge."

His logic is more ridiculous than the wrinkled shirt he's wearing. He kicks his feet up on the ledge of my desk.

I promptly shove them down. "Have some class, Jord."

He quirks a brow in my direction. "Shit, what's got your nuts in a vice so early?"

"Other than this unfortunate interruption?"

His eyes roll to the vaulted ceiling. "You'd be bored stiff without me stirring the pot."

"Unlikely. But I'm actually quite busy." I gesture to the stacks of files piled high beside me.

Jordan whistles. "Damn, you're buried. That's how you make the big bucks, partner."

I turn my attention to the open folder in front of me. "I'll get it done. Apparently June is a popular month to get divorced. Who knew?"

"I think we're in the peak for weddings." He scratches his chin. "But who the hell knows. Certainly not me."

I scribble a few notes in the margin. "Maybe there's a correlation."

"Don't go all Nerd Christmas on me. I haven't had enough caffeine."

"All right, out with it. What do I owe this pleasant visit to?" I lean back in my seat.

Jordan taps his fingers on the armrest. "Just wanted to check in on my buddy. Make sure you're taking care of the essentials. You know, listening to those natural instincts."

He's fucking snooping, and not being stealthy in the least.

"The detective gig doesn't suit you. But I'm good, thanks. How's business?"

"Oh, you know. A small startup was bought out by a major corp. Same old."

I drag a hand through my hair. "Sounds thrilling."

He makes a see-saw motion with his hand. "One of their associates is pretty hot. Didn't mind the eye candy. Speaking of, how's taffy girl?"

I hang my head. "Oh, here we go."

"What? It's an innocent question."

"Yeah and you're running for president."

Jordan barks out a laugh. "You can try tossing me off the trail, but I'll sniff that shit out."

I wave him off. "I haven't seen her since Wednesday. She watched Ollie for me."

He flings forward, snapping to attention. "I'm sorry, what was that?"

"Braelyn took care of Ollie while I was meeting with Don about the Guttenbarg case."

"The hot shop owner babysat your son?" His jaw is almost hanging on the floor.

I squint at him. "Are you deaf?"

"My mind is blown. I just… wow." He shakes his head. "Were you stoned?"

A dull pounding knocks at my skull. "What's the big deal?"

"You let a woman other than Mary help you."

I blink at him. "So?"

"This is huge." He makes a wide gap between his palms, demonstrating the size of precisely how big.

"It's really not."

Jordan points at me. "You're in denial."

"Dare I ask about what?"

"This Braelyn chick. She's totally getting to you."

"Didn't we already go over this?"

He crosses an ankle over his thigh. "That was last week. There's been new developments that, need I remind, you hid from me."

"You're such a girl," I mutter.

He thrusts his hips. "That's not what your mom said last night."

I slam my hand down, rattling everything within a mile radius. "Fucking low blow, Hughes."

Jordan winces. He has the decency to look guilty as fuck. "That was a dirty hit. I apologize."

I blow out a heavy breath. "It's fine."

"You know I'm just fucking with you."

"Yeah, real fucking funny. Hardy-har-har. Anything else you wanted to discuss during gossip hour?"

"Other than your girlfriend? No."

"Keep the jokes coming, you're on a roll."

"Just admit you can't stop thinking about her."

"Not gonna happen. I prefer to live honestly."

But he's the one speaking truth. Braelyn is rarely far from my thoughts. To make matters worse, she's the prime source of spank-bank material. I can't jack off without seeing her angelic face. Her mossy eyes stare into my soul, begging for more of me. In the darkest hours, she finds me waiting. I give in and let desire take control. Potent heat slithers under my skin.

Fuck, this is the most inconvenient place to get hard. At least my dick is out of sight. The chance of me standing up in the next thirty minutes is real slim. I tug at the collar of my shirt. Dammit, that woman is the devil. I stretch my legs to ease the pinching strain.

A low chuckle bursts through my untimely arousal. I lift my gaze to find Jordan smiling wide. I'm totally busted.

"Fucking called it," my friend gloats.

I don't dignify that with a response. He's goading me. I know this. Doesn't stop my muscles from flexing. My neck is so tight I'm likely to pop a button.

Jordan leans forward on his elbows. The smirk curving his mouth says it all.

"You don't know shit," I finally spit in return.

"It wouldn't bother you if I went to visit Thicket over my lunch break? I'm having a craving for something sweet." He smacks his lips.

The pen in my hand threatens to snap. "Are you done?"

He grunts. "Hardly."

"Is there an actual point to this riveting visit?"

"I came to collect you for the board meeting." He nods toward the conference room. "Ready?"

"Are you done messing around?" I counter.

"For now. The afternoon is fair game."

I stand and take a lingering glance at the piles of untouched case files stacked on my desk. My time could be much better spent. But it's not my place to argue. Yet.

We walk the short distance in silence. Jordan opens the door and motions me inside. Natural light floods the spacious area. Several people are already situated around the glossy wood table. We take our usual seats near the head.

Kathy appears beside me with a steaming mug of fresh coffee and a legal pad. "You took off before I could catch up. Anything else, sir?"

"This should do it. Thanks for bringing these, Kathy." I offer her a curt nod.

She fumbles for a moment, almost tripping over her feet. I raise a brow, and she ducks her head, dashing off without another word.

"Fucking women," I mutter.

"You caught her off guard by being somewhat pleasant for a change." Jordan's observation gives me pause.

"What are you talking about?"

He waves me off. "Never mind."

A hush falls over the room when the three partners trail in. Don, Gary, and Steve are all in their mid-sixties with a stature that demands respect. Their presence alone commands the large group huddled in front of them. One day, hopefully soon, I'll be standing beside them. Fresh blood and all that. I puff out my chest, letting the power infuse me. It's a feeling I'm comfortable with.

"Hello, everyone. Thanks for joining us," Gary begins. "We've had an impressive start to the summer quarter."

All three of them form an intimidating line in front of us. They started the firm, way back when, with a dream and a sliver of capital. I've heard the story a hundred times over bourbon at evening meetings. Steve especially loves to drone on about their glory days.

But standing before me in this stuffy room is a trio of old men past their prime. They spend more time on the golf course than in the office. Not that I blame them. They built this company from the ground up. But retirement is calling them. I'm ready for them to move over and let me lead. Getting partner at twenty-nine would be a feat, even for me. I'm chomping at the proverbial bit to get that promotion before hitting the big three-zero.

Don is waxing on about exceeding last year's gains. I tap my foot to the beat of his wheezing breaths. He points to a dozen charts on the projection screen. The facts and figures blur into a colorful clump. I barely bite back a groan. Don't they understand this is a waste of resources?

I glance around at my co-workers. Most of them are half-asleep, drooling, and with their eyes glazing over. Fucking awesome. Not that I blame them. These meetings are boring as hell and a total snooze-fest. With a motivated team, I can turn this firm around and quadruple our profits. The picture of perfection I'm sketching in my head is ruined by incessant scribbling next to me. I glance over and find Jordan jotting down copious notes. I'm sure my expression is the epitome of flabbergasted.

When did he become interested in keeping track of this shit?

I crane my neck further, the chair squeaking in protest. On closer inspection, he's doodling pieces of candy. What the actual shit is this? Fucking Braelyn, that's what. I never get a reprieve. Ollie and Mary have been hounding me. I can't even get my best friend to stay loyal. I'm fucking surrounded and outnumbered. Unfortunately for them, I'm a stubborn asshole.

Jordan gets an elbow to his ribs from me. He doubles over with a sharp inhale. His narrow gaze finds mine. Serves him right. I smile, proud and wide. Jordan rubs his nose with a middle finger.

I turn my attention to Steve, immediately regretting the decision. The density of his monotone chattering makes my shoulders slouch. A tap to my arm has me twisting back around. Jordan points to his piece of paper. I roll my eyes at his barely legible scrawl.

Just give her a taste.

Passing notes in a board meeting is a new low, even for him. What are we? Twelve? I shoot him a scowl, hating to admit how appetizing his words are. Stale coffee lingers on my tongue. Something sweet would hit the spot. Jordan's words from earlier circle in my brain. I could grab lunch at that dinky cafe next to Braelyn's store. If I happen to see her, so be it.

A loud grunt grinds from my throat. I force out a cough to cover the disapproving sound. Even I don't believe that pile of bull. There's something about Braelyn. No use denying it. Her soulful gaze is cloaked in secrets. The urge to ask her why curls on my tongue more often than not. I want to rip apart the mask she's wearing and see what's hiding beneath. Among other things. But surface shit comes first.

An abrupt clap drags me into awareness. The dynamic trio is wrapping up, and I've managed to miss the majority of their updates. Score one for me. And my decision is made.

"Thanks for your dedication. Keep up the good work, everyone." Gary gives the group a thumbs-up.

Steven flicks his wrist. "Meeting adjourned."

I'm out of my seat before Don opens the door. I hear Jordan chuckling and fight the urge to flip him off. I'm already putting on a show by rushing from the room as if someone's chasing me. An hour ago, I was lecturing him about being professional. The irony isn't hard to grasp.

My shoes skid on the carpet as I dip around the corner. Kathy is flagging me down, but I don't pause.

"Mister Stone? Sir?" Kathy's footsteps follow me toward the elevators. "Darcy Gorden is on hold. She says it's urgent."

"I'll call her back later."

I hear Kathy gasp but don't bother turning to catch the shock that's certainly splashing her features.

"But she sounds upset," she pushes.

"Don't care. I'm not her therapist." An idea strikes me. "Transfer her to Jordan Hughes."

Kathy's hot pursuit stops. "From mergers and acquisitions?"

"Yep, he's her man. Tell him I sent her." I smile, the expression feeling almost comical.

"Where are you going?"

The metal doors slide open in front of me. "To get some taffy."

chapter twelve

BRANCE

PUSH

THE STOP LIGHT FLASHES GREEN, AND I GUN THE ENGINE. I GRIP the steering wheel in a tight fist, cranking hard to the left. Maple Street has never been such a welcome sight. I slam on the brakes, squealing tires announcing my hasty arrival. The mapped route was expected to take twenty-five minutes. I made it in under fifteen. The lead in my foot gets a gold star.

I leave the air conditioner blasting. Without the arctic air pelting my face, I'd likely go up in flames. The damn summer heat is getting to me. I can barely breathe without igniting a fire in my lungs. And my tie is too fucking tight. I loosen the knot, undoing the top button on the collar.

What the fuck am I doing?

Lingering in my car, flipping shit, is far beneath me. This chick has me riled up and I haven't seen her yet. But the upper hand will be mine, as always. I'll get answers and expel this weakness. I'll just stoke Braelyn's temper and solve this shit. In and out. That's it.

I turn off the ignition and step out onto the sidewalk. No one else is parked in front of her store. That'll give us privacy. Burnt rubber stings my nostrils, but all I smell is sweet relief. There's no escaping this.

My stomach is ravenous, but I don't spare the restaurant a glance. They don't serve what I'm after. A switch flips, and I'm on autopilot. My sole target is Thicket and who's waiting within. That glowing lollipop is mocking me, beckoning me inside with each perfectly timed blink. It might as well be a red flag taunting a bull. I hear that loud and shrill.

I yank open the door with zero finesse. The frame clangs against the jamb but I hardly hear it over that damn chime.

Ready or not, Braelyn. I've arrived.

We've never touched, but my skin hums the instant I step into her sanctuary. Freshly spun sugar clings to the air. I breathe in deep, my blood buzzing.

Braelyn is crouching in front of a display case when I stalk in. I'm hyper aware of my surroundings, a predator on the hunt. The fabric of her baggy shorts is stretchy, giving me a nice view. I had a hunch she's been hiding curves. My body is strung taut, ready to snap at any moment. Braelyn is soft, too sweet. I'm going to ruin her. Too bad I can't find it in me to care.

She pivots toward me without rising, a warm smile curving her mouth. I catch the instant she realizes who's stomped into her space. Those green eyes go wide, that smooth jaw slackening. The surprise melts off her face quick enough.

She springs to her feet. "Brance."

My grin is anything but friendly. "Braelyn."

"What're you doing here?"

"Just browsing. Is that a problem?" I toss out the dare, raising the stakes with a quirk to my brow.

"It's one o'clock in the afternoon. Shouldn't you be at work?"

I glance at the window, rays of midday sun filtering in. "I'm taking a long lunch."

"Yet you're here."

"A slight detour."

"One that didn't include picking up Ollie?"

I frown, the thought not occurring to me until this moment. My son will forgive me. Hopefully. "I didn't plan this out. It was a last-minute decision." Lapse in judgement is more like it.

"He's going to be disappointed to find out you stopped by without him."

I wave off her words. "Who says he'll find out?"

Depending on how this turns out, Braelyn might prefer to keep my visit a secret.

She purses those Cupid-bow lips. "Is there something I can help you find?"

I steeple my fingers in front of me, keeping the endless stream of possibilities from spilling out. Braelyn stares at me, waiting for whatever bullshit I decide to spew. But I like to keep her guessing.

Any good sense remaining fizzles as heat coils in my lower body. I shuffle backward until my fingers brush the door's cool glass. I'm about to make a big statement, but pause before pulling the trigger.

A significantly delayed thought occurs to me. I take stock of our positions. Braelyn's stance is defensive. I'm much larger than her. I won't deny being an asshole, but I'm not interested in having this woman fear me. I'm crowding the doorway, blocking her exit. My presence might be considered intimidating. That seed of concern plants itself in my brain and sprouts roots.

"Is it okay that I'm here?"

Braelyn cocks her hip. "Why wouldn't it be? I can't afford to turn away customers. Even if you're surly and rude."

Her snide response is less than helpful. I pull in a lungful of patience and try again.

"Are you scared to be alone with me?" For some reason, her confirmation feels vital.

Her smooth forehead creases. "No? Why would I be?"

I ease toward the door, Braelyn's fiery stare tracking my movements. I flip the lock, then switch off that obnoxious neon sign.

Her narrow gaze flashes at me. "What the hell are you doing?"

"You're closed."

"Are you trying to freak me out on purpose?"

"No. We need a few uninterrupted moments alone." My dick is halfway to solid steel just staring at her.

She parks two fists on her slim hips. "You might have a weak work ethic, but I sure don't. I have a business to run. I can't just fuck off whenever I want."

I steamroll over her snark. "We need to talk."

"I can't imagine anything you're gonna say is important enough to shut my store down."

"Guess I'll have to change your mind."

I stride toward her with purpose. She makes a hasty retreat, knocking into the shelf behind her. Stacks of colorful bowls and matching cups rattle.

"Do you get some sorta rise outta this?" I take a measured step forward.

The furrow between her brows deepens. "Are you speaking in riddles again? Just a heads up—I don't comprehend."

I erase another foot of space between us. "Do you like fucking with my head?" I almost make that word plural but don't want her to bolt.

"Not sure what kind of mental manipulation you think I'm capable of performing. But either way, the answer is no."

"Is that your final answer?" The smirk covering my mouth is ten shades past filthy.

Braelyn blinks at me, her lashes lowering in slow motion. "Um, yeah. Pretty positive about that."

"You're playing a wicked game, Braelyn."

She stays silent for a moment, tugging at the messy bun the top half of her hair is piled up in. Her sandaled feet brush against the floor. I let her stall, enjoying the show. She eventually peers up at me with heavy lids, looking the opposite of innocent.

"Not sure what you mean. I haven't done anything." The breathy undertone to her voice wraps around my cock. Fuck, she's good.

I straighten against the strain in my pants. "Everyone gets a smile but me. Each and every person who walks through that door gets a pleasant greeting. All I get is a fake-ass grin and plastic attitude."

"Pretty sure you've earned that."

"Maybe. But that doesn't matter. I've come to collect some pleasantries."

Her lips twitch. "Didn't realize you noticed."

"Impossible not to. You throw hate my way with rapid fire."

"That's filthy rich coming from the master instigator. I wouldn't have reason to defend myself if you weren't always on the attack."

I hand over some truth. "You seem to make it worse."

"Wonder why."

"Me too."

"What're you gonna do about it?"

I run a palm over my jaw. "Haven't decided."

Temptation dances in her green eyes. "Need suggestions?"

I picture her writhing beneath me. Those green eyes wide and dazed. Long blonde waves spread in every direction. Lips parting in pleasure. Lust pounds in my veins. Hell to the yes.

"Pretty sure I can manage." The words grate from my throat.

"Yeah? Care to share your plans, then?" She's focusing on the bulge behind my zipper. Her interest is even more obvious than the flush racing up her neck.

"That's for you to find out," I murmur.

"Are you just gonna tease me? Or actually do something?" She's bold, and I'm ridiculously aroused.

I narrow the gap between us, and her legs tremble. "I like seeing you squirm."

She lifts her chin. "I enjoy watching the steam billow from your ears."

I find a sliver of space to move closer. "Wanna hear a secret?"

"Always," Braelyn purrs.

"You're a damn distraction."

She snaps her fingers. "Guess it sucks to be you."

Her tactics don't deter me. "All I can think about is wiping that sad look off your face."

"I'm fine, other than these inconvenient visits from you." Her guarded eyes skitter away from mine.

"Don't lie. You want me. Just once would do. I'd turn that frown so far upside down, you'd never stop smiling."

"Cocky asshole." She dips her chin, but I catch the blush staining her cheeks.

I close the distance between us by another foot. "I'll lick your clit until you scream my name. Then it'll be my cock's turn to pleasure you. Over and over until you beg me to stop."

Braelyn clears her throat, but there's no disguising that husky rasp. "You have quite the imagination."

I'm hovering on the edge of her personal space. "That's just the start."

"Thought you weren't volunteering to give me an endorphin boost?"

My shoulder brushes hers when I shrug. "Changed my mind."

"So glad I could persuade you to fall under my voodoo spell." Sarcasm coats her words.

"Happy to hear you finally owning up to it." I sweep some hair off her shoulder, exposing bare skin.

Her breath hitches. "I admit nothing."

"You don't have to. I read it on your beautiful face."

"Maybe that's part of my ploy. I'm just waiting for you to step in my trap."

"You've got a smart mouth." I flick my eyes to her pouty lips.

Her tongue darts out, dragging slowly across them. I track her sinful movement. We're close enough to touch.

"And you know just what to do with it," I add.

The veil lifts from her eyes, those mossy depths reeling me in. I'm helpless against the pull.

"Do you like that about me?" she whispers.

"More than I should," I tell her honestly.

"You don't sound too unhappy about it." Her rapid breaths puff against my neck.

"Because I'm not."

"This sure is an interesting turn of events."

"Don't go turning this into some grand gesture. You'll be sorely disappointed."

Braelyn huffs. "Trust me, I won't lose any sleep over you."

"Tell me what's happening up here?" I gesture at her temple.

She leans into me, ever so slightly. "Too much. I can hardly see straight."

"You dating anyone serious, Braelyn?"

She doesn't speak, just shakes her head.

I press against her, our chests rising and falling in tandem. "Good, that'll make this less complicated."

chapter thirteen

BRAELYN

CHEMISTRY

Who's the hussy exchanging seductive lines with this man? Urging him on, feeding the flames? Oh, that'd be me. I'm having an out-of-body experience. Or this is a dream. Maybe both.

Before I can process this surreal development further, Brance pounces and seals our mouths together. My ass slams against the shelf behind me, but I hardly notice. All I feel is him. He growls against my lips, demanding entry. I open for him without pause and moan when his tongue slides along mine. He tastes like peppermint and midnight fantasies. I'm already certain the combination is highly addictive.

He nips at my bottom lip, only to lick away the sting immediately after. I flutter my lashes at the heady sensation and reach out for something to hold me steady. My palm lands on Brance's torso, the muscle bunching on contact. I curl my fingers into the rich fabric of his shirt. He steps into me, erasing distance I didn't realize was there. His body aligning with mine sets off a round of sparklers in places long abandoned.

I want to question his intentions, but shove that curiosity under layers of arousal. It's not important and won't change anything. I focus on the inferno overhauling my neglected system. Brance surrounds me, stealing any shred of lingering doubt. A roaring blaze ignites under my skin, the thermostat ratcheting to dangerous levels. His mouth demands more of mine. I'm all too willing. He can take everything. Being in this position, feeling this heat, is something I've been depriving myself of. I haven't kissed anyone in years. Not since—

I squeeze my eyes shut and force that thought away. Instead, I clear my mind and get lost in Brance's hard edges. Nothing about this man is soft. Everyone else is cautious with me, almost to a fault. Brance is different. And I like that a lot.

My guard shatters when his body vibrates with a rumble. I angle my head and welcome him deeper. He delves in, taking what I'm offering up so freely to him. I don't realize my mistake until it's too late.

Try as I might to remain locked in this moment, inky memories swoop in. I choke on the past clawing up my throat. The onslaught is just too much, all at once from every direction. A single droplet escapes and zigzags a path into my bliss. Something cracks inside of me, but it doesn't hurt. Just the opposite. I toss off the chains and dive into the pleasure.

When his big palm cups my cheek, our connection sizzles. Brance tenses and rips his mouth off mine. His wild eyes study my face, wet with tears.

"The fuck?"

A jolt zips up my spine at his gruff tone. I tug him toward me by his tie. "I'm fine. Keep kissing me."

He begins prying the silk from my grasp. "The hell I will. You're crying."

I strengthen my hold. "It's nothing. Please don't stop. I need this."

Brance shakes his head. "Are you stoned? You must believe I'm some sort of sadist. Sorry to disappoint, but even I have boundaries. This is a hard limit for me."

"Please, Brance," I beg again. "I'll explain later. Kiss me. Make me break. I wanna see stars again."

He hesitates but I feel the moment his body wins against whatever conscience is trying to stake claim. The fight leaves his flexed muscles. He dips down and murmurs, "You better tell me all of it."

I'm nodding even before he finishes speaking. He's not asking and the why will come eventually. There are far more important matters to address, right the eff now. I yank on his tie, and Brance folds around me. When his lips press against mine, I'm not a hollow shell pieced together by sorrow and pain. In this instant, I'm a woman being desired and devoured. I get seriously turned on by it.

"You want to feel?"

I manage a jerky nod.

"You'll tell me if it's too much?"

"Yes," I murmur. The fact that he's checking on me, asking about crossing this line, somehow makes this more tender and intimate. But I'm not fooling myself. When this bubble pops, we'll return to business as usual. I'll ride this wave until we crash.

"Might as well make it real fucking good." His rasp ricochets off my parted lips, and I swallow it down.

I shiver when Brance's hand begins to wander. His fingers drift along the bare skin of my inner thigh. The loose fit of my shorts grants him easy enough access. I sag against the shelf when he reaches my center. Brance shoves my panties to the side with masterful precision. He glides through my slick heat, turning me into a quivering mess. He doesn't waste time teasing with me, zeroing in on my clit with sure strokes.

Brance rips his mouth away with a snarl. "You're wicked. This shouldn't be happening."

"But it is," I whisper.

"We should stop."

I reinforce my hold on him. "No, that's the last thing we should do."

"You make me weak," he admits.

I arch my back. "Good."

"I can't do this with you. There are complications." His words are harsh and meant to sting, but my body only burns hotter. A slice of forbidden never sounded good until now.

"Regret can come later." It's my turn first for once. That selfish bitch of an emotion has stolen enough from me.

His lips ghost over the corner of mine. "Easy for you to say."

Rather than stop, Brance's fingers pick up speed and take me higher. Molten heat boils in my lower belly, and I'm almost there.

I choose to stay silent, letting him fight through this battle on his own. When he presses his mouth against mine, I smile into the kiss.

"Fuck, you're too much," he mumbles.

I snag his bottom lip between my teeth. "You're welcome."

His tongue and fingers follow the same swirling pattern. I'm spinning past the point of recognition. I widen my stance and shamelessly rock into his touch. Brance presses his hardness into me. I garble out some semblance of a gasp at the size of him. But I'm more than likely imagining things.

"You're not the only cocky one," he chuckles.

Shit. Did I say that out loud?

His mouth veers off my lips, traveling lower. Sucking

down my jaw and neck. I tip my chin up, giving him a wider expanse to explore. His tongue lashes at me. He drags his teeth across the sensitive skin of my throat. I'm being torn in half, split open to make room for a new me to flood in. The one who lets handsome men in suits ravish her and plead for more.

I spear my hands into his hair and tug him closer. Brance responds by pushing forward until we're plastered together. In a rare show of concern, he cradles the back of my head so it doesn't ram into the shelf. The move makes me want to straddle his lap.

Before I can suggest it, Brance doubles his efforts on my clit. He adds another finger into the mix and my brain turns to mush.

"Oh, f-fuck," I wheeze. "I'm g-gonna come."

"About fucking time," he growls into my ear. His lips return to mine for a bruising kiss. Tingles shoot up my legs, and I'm tripping over the edge. With his final swipe along my slit, I explode with a soundless scream. Streaks of white blur my vision. I'm a ball of cosmic energy soaring straight into the galaxy, and the stars have never been brighter.

Hello, twinkling goodness. I've missed you.

The haze slips away, and I float down from the clouds. Brance wrenches his mouth off mine. I blink into awareness. His panting breaths caress my lips. My chest rises and falls rapidly against his, the pounding of our hearts echoing between us.

"I need to stay away from you," he mutters.

I almost laugh considering our current position. "You should probably put forth a bit more effort."

Brance's expression hardens and I hold my breath, waiting for the inevitable blow. I've come to expect them, almost look forward to his scorn. Pushing his buttons is an intense shot of adrenaline. Watching the blue fire build in his gaze gets my blood pumping hotter. He's bringing me back to life without even trying.

We stare at each other, the silence between us stretching. I'm prepared to wait him out. I won't be the one to explain whatever just happened. After another moment, Brance drops his hold on me and steps back. I use the opportunity to check him out. The man in front of me has become ten times hotter since striding through my door. I like seeing him disheveled.

Brance's suit is deliciously rumpled. A naughty gleam lingers in his eyes. Evidence of our kiss lingers on his lips, slightly swollen and red. His hair sticks up in sexy disarray, sections pointing in every direction. I curl my fingers, hiding the guilty offenders. But combing through those silky strands will be committed to memory. I want to do that again, multiple times. But I tamp my trampy side down. For now.

He makes quick work of straightening his tie. "You owe me a story."

A boulder drops in my gut. "Now?"

Brance sweeps the brown locks off his forehead, erasing more proof of our tryst. "Nah, gotta get back to the office."

"Already?" I'm still recovering from my orgasm.

He smooths the wrinkles from his shirt. "My schedule leaves no time for deviations. I have a full calendar every day. This indiscretion cost me several hours. I'll be working late to catch up."

"Was that a dig at me?"

"Does it matter?"

"Really, Brance? Just like that?"

"Were you expecting something else?"

I open my mouth, then close it. Was I? How could I? Brance smirks at my extended silence.

"That's what I thought." He tops it off with a wink for good measure.

"You're such an—"

"Asshole. Yeah, got it. I don't have time to rehash the details."

Any traces of euphoria left trickling through my system vanish. I bolt upright and cross my arms. "Glad you're being open and honest."

Brance takes a bow. "My pleasure."

"Feel free to show yourself out." I motion toward the entrance.

He takes a few backward steps. "Already on my way. And don't worry, you'll be hearing from me."

In the next beat, only five short minutes after flipping my world upside down, Brance turns and walks out.

I TUCK SEVERAL SIGNED CONTRACTS INTO A FOLDER, ADD IT TO THE pile, and slide everything across my desk. Another case wrapped up in record time. I shift in my chair, the gears protesting with a creak. It's barely noticeable over the deafening hoot from my client sitting in front of me.

A shit-eating grin spreads across Doug Thompson's face. He's liable to crack a cheekbone with that gleeful expression. Not that I blame the guy. We just finalized his divorce. As of today, he's a free agent.

He whips open the file and chuckles. "Damn, thanks again, Brance. I can't say it enough. You're a shark."

"Just doing my job."

"And you're damn good at it. You definitely followed the correct path in life."

I offer a half smile, chewing on the compliment. Ripping couples apart isn't glamorous. Most can't handle the conflict and confrontation on a daily basis. That's never been a problem for me. Considering the hostile environment I was raised in, it's a miracle there's an ounce of compassion left inside of me. But I accept his praise with a nod.

"Never considered another career," I tell him honestly. If my father had a decent lawyer, our lives would be drastically different for the better. I'd probably be a fucking preschool teacher. But I was destined to save sorry saps like Doug Thompson.

"Sure am glad my neighbor held onto your card. He couldn't sing your praises any louder. And he's not one to toss shit around lightly."

I scratch the back of my neck. Jovial bullshitting isn't my favorite. "I'm really happy to hear that. Recommendations are much appreciated."

Doug settles deeper in his chair, making no move to leave. "Hell, I'll tell all my buddies if their marriages take a nosedive."

"That's all I ask." I drum my fingers on the armrest.

He scrubs over his salt-and pepper-whiskers. "You can't plan for that shit, but it's good to be locked and loaded just in case. Having you in my arsenal before those damn vows would have been handy. I learned my lesson the hard way."

"But you're all fixed up now. Get out there and enjoy yourself." I almost stand to walk him out, but hold off a moment longer.

Doug leans forward. "Can I take you out for a drink? We've got reason to celebrate."

"I appreciate the offer, but there're some loose ends that still need tying up. I'll be stuck here finishing up for a bit." I give the stack of files next to me a harsh pat.

"Well, shit. I guess that gumption is what makes you so successful."

"No rest for this attorney." I rock in my seat.

"Glad I went into real estate."

I grunt. "Smart man."

He rises to his feet. "I'll get outta your hair. Thanks again for everything, Brance."

"My pleasure. Let me know if you're ever in need of my services again."

"You've got a deal." He extends a hand, and we shake on it. After a salute, he spins on a heel and heads out.

Fucking finally.

Once the door closes behind him, I allow my shoulders to sag. Doug was the final name on my long list for the day, but the night is young. I still have a load of work ahead of me, courtesy of Braelyn and her enticing allure. That woman is guaranteed to cause trouble. Hell, she already has. But I'm not done with her yet.

I grab a file off the towering stack, flip it open, and separate the packets. There're custody claims, a default judgement, child support orders, addendums to original agreements, and a slew of sloppy mediation records. Of course I had to choose the most complicated case to start with. What a fucking mess. After sorting through this disaster, I attempt to make sense of it all. Ten minutes later, I've read the same paragraph twenty times. I can't concentrate, and all the letters are merging together. The office is too damn quiet. Everyone already tucked tail and ran home.

Usually I'd be following close behind. It's getting late, and Ollie is probably eating dinner. A swift slice of guilt stabs at me in the gut. I should be the one preparing his meal, not stuck in the office until it's pitch-black outside. I groan into the cradle of my palms. Once I'm partner, things will be different. That's the promise I rely on. I'm almost there. I just have to push a bit harder.

A grin tugs at my lips when I think of putting more pressure on a certain blonde. I glance down at my fingers, flex and release. I've long since washed traces of Braelyn away.

But I swear her scent still lingers. Tangy and sweet, like the woman herself. She's a fucking puzzle I'm going to enjoy solving.

The mossy green of Braelyn's eyes fills my vision, and I let the afternoon resurface in my mind. I could have hung around Thicket and coddled her a bit. That's not my style, but I found myself wanting to. That's the main reason I ripped myself away and took off. It wasn't a lie that I had clients stacking up, but they can always wait.

I didn't move fast enough, catching the disappointment spreading over her features. Braelyn's frown is a fierce weapon. It made me want to bury my face between her thighs until she was screaming again. Fuck, she tastes better than the candy in her store.

Shaking those inconvenient desires away, I drag my focus to the papers strewn in front of me. That's how I manage to waste the next few hours. I bounce between cursing Braelyn's name and scanning over case notes.

A tentative knock echoes across the silent room. I drop the folder and check my watch. It's almost eight o'clock.

"Come in," I call.

Kathy pokes her head in. "Do you need anything before I leave?"

I figured she'd already left. Guess I'm not the only one burning the midnight oil. "What're you still doing here?"

"I had some invoicing to wrap up."

It seems this month is rough for everyone. I wave her off. "I'm good. See you in the morning."

She hesitates in the doorway, gnawing on her lip. "Sir?"

I lift my brow. "Problem?"

"There's a Miss Miller here to see you."

I'm sure my jaw hits the floor. What the fuck? I brush off the surprise and school my expression. "Show her in."

Braelyn appears out of thin air and steps into my office.

She's wearing the same outfit as earlier. Those sinful shorts taunt me as she strides further into my space.

I lean back in my chair, stretching my legs wide. "Here to return the favor?"

She bites the corner of her bottom lip. "Um, not quite."

"Need another go first?" I scrub a palm over my mouth. "Let me clear off a spot for you to sit."

Her breath hitches. "I-I really didn't come for that."

My chuckle is dark. "No shit. Pick a chair." I point to the matching set in front of my desk.

Braelyn plops down with a huff. "Thanks for the warm welcome."

"What can I say? My filter is weak on the best days. All bets are off when I'm stunned."

"You're not the only one who can drop by unexpected," she tosses out with a flip of her hair.

"Touché." I smirk, nearly adding a wink into the mix. "How'd you know I'd still be around?"

She lifts a shoulder. "Took a chance. I also recall someone not so subtly telling me they'd be working late."

I gesture around my sanctuary. "Guess your gamble paid off."

Braelyn flicks her gaze from one wall to another, taking in every square inch. I imagine viewing my office through her eyes. Gray carpet, dark furniture, tall windows, black curtains, a colossal desk. Can't forget the imposing man glaring at her.

She returns my stare. "This space is very fitting for you."

I shouldn't ask, but sensible rationality doesn't exist where this woman is involved. "How so?"

"Broody and crass, calculating and impersonal." She points to an abstract painting that resembles a Rorschach.

"Did you come all this way to insult me?"

"I thought this was me returning the favor?"

Fucking hilarious, this one. "I'm a busy man, Braelyn. I don't need to waste more time going back and forth with you. We both know how this goes."

"But it's okay for you to disrupt my routine?" She toys with the ends of her hair, and I imagine wrapping the length around my fist. Coming from her, even this insignificant action is a fucking distraction.

I see us getting nowhere, real quick, so I motion her on. "You came to spill your secrets. Out with it."

Braelyn flinches, and another knife lodges in my stomach. I almost groan. All I fucking need is for this chick to reach my soft spot. That place is solely reserved for Ollie. I steel my resolve with a deep inhale.

"I never made a will," she murmurs.

The chair creaks when I shift and lean forward on a bent elbow. "Okay? Not sure what that has to do with anything."

She clears her throat. "I was hoping you could help me."

My scoff might as well be a shout. "That's not my department."

Braelyn rolls her eyes. "Yes, I'm well aware. But this is a law firm full of attorneys. Surely there's someone who can help me."

I tap a finger to my chin. "Hmm, and yet you're sitting in *my* office."

"You're my jumping-off point. I figure you can guide me in the correct direction."

That earns her a laugh brimming with thunder and contempt. "Wow, you're a shitty salesman."

She's off the chair and on her feet before I can track the swift movement. "You're right. This was a mistake."

The fact Braelyn doesn't take my shit turns me on in a big fucking way. Her sassy words send a spike of arousal straight to my dick. But if I'm honest, almost everything this woman does gets me going.

I point to the seat she just vacated. "Sit down."

She crosses her arms, one of those cheap flip-flops tapping the floor. "I don't take orders from you."

Add temper tantrums to that rapidly growing list. I'm sporting a semi under my desk. I grind my molars. "Please."

Braelyn parks her ass on the very edge, not bothering to get comfortable. "Satisfied?"

"How old are you?"

A dent marks her forehead. "Twenty-five. Why?"

I twirl a pen around my fingers. "Just wondering why you're already putting a will together. That's very… responsible."

She lifts a hand to her chest. "Holy shit. Was that a compliment?"

"Don't read too much into it. What made you decide to do this now?"

"Why do you care? I thought you don't handle this sort of thing."

I concentrate on her stoic expression. "I typically don't, but we aren't in the habit of turning away business. I can get the ball rolling if you're willing to cooperate."

"Because I'm the one being difficult," she retorts.

"We'll agree to disagree for the sake of keeping things moving ahead. Tell me why you're concerned about handling this in the immediate future."

Braelyn glances out the window. "Life can end before you're ready. I'd like to be prepared."

"That's morbid." A thorny vine loops around my ankle and cinches tight. I jerk my knee and kick off the eerie sensation.

She picks at a thread on her shirt, still avoiding my eyes. "So is reality."

"Sounds like you have experience on the matter."

She blinks and looks away. "You might say that."

The sound of inevitable doom clangs in my ears. I steer this sinking ship into calmer waters. "We'll discuss this further over dinner."

Braelyn's gaze snaps to mine. "What?"

"I haven't eaten. You could always use two or three extra portions. Mary was already planning to stay late and get Ollie in bed." I'm already shoving all the loose paperwork into a haphazard stack.

"That's not necessary. I just want to set up a will."

"Which is a complex process. We can start tonight." I stare at her, my stony expression practically begging for an argument.

Braelyn collapses into her chair. "Fine. Whatever."

I stand and step out from behind my desk. "I was mostly done when you showed up. Let's hit the road. Have you been to Pour Spout?"

"Never heard of it."

"We'll go there. Good food, better atmosphere. We'll be able to talk without shouting."

"Super," she mutters.

"I'll drive. You can ride with me."

Her head whips back and forth so fast she transforms into a colorful blur. She visibly gulps. "U-uh, n-no. That's okay. I-I want to take my car."

I furrow my brow, an array of dots scatter in front of me without connecting. "Are you okay?"

Braelyn's chomping on her bottom lip but otherwise appears frozen. "Y-yeah. I have issues being a passenger. It's a long story. I need to be in control of the vehicle."

If I look close enough, there's perspiration dotting her brow. She's haunted by something. I can almost see ghosts swirling in her eyes. Her sheer terror is probably connected to the accident she mentioned before. She has a similar air of panic surrounding her.

I edge toward the door. "All right, forget I offered. Drive yourself."

"Thank you," she whispers.

This meek version of her awakens a piece of me that I'm uncomfortable giving a voice to. I'd like to dissolve that weakness in a tub of acid. Since that's not readily accessible, I lash out the easy way.

"Before you get any ideas, this isn't a date. It's a means to an end." I clutch my keys, their teeth digging in with a sharp bite.

Braelyn seems to snap out of the trance, her gaze clearing. She grabs her purse and shuffles over to me. "Wow, way to sell me on it. I can probably find a different lawyer who'll make this ordeal less painful."

I hitch a thumb over my shoulder into the dark corridor. "By all means, go get one. You'll still owe me the truth behind your extreme reactions."

She huffs but doesn't dispute what we both know is true. We make quite the fucked-up pair. I decide to let her off the hook, for now. Braelyn gasps when I switch off the lights and we're blanketed in darkness. A dry chuckle escapes me.

I yank open the door and guide her into the hallway. "Stick by me, and you won't get lost."

chapter fifteen

BRAELYN

TALE

I FOLLOW BRANCE ALONG THE WINDING ROAD AND ATTEMPT TO get my breathing under control. My palms keep slipping off the wheel, ensuring I remain hovering over the edge of a nuclear meltdown. Something sharp shifts inside of me. My heart is still pounding at an unhealthy rate. Why couldn't I let him drive me? It's such a simple, mundane thing. But to me it's often the crux of a panic attack. Just thinking about it makes me twitchy, which is the last thing I need at the moment.

Without looking away from his taillights, I wipe the sweat from my hands. We're traveling far below the speed limit. I'm not sure if Brance is always a terribly cautious driver or if this is for my benefit. Either way, I appreciate the snail pace. My days of joyriding are long gone.

A whoosh of toxic air blasts from my lungs when we pull into a mostly empty lot. Arriving at our destination is a soothing balm over my blistering skin. The trip was under ten minutes, effectively slamming a lid on further threat. That suits me just fine.

I park in front of the understated building and glance around. I figured Brance was more of the swanky restaurant type. This place looks like an industrial factory. But there's a lake out back. Must be one of the perks. Finding beauty in concrete blocks is more challenging.

This will be fun.

After turning off the ignition, I leave the comfort of my air conditioning and wait for Brance to approach me. The temperature is balmy, even as the sun slips further down on the horizon. I shake out my hands, chasing off the last fringes of fear. It's a small miracle I didn't have a full-blown episode.

"Did you handle the journey all right?" There's a hint of a grin lifting Brance's lips.

I dust myself off. "Still in one piece. Thanks for your concern."

"As your interim attorney, I take a sliver of responsibility. Wouldn't want any guilt on my conscience."

"Heaven forbid," I mutter.

Brance dips his chin. "That's the idea."

I make the mistake of looking at him and get a bit tongue-tied. The spotlights give him a celestial glow. He ditched the suit jacket and tie. The collar of his shirt is unbuttoned, the sleeves rolled up. My focus drifts to his exposed forearms. Tan and dusted with dark hair, they're sculpted with lean muscle to fend off opponents. Even with nightfall fast approaching, I notice two prominent veins snaking down his left one. My fingers twitch to trace those viral lines. Gah, he's too sexy.

The sound of a throat clearing yanks me from my erotic reflection.

"Still in a state of shock?"

I snap my gaze away from his arm-porn. "Uh, no. I'm good. Yeah, really great."

Brance chuckles, and the sound makes my belly do a stupid flippy-dip. "Seems that way. Shall we go in or continue loitering?"

I gesture to the entrance. "Lead the way."

"Ladies first."

His palm settles on the small of my back. The simple touch settles me more than I appreciate. After one small taste, my body is turning against me. Freaking harlot.

When we step inside, I do a double-take. The interior is stunning and unexpected to the extreme. Warm shades of red and orange blend seamlessly with light wood accents. Cozy booths frame the perimeter. The center consists of tables with comfy chairs. There's an oval shaped bar along the far wall. I let my mouth hang open while taking it all in.

"Pretty sneaky, huh? Keeps the riff-raff off their case. Only those willing to take a chance get to appreciate this hidden gem." Brance's voice is missing the harsh edge, exposing a smooth timbre. If I didn't know better, I'd think he was teasing with me.

I peer up at him. "And how'd you find this treasure chest?"

"A client recommended it for a meeting."

"Thanks for paying it forward."

He scratches the fresh stubble on his jaw. "I like to be decent every now and then. Makes me more mysterious."

I nudge him with my elbow. "I'll get back to you on that one."

A hostess shows us to a booth in a shadowed corner. If Brance wasn't the man beside me, I'd assume we had an intimate evening ahead. In our case, there's nothing other than bumps and bruises waiting.

He motions for me to choose a side, then sits down on the other. A server drops off glasses of water, and I eagerly take one. The cool liquid eases my throat. I shift along the leather seat and grab the drink menu. I'm going to need wine. A single glass will do. Any more than that, and I'll have to stick around until the alcohol wears off. That would defeat the purpose.

I'm busy looking at everything that isn't Brance. His foot taps mine, drawing my purposely wandering attention.

"Nervous?"

I tuck some hair behind my ear. "No. Should I be?"

"That depends." His blue eyes twinkle under the pendant lamp.

"Do I dare ask on what?"

Brance rests his folded hands on the table. "How much you're willing to share with me."

My stomach seizes at the impact of his words. I shove past the knot, inhaling the longest breath possible. "Can we order first?"

"I recommend anything on tap. They brew their own."

I shake my head. "I prefer grapes, especially of the white variety."

"Whatever gets you talking faster," he mutters.

When the server returns, I throw caution to the wind and get a stout.

"Nice choice."

The pause that follows is nine months pregnant. I drum my nails on the glossy wood edging. Brance watches my fingers with rapt focus. When our drinks arrive, we share a sigh that borders on comical.

I take a very unladylike gulp of my beer. The dark color is appealing, but the taste is better. "This is delicious. It's so rich and thick."

He wags his brows. I snort into my glass, bracing for the worst.

"Sounds like what you were grinding on earlier."

That earns him a genuine laugh. The man doesn't

disappoint. That's for certain. "Yeah, yeah. That was shameless."

Dimples dent both of Brance's cheeks. I never noticed those panty-killers before. Guess that's where Ollie gets them from. Good grief, could he be more attractive?

"I'm not complaining." He lifts his beer to mine.

I accept his cheers with a clink of our glasses. "What a relief."

Brance takes a long swig. "Since we're on the subject, what's with the tears?"

I glance at the ceiling and exhale the weight on my chest. There's no point trying to avoid this topic. The man sitting across from me has proven to be quite persistent.

"Promise not to be a brutal asshole after I tell you all my shit?" I shoot him a fierce glare.

He holds up a palm. "I'll do my best to curb the snark."

"Thanks." My smile is forced, wobbling at the corners.

Brance watches me, his eyes bright and full of mirth. I drop my gaze from his. Getting lost in those blue depths will make trudging into the past more difficult. There's a candle at the center of the table. The flame makes a safe focal point. I allow the numb to take hold. Ice clots my veins, the freezing layer familiar and almost comforting.

"I met Devon my freshman year of college. We ate lunch in the cafeteria at the same time and eventually got to talking. He was a junior and very charming, swept me right off my feet. We had a lot in common, especially when it came to escaping our families. Devon came from nothing. He was always trying to prove himself. He believed that landing the right job and getting a big paycheck would solve everything. Others would finally accept him. It didn't matter that I always had. He was searching to fulfill that bigger picture."

My beer trembles, vibrating on the wood surface. I belatedly realize the hand holding my glass is shaking. "It became obvious Devon had a very skewed mentality. But I understood that. Hell, I lived it. It's hard to pull yourself up when everyone shoves you down. We sink or swim, right? Well, Devon worked himself to exhaustion on the daily. It got worse after he graduated."

Why am I so parched? I lick my lips, a slow stroke to wet the dry skin. After taking a sip of my drink, I dig deeper. "Devon got hired by a huge corporation. He was one of thousands, but opportunities to climb the ladder were handed out like candy. That was all it took for him to go all in. The change started slow, but soon enough I'd go days without hearing from him. I didn't let it bother me because he had good reason. Plus, he always made it up to me. We worked through the strains and looked forward to our future."

Brance remains silent across from me and I'm thankful for it. I guess he's respectful when it truly matters.

I pull in a slow breath and dive under. "The night of the accident, Devon was taking me somewhere special. There was a surprise he wanted to share with me. I could tell something was off with him. He was acting more unsettled than usual. I remember his knee bouncing so fast while he drove well beyond the speed limit. Devon blamed it on stress and some big project. When I pressed him on it, he admitted to taking caffeine pills. Apparently he wasn't sleeping well and wanted to be alert for our date."

The restaurant is quiet, allowing me to hear everything from that night. Tires squealing and the windshield shattering. The blast of shards splintering pierce at my ears. Smoke fills my nostrils when I inhale. I cough, but it only gets worse. Searing heat blurs my vision as I watch it all unravel.

"The turn was sharp and sudden. Devon didn't see it coming. The car flipped several times before crashing into a tree. The impact was on his side, killing him instantly. I was stuck in the car for hours. My vocal cords were ripped to shreds when they found me. I'll never forget that feeling of being trapped. But the vision of him hanging lifeless in front of me is what keeps me up at night."

Brance's face has paled considerably, but I don't let that stop me.

I wipe the tears off my cheeks. "The police found an engagement ring in his jacket pocket. Devon never got the chance to ask. I lost my shit when the doctor handed me that blue velvet box. He'd left me something to always remember him by. I slipped the band on my finger and didn't take it off for a year. I wasn't his fiancé, but wearing that ring meant everything to me. It became a symbol of him, I guess. My therapist said that was a normal reaction. Holding onto the possibility or whatever. Makes me sound more crazy. But having something of him close gave me a significance to grasp. Devon loved me enough to buy a diamond. That's the type of boost a very grief-stricken girlfriend needs."

I sniff and finish off my beer. "After the accident, they diagnosed me with post-traumatic stress disorder. Can't leave out insomnia and anxiety. Pretty much all the good shit. I was in therapy to learn how to cope and deal with my new normal. The first year was horrific. I was a shell. My friend, Sadie, is solely responsible for keeping me alive. I'm better these days. Most of the time, I can control the episodes. I still suffer from panic attacks, nightmares, and flashbacks. But not nearly as often." I slouch in the booth, depleted and done.

Brance scrubs over his mouth. "I'm not sure what to say, which might be a first for me."

I give him a watery smile. "I'll accept that."

"Shit, Braelyn." He grunts and shakes his head. "The fact you're sitting here is incredible. You could have died."

"So I've been told."

"And you've been able to move forward?"

I shrug. "Mostly. I have certain triggers."

"Like riding shotgun?" he asks.

"Driving in general." I feel my lips wobble, recalling that dreadful conversation at Thicket.

Brance nods. "That explains a lot."

"The triggers are a rolodex, spin the dial and see what pops up. Trauma is fucking hilarious like that. I'm a mess." I trace a liquid ring on the table.

"No, you're not."

"And you're just trying to be nice."

He barks out a laugh. "We both know that's not true. Not sure I've tried to spare anyone's feelings other than Ollie."

"Yeah, that was pushing it." A quiet giggle escapes me.

"For what it's worth, I'm really fucking sorry."

"Thanks. It's super tough, but that's my life."

"You survived," he murmurs.

I suck my bottom lip between my teeth. "Barely."

Brance stretches an arm out along the back of his seat. The massive watch on his wrist gleams and catches my attention. There's a reflection from the overhead light, the possibility of blinding someone at any given moment is very likely. I follow the glowing circle while our silence stretches. My mind is a soggy sponge. I'm not sure where to go from this point.

From within my murky sludge, a flicker of sunshine breaks through and rises to the surface. The illumination spreads, sparks igniting with a simple strike of flint. The heat cocoons around me, but the emptiness remains.

I'm flayed open, exposing the most vulnerable parts. It only seems fair to return the favor, asking him for a piece of his why. I glance up at Brance from under my lashes. "Will you tell me about Ollie's mom?"

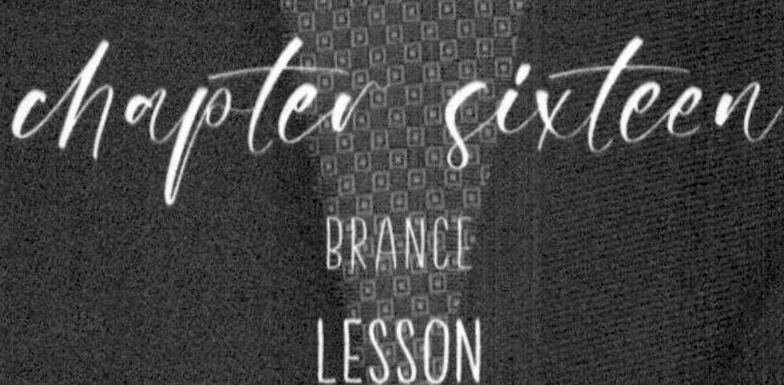

Braelyn's question is a cheap shot straight to the nuts. But I've been expecting it all the same. I don't blame her. She just finished ripping her wounds open. The least I can do is spill a few guts of my own. I won't let her bleed all over the floor alone.

There's already pressure building in my skull. I'd rather sleep on a bed of nails than talk about Veronica. She's been out of my life for over five years. If I had my way, her name would be torn apart and diluted until unrecognizable. But that bitch always finds a way to haunt me.

I press on my temple, but the pounding gets worse. "For the record, this is my least favorite topic to discuss. And that includes my mother, which is another clusterfuck entirely. Consider yourself lucky I'm even considering it."

"You don't have to," she murmurs.

I barely catch the words, leaning closer to eliminate mis-understanding. "I'm well aware, thank you." I release a harsh exhale. "Shit, sorry. Thinking about her makes me meaner than usual."

She offers a limp nod. "Maybe we should skip it."

The green of Braelyn's eyes is muted and dull. Fuck. If telling her about the nightmare that is Ollie's mother will lift the shadows, I'll rank us even.

"Nah, I'm already in the fucking trench." I rake through my hair, tugging on the roots until it burns. "Might as well make it count."

The server stops over, and I dismiss her with a flick. There's no chance in hell I could eat after Braelyn's story. Add in a putrid scoop of Veronica, and my stomach goes on strike. Revolt. Fight back. I'm more likely to blow chunks. My appetite has been replaced with a revolting gurgle that might require antacid. That describes Veronica quite perfectly.

Braelyn quirks a brow. "Are you all right? You look a little green."

I swat her concern away. "I'll be fine when this is over with."

A muscle clicks in her jaw. "Am I that impossible to be around?"

I run a hand over my mouth to hide my sudden grin. That damn sass is too sexy. "Call off the firing squad. I'm not referring to you."

"Hopefully you understand why that's my first assumption."

"Yeah, sure. It's a decent guess. But in this case, you're wrong."

"Could've fooled me," she mutters. My patience is a ticking bomb. "The window of opportunity is closing. You want to hear about her or not?"

"If your fangs will only get sharper, the answer is no."

I point at her with my middle finger. "Now it's your turn to curb the snark."

"Gentlemen first," Braelyn retorts.

"Good thing there aren't any at this table."

She huffs. "You're impossible."

"That's my job."

Her gaze flares, the green almost electric. Ah, there she is. Mission fucking accomplished. She parts her lips, and I hold up a hand. Braelyn pins me with a glare, but remains silent.

"Shit, where do I start?" I blow out a long breath. "I met Ollie's mother at a bar near campus. Veronica was striking—beautiful but frigid. It seemed fitting that she was studying medicine. We were dedicated to our fields. There was no time for relationships, not that I ever wanted one. We'd hook up whenever our schedules aligned, which was rare. That suited me fine. Our arrangement was easy and convenient."

I pinch the bridge of my nose. "We kept this going for almost two years, until Veronica got pregnant. The day she found out was the true beginning of an agonizing end. The arguing started almost immediately. The last thing I wanted was a woman connected to me for the rest of my life. But that baby was mine, and I was prepared to raise him. Veronica felt the complete opposite. She planned to have an abortion the moment a doctor approved the procedure. Don't get me wrong. I'm supportive of the woman's right to choose. Unless, of course, that decision involved killing my child."

An erratic stampede thunders in my ears. There's not a reality for me where Ollie doesn't exist. It's simply not a feasible thought. I clench my eyes shut and picture his smiling face. He's the only good I have.

Braelyn's hands are curled into trembling fists. She looks ready to spit bullets. Not sure if her expression is aimed at me or Veronica. I'm guessing the latter. Either way, she gives me the fire power to continue traveling along this road paved in cruel memories.

"By some miracle, I convinced Veronica not to terminate the pregnancy. It was a bloody battle. She made me miserable for nine months. Carrying him full term was a death sentence to her. As punishment, she set out to humiliate me whenever physically possible. She could write the book on manipulation. Veronica held everything over my head. Nothing was off-limits. She'd come to my office. Hound me at home. Come to the bar when I was out with friends. Wake me up at three o'clock in the morning with a list of demands. If I didn't give, she'd threaten to call the clinic. That bitch had their number on speed-dial."

A tremor snakes up my limbs, making me shiver. "Veronica used our baby as a weapon against me. Once she was further along and showing, things went from bad to unbearable. She went legit psycho. I honestly don't understand how she ever appealed to me. Whenever we were in public together, she'd fight with me on purpose. The ugly kind, like a wreck you can't look away from. I was the worthless bastard who knocked her up. She let anyone within listening range hear about it. I'm thankful Veronica was stuck in town for med school. Even though I was in hell with her around, the alternative would have been worse. She would've left just so I'd have to chase her. Her tolerance for me shrank to nothing by the time Ollie was born."

I swallow the bile rising in my throat. "He was wailing with all his might, but Veronica wouldn't even look at him. She left the hospital mere hours after giving birth. The doctors strongly advised against it, but there was no reasoning with her. She took off without a word, and I let her go. When the door slammed behind her, it was disturbingly clear that Veronica would only be known as an egg donor."

The restless air shifts and settles around me. A familiar numbness seeps into my pores, the haze of indifference expanding. "I had Ollie, and that's all I cared about. For his sake,

I try to remain civil whenever he brings her up. He wants to know about her and why she left. It's the hardest thing I've ever struggled with. I could give a rip how she treated me. But Ollie deserves better." My exhale is rough, purging the remaining debris left inside of me.

"So, there you have it." I dust off my palms. "Veronica shoved my empathy and compassion through a meat grinder. That shit is a pulverized mass, hideous and beyond saving. Not that there was much to begin with. Living happily ever after is a myth. That notion belongs in fairy tales and bedtime stories. Reality is a twisted, mangled version. The sanctity of marriage is a farce. My parents were stellar models for that sham. If the concept wasn't already lost on me, Veronica would have finished the task. That's what makes me a successful divorce lawyer."

Braelyn's throat bobs with a gulp. "Well, now I'm the speechless one."

"We're fucked up, huh?"

She nods. "Sadly, yes. I'm not sure who's worse off."

She is, of course. But I don't dare voice that. "It's not a competition."

"No shit?" Her eyelashes flutter shut, hiding that stunning gaze. But those mossy pools are fixated on me again a moment later. "Is Veronica gone for good?"

I sneer at the sound of that woman's name spilling from Braelyn's lips. "She's in California for her residency. I'd prefer Australia or Africa, but a few thousand miles between us is good enough for now."

"Do you think she'll try to gain custody of Ollie?" The wobble in her voice is a punch to my solar plexus.

Thick tar gurgles in my gut, staining everything with a black hue. "She'd be batshit to try taking me on. I'm a damn good attorney. My case against her would be bulletproof. Veronica wouldn't survive the battle I'd rain down on her. All she cares about is her career. I'm sure she'll make the best surgeon. Ripping out hearts with her bare hands is a specialty."

"I don't get that. What kind of life will she have?"

I'm quiet for a moment. Past and present collide with the future in my mind. "An isolated one. That type of solitary existence is what I always imagined for myself. Ollie changed that. He's fulfilling dreams I never allowed myself to have."

Her sigh is a pleasant tune. "See? That's what I mean. He's everything to you. Why wouldn't Veronica want to meet Ollie?"

Pondering her question isn't necessary. My response is split-second. "She's callous and senseless. I sent her pictures from his first birthday, trying to be nice for Ollie's sake. Maybe she'd want some semblance of a relationship with her child, right? Any sane mother would. Well, the sealed envelope was returned with a big note clearly stating not to contact her again."

Braelyn slaps the table. "She might be the worst human ever."

I grunt. "You haven't met my mother."

Her jaw drops. "No wonder you have issues with women."

I cradle my throbbing skull. "We're not getting into that tonight."

She hums. "That's fair. I think we've made a lot of progress already."

My scoff bounces off the walls. "What?"

Braelyn motions between us. "We have a better understanding, right? Bonded through pain or grief or whatever this is. Life has not been the smoothest ride. We get each other on a level most cannot reach."

"That's some fluffy ass shit, Braelyn."

Her smile sparkles. "Just go with it. I'm feeling sentimental."

The last thing her damaged psyche needs is a man like me. But who am I to deny her? "Kindred fucking spirits. Awesome."

"I'm glad we're on the same page," she giggles.

The fact this woman can laugh after what she's suffered through is a testament to her character. The center of my chest grows warm while I listen to the joyful sound. I rub at the tingling sensation and curse that soft spot for spreading. Exploring these feelings is more dangerous than dwelling on the countless ways my mother fucked me up.

I adjust my watch, clocking the late hour. "Enough of this sappy shit. Let's get to the reason we're here."

Braelyn's eyes are twinkling. "You wanted to take me out on a date?"

"That's hilarious." My flat tone reflects zero amusement. I open the notepad app on my phone. "We'll begin by reviewing your assets."

"Is that a sneaky way of asking to see my butt?"

I almost choke on my tongue. "Strictly business, Braelyn."

She rests her chin on a closed fist. "Since when? That's no fun."

"Writing a will isn't meant to be." A thought occurs to me. "How did you manage to open Thicket two years ago? You were what, twenty-three?"

Braelyn lowers her gaze. "Devon had a will and left everything to me. That turned out to be more than enough capital to start Thicket. He included a simple note that told me to follow my heart. So I did."

Every ill word I've thrown out about that store slaps me in the face. Shit, I'm an asshole. I swallow a massive bite of humble pudding, which is far worse than pie. "I'm glad you were able to do that. He made sure you were taken care of."

"He really did," she murmurs.

I almost reach for her hand, but stop myself at the last second. "I'm sorry he's not here to see what you've built."

"He is in his own way." She spins the bracelet on her wrist. The rainbow colors are faded with age.

The pressure in the room increases tenfold, and I find it hard to breathe. It's becoming painfully obvious how bad of an idea this was. I have no right to get involved with her personal dealings. I open my mouth to diffuse this lit stick of dynamite, but she beats me to it.

Braelyn pulls something out of her purse and sets it on the table. "Before I forget, these are for Ollie. I got a new flavor of taffy. He wasn't in today so I figured you could give this to him." She pushes the wax paper package closer to me.

A torrential downpour wreaks havoc on the deserted lands that makes up my entirety. The concrete surface soaks in the moisture and groans for more. With a simple gesture, this woman ends my drought. She's already busy planting ideas and sprouting possibilities. The desert in my chest will be a thriving rainforest if this continues.

All I can do is stare at her offering and the implications waiting inside. Her eyes are searching too close, watching my inner storm pass and clouds lift. There's more damage being erased with every blink.

I lift the hefty sack of candy. "That's a lot of sugar."

She shrugs. "He's had a lot more on many occasions."

I clear the shrapnel from my throat. "Well, thanks. Ollie will love this. Maybe it'll help him forgive me for hanging out with you when he wasn't around."

Braelyn laughs. "We'll just have a redo. The second time around will be better."

Dammit, she's digging deeper into me. I just might let her.

chapter seventeen

BRAELYN

CROSS

TIP MY FACE UP, ALLOWING THE MIDDAY SUN TO SHINE DOWN ON me. Is there anything better than kicking back while soaking in natural vitamin D? At this moment, I'm going with no. My new sunglasses paint everything in a rosy tint. The bright hue matches my mood. I'd stay here for hours and bathe in this cheery goodness. It's a beautiful afternoon to be outside.

The bench creaks beneath me when I cross my legs. Even though the wood is weathered and worn, this is my favorite place to sit. I release my hair from the confining bun. With a swoosh, long waves spill down my back. The breeze picks up, and golden strands swirl in every direction.

All around me, the park is bustling with activity. Probably due to the temperature being that optimal blend of warm and balmy. A group of teens whip a frisbee around, chasing the disc back and forth. There're countless children climbing all over the playground equipment. An adorable puppy scampers by with a young girl holding the leash. I smile at the pair.

"I always wanted a dog. I begged my parents incessantly to no avail. They didn't want another mouth to feed." I wrinkle my nose, the stench of those memories a sour burn.

Sadie tilts her head toward me. "What's stopping you?"

I pick imaginary lint off my shorts. "I'm cautious to accept that level of responsibility."

She quirks a brow. "You own a business."

"That's different. Thicket isn't a living, breathing being."

"You could kill it off just the same."

I choke on a gasp. "Harsh."

"Truth." Sadie lifts a shoulder. "And we both know you'd adopt Ollie in a heartbeat."

I part my lips, but nothing comes out. How do I respond to that without giving myself away? The mere suggestion of having that adorable boy around permanently is too much. My fractured spirit can't handle that as a feasible possibility, so I settle on whispering, "That'll never happen."

Sadie huffs. I imagine her eyes rolling behind those mirrored shades she's wearing. "Don't get mopey on me. We're focusing on being positive."

I nudge her side. "I'm all good."

She slides her sunglasses down, giving me a once-over. "You're different."

"Jeez, thanks. Not like I didn't already know." I feel a strain locking up my body, preparing to battle whatever threat crops up.

She shoves me. "Not like that. You're acting like the old Braelyn. I should have used the word better or cheerful. You're the girl I met in advanced marketing our senior year."

With her observation, the tension in my muscles ease. I blow out a long breath. "Thanks. I like to think so. It's been over a month since I've had a really bad attack. And that class was brutal. I wouldn't have passed without you."

Sadie purses her lips. "Um, no. It was the opposite, and we don't need to lie. You carried my ass that final semester."

I track a puffy cloud through the blue sky. "Just trying to give you a boost, Dee."

She taps her chin. "Well, in that case, how's Mister Tall, Broody, and Sexy?"

"Really? Talking about him will make you happy?" It takes a ton of effort to keep my voice level. Just hearing that man's nickname makes me squirm.

Sadie bobs her head. "Oh, yes. Super-giddy. Let me live vicariously."

Traitorous butterflies wake up and take flight in my belly. "I guess he's fine. We've reached somewhat of a civil agreement." If nothing else, I have a better understanding of his rude attitude and abhorrence to women.

She begins to fake-snore at maximum volume. The grating noise attracts attention from people nearby. I dip my chin and look the opposite way. Sadie scoots closer, shutting down my plans for escape.

"Was that snooze-alert too subtle? I expect more than that." She twirls two fingers, motioning for me to spill.

"Such as?"

"He storms into Thicket and ravishes you," she replies.

Tingles dance the Cha-Cha up my legs. My breathy sigh gives me away. "That was a great day."

"Mm-hmm, I need a deal like that. My lips haven't been sucked on in months."

I laugh. "A kiss would suffice."

"Nope. I want passion all up in my lady bits."

"Sorry to disappoint, but that appears to have been a one-time thing. Brance hasn't given any indication of another round."

She slaps her thigh. "That's bogus. How long has it been?"

I flip my hand top to bottom. "Two weeks?"

"But he's been by?"

"Yep, with Ollie." A smile lifts my cheeks.

Sadie snaps her fingers. "Damn. I want another juicy rendezvous."

"Me too," I whisper.

"Maybe he's playing hard to get?"

My snort is loud and cracks through the boisterous ruckus streaming from all corners of the park. "That'd be a big hell no."

She reaches for her drink. Most of the ice is melted and condensation drips down to her lap. "I might as well order my tea hot in this weather."

I grab my own beverage and take a sip of the lukewarm liquid. "We can go for ice cream in a bit."

As if hearing our plans, a bolt of youthful energy zooms toward us. That bundle of vibrant color comes to a screeching halt in front of me. I blink, and Ollie appears from the blur of dust.

"Miss Braelyn!" The wide grin he's donning reveals all of his teeth. "What're you doing here?"

I bend forward and ruffle his unruly mop of hair. "Hey, Ollie. What a nice surprise. I'm enjoying the great outdoors with my friend." I look to her, nodding at him. "Sadie, meet Ollie. He's my best customer."

He preens with my praise, puffing out his chest. "Thicket is my most favorite shop ever."

Sadie beams at him. "Doesn't Braelyn have the best candy? I love it."

Ollie bounces on his toes. "So do I. Sometimes on Saturday she gives me extra."

"Lucky duck. You must be super-special." She winks at him, and they exchange a high-five.

"I sure am." He does a little jig, showing us his best moves. There's not a shy bone in this kid's body. "Right, Miss Braelyn?"

"Absolutely, buddy. I look forward to your visits the most." And that's the honest truth.

"Really?" Wonder rattles in his tone. Ollie steps closer, and I lift my arms to wrap him up. But I stop short of looping them around his shoulders for a hug. That'd be inappropriate. Or maybe not. I'm still figuring out the lines. At the last second, I yank my hands away and nod instead.

"Yes, of course. So, what're you doing here, sweetie?"

He hitches a little thumb over his shoulder. "We're gonna play."

I don't have the chance to ask who's with him. Brance appears out of woodsy-scented air, looking hot enough to drop panties all across town. I'm well aware he rocks a suit better than any other man in the history of humanity. But Brance dressed down in a plain tee and faded jeans? Oh, Lord. Denim has never looked so appetizing. And let's not leave out the two-days' worth of stubble. He's certifiably combustible.

The pleasant temperature spikes a thousand degrees, and I'm boiling in lust. Next to me, Sadie makes a high-pitch noise in her throat. Her jaw is hanging down to the gravel. Guess I'm not the only one affected.

"Holy shit," she whispers. "Is that Brance?"

I squeeze my eyes shut against a thrashing wave of arousal. "Yes."

"Wow. And why aren't you hitting that? I mean, how do you refrain?" Sadie has a death grip on my arm. I wince and peel her fingers off me.

"Will you keep your voice down?" I shush her and suck in a hiss through my clenched teeth.

Brance's knowing grin spreads wider the more we talk. Those dimples make a rare appearance. My hormones spill out in an embarrassing puddle at his feet. I'm so screwed. This man is a walking advertisement for orgasms.

"Ladies," he greets.

"Hi." My voice is barely more than a squeak. I hitch my

shoulders up, as if that'll protect me. Sadie's elbow bumps me in the ribs. I clear the lust from my throat. "Uh, this is my friend, Sadie." I'm sure my cheeks are the shade of a tomato. I fan my face, desperately needing a reprieve.

Brance pays very little mind to my friend. After a quick nod in greeting, his rapt attention returns to me. His eyes are covered by a mirrored pair of aviators, saving me from receiving the full impact. But at this point, it doesn't matter. I feel the heat of his stare to my very core.

A man I haven't met before strides up next to Brance. "Dude, your kid has wheels. What's the big hurry?"

Brance gestures to me. "Ollie saw a familiar face. This is Braelyn." He flicks a wrist at Sadie. "And her friend."

The stranger bounces his brows at me. "Ah, we finally meet. I'm Jordan. This guy's best friend"—he claps Brance on the back while jutting his chin toward Ollie—"and that little man's godfather."

Brance grunts and shakes off his friend's touch. "We went to law school together and practice at the same firm."

"We're tight like that," Jordan adds.

"Oh, sweet baby Jesus," Sadie mumbles under her breath. "Thank you."

When I peek over at her, she's pointing to the sky. I laugh, her reaction releasing the pressure in my straining lungs.

She leans closer to me, her whisper tickling my ear. "Did they walk straight off a model shoot for GQ? Good grief."

I bow my head to hide the telling smile. "You're being really obvious."

"That's the goal." She sends a flirty finger wave to Jordan. "Hey there, handsome. I'm Sadie."

He moves closer, taking her hand and placing a delicate kiss on the top. "It's a pleasure."

Sadie melts into the bench with a fluttery sigh. "Whoa."

I bite my tongue to trap the giggle that's bubbling up.

At least one of us is getting properly romanced. I shift away, attempting to give them some semblance of privacy. Their chemistry is setting off sparks in every direction.

When I look up, Brance is scowling at them. No surprise there. Ollie is standing beside his father, quiet to a point of concern. He's busy studying all of us. I'm sure this kid sees everything. A furrow dents his brow, but the lines clear quick enough. He hops toward Jordan.

"Uncle Jordy?" Ollie tugs on his sleeve. "Will you push me on the swings?"

Jordan clasps their palms together. "Absolutely, buddy."

Ollie smiles at Sadie, the blue of his eyes sparkling. "And Miss Sadie? Will you help him?"

My friend leaps to her sandaled feet. "I'd love to."

I inch forward, waiting for my invitation. But Ollie is staring at Brance.

"Daddy?" His tone is sugary sweet. "Stay here and keep Miss Braelyn company, okay?"

Brance stills. For a moment, I'm certain he's going to reject Ollie's wishes. But then the tension deflates from his posture. "Sure, kiddo. Go have fun."

The trio take off for the playground without a backward glance. With just the two of us left, the atmosphere grows thick and hazy. My pulse is going haywire. I do my best to avoid Brance's electrified presence in front of me. He's giving off some seriously pissed-off vibes.

After a full minute passes, he mutters something unintelligible and takes a seat next to me. The wood groans with his weight. I stifle a laugh.

A rumble rises from his chest. "Yeah, real funny. My son makes a terrible matchmaker."

"Ouch. Thanks for that. My self-esteem is flimsy enough." I put more distance between us. He flings a variation of abrasive shit at me on the regular. I'm more than accustomed to the stench. But it's extra potent this afternoon. Probably due to him looking extra delicious and smelling like a sinful fantasy. He makes me weak in the filthiest of ways.

Brance scratches over his weekend growth of scruff. "My feelings on this matter have always been clear."

"I was never in doubt."

"Glad we're on the same page."

"Yep, got it." I search the grounds for an available space to sit. My favorite spot is being tainted.

He yanks off his shades and glares at me. "What brings you to this area? Isn't it a bit out of your way?"

"Because you know where I live?"

He doesn't have a response to that. I grin, my expression probably dripping with smug satisfaction. My bruised ego raises her head, a sneaky plan taking shape.

"Maybe I'm here meeting someone."

He doesn't have to know I'm referring to Sadie.

"Bullshit," he spits.

"Is that so hard to believe?"

"Yes."

"Well, I'm single and ready to put myself out there." I just wish the man sitting next to me would be more receptive. Another release or two from him would do the trick. I feel like we share some version of a mangled bond. A deep-rooted understanding only a catastrophe of pain leaves behind. But I'm foolish for thinking Brance is looking at me with anything other than thinly veiled indifference.

"Pretty sure you already are. Do you recall being ready to fuck me a few weeks ago?"

"That's ancient history."

"Is it?" Suddenly he's so close that his breath is hot on my neck.

I can't stop the shiver from wracking my limbs. It takes every ounce of self-control to keep my eyes trained straight ahead. Blistering flames race through my veins. I gulp and silently recite the alphabet. Am I a coward for not facing him? Most definitely.

The bench creaks when he shifts out of my personal space. "Don't look so terrified. We both know you're not repulsed by my touch."

The truth parts my lips. I'm two seconds away from suggesting a secluded location more suitable for straddling his lap. There has to be an abandoned lot nearby. But no. That would be very bad. I scramble for a distraction.

"Is it all right for me to hug Ollie?" I blurt.

"What the fuck kind of question is that?"

"A serious one. Earlier it seemed like he was swooping in, but I wasn't sure that'd be okay."

"Please don't deprive my child of affection, Braelyn. If he wants a hug, give him one. You'll likely shatter his heart by denying him."

"What? Why?"

Brance flails his arms in a wild circle, the answer waiting right there. "Because he's crazy about you. Pretty sure running into you today has made his entire month. If he asks me to marry you one more time, I'm likely to go insane. He'd have you living with us in a second."

I'll never admit how breathless that possibility makes me. "That's silly."

"But it's the truth."

My heart pounds so hard it's liable to burst. "That might be the nicest thing you've ever said to me."

He rubs his temples. "Give my son the credit. This is not my doing."

The lash of his words doesn't strike. I'm protected by the comfort of hearing Ollie likes having me around. This bit of information is exactly what my wounded pride needed. I smile at him, probably looking like a loon. "Thanks."

Brance twists toward me. "For what?"

I kick at the gravel, sending tiny rocks flying. "Telling me how he feels. It's good to hear that. But us getting married is off the table."

"I'm sure he'll ask you sooner or later. I'm not giving him the desired response."

I cough over a gasp. How the hell would I get out of that pickle?

Ollie bounds up to us, intervening without realizing. "Daddy, guess what? Uncle Jordy told me we're going to Five Squares for dinner. Braelyn and Sadie can come with us." Ollie's twinkling gaze flings to me. "I can show you how to play the ducky game."

I peek at Brance from the corner of my eye. His jaw is locked. A muscle twitches from the effort. I can practically hear his thoughts stewing. It doesn't appear he's planning to respond.

"That sounds great, sweetie." I have no intentions of denying Ollie anything. Deep down I know Brance agrees with me, happily or not.

chapter eighteen

BRANCE

GOOSE

I unbuckle Ollie from his seat, and he wiggles free of the straps. Before I can blink, he jumps down and begins spinning in circles on the sidewalk. Jordan steps out from the passenger side and joins me. We watch my son entertain himself with an imaginary sword. If I could bottle his energy, we'd make a fortune.

"Ah, to be young again." Jordan leans against my car.

I ignore his sentiment. "Thanks for the fucking set-up."

He straightens off the fender and crosses his arms. "How long have you been holding that in?"

"The entire ride over here."

"Don't pretend to be mad." His placating tone grates on my already shot nerves.

I flare my nostrils and force out a cleansing breath. "I'm beyond livid. Thanks for using Ollie against me."

"Oh, this was entirely his idea." He points to the restaurant, which appears warm and inviting in front of us. I feel the complete opposite.

"Why am I not surprised," I mutter.

"Your son had the right idea."

I exaggerate my snort. "Hey, broken record. We've already been over this. And countless times at that."

Jordan scuffs his shoe over the concrete. "My pestering has been proven effective."

"Yet my decision remains the same."

"You're so fucking stubborn."

My chuckle is pitch black. "I'll take that as a compliment."

"You shouldn't."

"It's served me well."

Ollie crashes into me, wrapping his arms around my leg. "Daddy?"

I pin Jordan with a glare before smoothing my features. "Yeah, buddy?"

"Are you done arguing?"

I swallow the ball of frustration aimed at my friend. All Ollie will see is a strained smile. "Yes. Jordan is being goofy garbage."

My son gasps. "Uncle Jordy, stop being stinky."

He holds up a palm. "I'll take a shower later."

His response seems to appease Ollie and provides a detour out of this conversation.

"No woman worth keeping will stick around if you smell bad. And we know how bad you

want a girlfriend." I paste on a grin with my advice.

Jordan barks out a laugh. "You're digging in the dirt, man."

I grip his shoulder. "Quit making it easy on me."

He rolls his eyes. "This isn't over."

"We'll see," I mutter.

"Can we go inside? Please?" My son yanks at my jeans.

I run my thumb down his smooth cheek. "Of course, little man. Lead the way."

Ollie runs to the entrance without a beat of hesitation. Jordan and I follow close behind, chewing on his dust. I open the heavy metal door and usher them inside. The restaurant appears low key, which isn't surprising at four o'clock on a Sunday. Five Square is a causal joint that we frequent often enough. Ollie goes bonkers for the sorry excuse of an arcade they have hidden in a back corner.

The women are waiting in the lobby, chattering away. Their conversation comes to an abrupt end when they catch sight of us. Sadie is directing a blinding smile at Jordan, which he returns in spades. Braelyn holds up a hand, and Ollie slaps their palms together. I stand off to the side, already counting the minutes until this disaster is over.

How in the hell did I get roped into this? It smells like shit is about to hit the fan. And here I am, plowing in with my eyes wide open.

I glance around for the most accessible exits. On the plus side, there appears to be several. More importantly, the bathroom is easy to find along the far wall. The bar is separated from the dining area. I'm tempted to down a few shots of something strong before attempting to survive this family-style meal. That should take the edge off.

"Come on," Jordan says. "I'll buy you a beer at the table."

Fucker knows me too well. I offer a grunt and trudge behind him to a circular five-top. Usually Ollie prefers sitting in a booth, but I don't comment. Nothing about this situation is what I'm accustomed to. I'll let him handle this oversight on his own.

Without pause, he snags a chair in the middle. "Will you sit by me, Miss Braelyn?"

A belt cinches around my chest at his words. My son is too damn attached to this woman. What's going to happen when she inevitably fucks us over? I scrub my forehead, unable to process the clusterfuck it will cause.

Sadie and Jordan settle in, leaving me the other spot next to Ollie. I wedge myself into the tight space with a grunt. The rickety chair almost topples under my weight. I bang my elbow in an effort to remain upright and not fall ass over backward. That'd be extremely fitting for the occasion.

Jordan coughs into his fist. "Smooth, dude. Keep that shit up. You're making me look like a rockstar."

I almost punch him in the arm. "Don't curse in front of Ollie."

He has the decency to wince. "My bad, sorry. But little man is totally distracted."

I follow his line of sight and find Ollie immersed in a coloring project. His tongue pops out from the corner of his mouth. Concentration crinkles his forehead. The red crayon in his hand moves at breakneck pace.

"Whatcha making, buddy?" I lean in for a better look.

He lifts his eyes to my face. "A dinosaur, duh."

I laugh at his no-nonsense tone. "I like his horns. Very scary."

"Those are teeth," he corrects.

"Ah, right. The better for him to eat with." What am I saying? There's a sharp thorn cutting into my hip, stabbing deeper with every subtle movement. Having Braelyn so close is messing with my mojo. I'm losing cool-points by the second.

Ollie's pinched expression reflects my thoughts. "Um, sure, Daddy. He's having a salad for dinner."

I grin at his creativity. "That's very humane."

"Huh?" His face twists into a more complex knot.

"Never mind." I let the bad joke roll off my shoulder. That stiff drink is sounding more appealing by the instant. But that would be admitting defeat. I don't lose.

Ollie shrugs and returns to his picture. He picks up a crayon and passes it to Braelyn. "Wanna color with me?"

The green in her eyes is super-charged. That pleasing color is sending out happy vibes to anyone in a fifty-foot radius. I won't deny soaking in a few. This woman cannot be ignored, try as I fucking might.

Braelyn gets to work filling in a small section of Ollie's paper. He watches her with more interest than his favorite cartoon. Is he that starved for female interaction? I'm really hoping to avoid further mommy issues where he's concerned. If Braelyn fills a temporary gap, this battle is steeper uphill than I predicted. But there's no need for a white flag. At least not yet.

Realization dawns that I'm gawking at her just the same as my son. Our intent couldn't be further apart. Mine is of the X-rated variety, extremely inappropriate considering our current position. A harsh bite clamps in my gut. I snap my gaze off those bee-stung lips, hard as it might be. Jordan is shaking with silent laughter, almost collapsing to the floor. I flip him the bird under my armpit.

A beer gets placed in front of me. I shift my focus to the server as he drops off Ollie's milk and Braelyn's lemonade. His attention snags longer than appropriate on the luscious gold waves spilling down her back. I clear my throat, loud and annoyed. His eyes lift to mine and expand to saucers after noticing my glare. A cringe tightens his smile. He nods and scurries away with a pissed off bull chasing his heels. Pansy-ass bastard.

But what does that make me?

"Scaring off potential competition? Bravo, brother. You're making me so proud." Jordan's jovial timbre is worse than nails on a chalkboard. His humor is wasted on me.

I scowl. "Will you drop it already?"

"Tell me what I wanna hear." He cups his ear and edges toward me.

I flick his lobe. "Knock it off."

"Oh, you love me."

I shove him out of my personal space. "Quit hitting on me. Your date will get jealous."

"Nah, we're solid." Jordan twists toward Sadie. She snuggles against his arm and bats her lashes. That was easy.

With them occupied, I'm free to spy on Ollie and Braelyn. He's resting his cheek on an open palm, fascinated by whatever she's doing. Braelyn is bent over the paper and scribbling with broad strokes. She's using three crayons at once. I can't tell what she's drawing from this angle. As if encouraging my creeper status, Ollie slouches lower and opens a clear path for me to see.

"That's really pretty, Miss Braelyn."

"Thanks, sweetie. I find peace in rainbows."

I catch the slight zigzag twisting his mouth. That's a curious expression I see a lot. She must notice his delay in response.

Braelyn lifts the crayons from the page. She traces the lines with her finger. "There's something soothing about the colors. Bright and vibrant and promising. The arch is a guide I can follow."

"That's some deep shit," Jordan mumbles from beside me.

I elbow him in the gut. He retreats with a groan. Braelyn's green eyes land on me, pooling with something I can't quite read. Her lips twitch with a half-smile, and I'm sunk.

The server swings by to take our order. Braelyn gets a burger with fries. I find myself repeating the same. This gets another round of snickers from the peanut gallery next to me. I choose to ignore them.

"Miss Braelyn?" Ollie wiggles on his chair.

Her hands hover over his shimming shoulders. The protective move makes me grin. He senses her touch and settles on his butt.

She relaxes in her own seat. "Yeah, sweetie?"

"Can we play the ducky game until our food is ready?"

Braelyn lifts her gaze to find mine. A question quirks her brow. I shrug and point to the claw machine. Her face lights up brighter than the arcade's fluorescent bulbs. I hide my dick's reaction under a napkin.

"Will you teach me? I never win." Braelyn's pout is worthy of an Academy Award.

Ollie's nod is vigorous. "I'm super-good at it. My daddy taught me."

She winks at me. "If that's the case, I imagine we'll be very lucky ducks."

My son giggles. "You're so funny."

Glad he laughs at someone's jokes.

Ollie grabs Braelyn's hand and they skip off to the corner alcove.

"She's so good with him," Sadie coos.

Jordan smiles. "He loves spending time with her. They're so happy."

The instinct to bang my head against the table rips through me. "Seriously?"

They exchange a glance. Sadie is smart enough to avoid my glare.

"Why deny the obvious?" Jordan juts his chin in the direction they went.

Braelyn has her head thrown back, laughter pouring from her lips. Ollie jerks the joystick this way and that, determination set in his no-nonsense posture. There isn't a pinch of doubt they're having a blast. It's more than likely I'll have to drag them out when dinner shows up.

"We'll never reach an agreement on this." I sag against the back of my chair. My legs are stretched out wide. I keep my features flat, masking the conflict waging a war inside of me.

Jordan holds up a finger. "As Ollie's godfather, I vote for giving Braelyn a chance."

"I second that," Sadie echoes.

I roll my eyes to the ceiling. "Not your choice."

"He's practically begging her to be his mama." There's not an ounce of amusement in Jordan's voice.

Venom sizzles under my skin. "That's a ballsy low blow."

He clicks his tongue and faces Sadie. "You'll have to excuse my friend. He's a bit tense about a certain meeting tomorrow. The wait has him edgy as fuck."

My head whips toward Ollie at the claw machine with Braelyn. He's safely out of listening range. I turn my glare to Jordan. "Watch your fucking language."

He brushes off my concern. "My bad," he deadpans. "It's hard to remember the rules with such a stellar role model around. I'm not sure what gave me the idea it was okay to curse."

Sadie's gaze bounces between us, settling on me. "What meeting?"

"The partners at our law firm are deciding who's joining them up on top." I rub at the knot in my throat.

"And our guy here is the front runner," Jordan adds.

That earns him a smirk. "Thanks, man."

He nods. "I'll have the whiskey on ice in your office to celebrate."

I chuckle, but the sound is forced. "I can hardly wait."

Sadie taps her chin. "Speaking of that, having a significant other to share the joy with makes it extra special."

I drag a palm over my mouth, muffling the growl gaining strength. "Thanks for the suggestion, but I'll manage without."

Jordan rolls his neck toward Sadie. "He doesn't realize the perks. My man has never been part of a healthy functioning duo."

She rubs her nose along his. "Should we try harder to convince him?"

Once again, I'm surrounded by Braelyn fans. If I strain my ears, there's a roar of applause rooting from her corner. Everyone loves her. I should be used to it. But I'm not ready to climb onto the bandwagon.

"Hello?" I wave in front of them. "We're in a family space, and I'm sitting right here."

They stare at me, waiting for my willpower to collapse. Fucking traitors.

I grip a fistful of my hair. "I'm playing nice enough. I bring Ollie to her store without complaint. I tolerate her overly sweet demeanor. I abstain from the temptation she inadvertently flings my way. She's everything I've spent my life avoiding."

The list continues to compile in my mind. Her natural beauty is a nuisance. The effortless connection she has with Ollie threatens to break me. I can't lower my guard. If I do, everything will crumble. But my arsenal is scraping bottom. She's bound to be the catalyst of my ultimate destruction.

This game is rigged. The deck has been stacked against me from the start. They're rooting her on without considering my feelings. Not that I blame them. But they should want better for her. *I* certainly do.

Red fringes along the edge of my vision. I blink the anger away with a grunt.

Sadie scoots to the edge of her seat. "All signs are pointing to yes. Just give in. It could be one night only."

Jordan gets out his pom-poms. "Have you asked what she wants?"

I scoff. "No. And I'm not going to."

The noise he makes calls my bluff. "Wanna bet?"

I lean back and cross my arms. I've never been in the business of losing money.

chapter nineteen

BRAELYN

SWAY

SWING MY HIPS TO THE SWOONY BEAT THAT'S CROONING FROM THE speakers. With a pep in my step, I strut by the front display cases while snagging misplaced items. Before disappearing from view, the setting sun makes a last-ditch effort to blast me with warm rays. A crystal wind chime dangles from the window, reflecting rainbows all across the floor. I follow the colorful path and shimmy down the far aisle.

I'm still buzzing from yesterday. Having dinner with Ollie, Sadie, and Jordan was great. Exchanging fervent glares with Brance was better. His scorching blue gaze barely left me during the entire meal. That amount of blatant attention from him had me flustered and bothered. Just when I think we've established a truce, he stomps on the flimsy agreement and rips it to shreds. That man is something else, and I want more.

The clock strikes seven o'clock, alerting me that it's officially quitting time. I glance toward the entrance where the open sign is still blinking bright. The store has been empty for almost an hour. I could've closed early. At this point, I doubt anyone will be strolling in. A Dapper sundae will be mine in less than twenty minutes if I hurry. The promise of ice cream has me restacking these shelves with gusto.

Not even a minute later, the welcoming chime calls out. I turn toward the front to greet the customer. But no one is there. Until *he* is.

Brance appears from behind the counter, donning a dark gray suit. It's no surprise he took the liberty of switching off my lollipop light. I'm sure he flipped the lock in the same beat. He saunters over with all the ease and confidence only a powerful man possesses. His light blue shirt is open at the collar, no tie in sight. My fingers itch to rip at the remaining buttons.

The shock of seeing him leaves me breathless. I'm slack-jawed and openly ogling. Is he here to deliver a gift or punishment? As if it actually matters. It's impossible not to stumble over the last time he dropped by alone. The memory swirls to the forefront of my mind. I swallow the saliva pooling in my mouth.

"Can I help you find something?" My voice resembles a purr.

Brance licks along his bottom lip. "I certainly hope so."

I tuck some hair behind my ear. "Where's Ollie?"

"At home."

"With Mary?"

A sharp jerk of his head. "Nah. Jordan offered to watch him."

I scrunch my forehead. "Why?"

"He wanted me to celebrate."

"What's the occasion?"

"I made partner."

A hitch stutters my breath when he stalks closer.

"Wow, that's great. Congratulations."

"Thank you."

I fidget with the hem of my skirt. The shorter length didn't bother me until this moment. Do I appear desperate? Or not bare enough? I bite the inside of my cheek. There's no use denying I want to hike the fabric up or strip it off completely. The neglected hussy inside of me fluffs her flouncy hair. She might get her way.

An insistent ache is already building inside of me. I squeeze my thighs together, but that only makes it worse. "Too bad I sold out of cupcakes earlier. I would've offered you one."

"I'm in the mood for something you wouldn't give to just anyone. At least, I hope not." Brance's long stride is impressive. He covers the distance between us in mere seconds. Before I can gasp, we're separated by a few short feet.

"You're back for more?"

"Much."

My nipples pebble from the rasp in his tone. The abrasive grit scrapes against my sensitive flesh, and I shiver. I flare my eyes, devouring every inch of his impressive form. Brance is all male, and my body is yearning for satisfaction. I'm a quivering mess just thinking about him using that dominating presence on me tonight.

Brance hovers just out of reach. "I tried so fucking hard to stay away from you."

"Why?" I drag in a deep inhale, savoring his spicy cologne.

"Because you deserve better."

Only an arm-length keeps us apart. I could lean forward and grab him. "Says who?"

"Me."

"What about my opinion?"

His taut jaw pops. "Overruled."

A ball of fiery lust burns in my throat. "Seems to me an appeal is in order."

I bump into the wall when Brance stalks closer. The solid surface behind me offers stability to my wobbly knees. He doesn't stop until our chests bump. Rather than cower and feel a prickle of fear, searing heat explodes across my limbs. I lift my chin and face his menacing glare.

"You looking for a rough fuck, Brae?"

I don't overthink his use of my nickname. I'm too busy drowning in desire. A heady dose of carnal pleasure gets injected into my veins. My lashes flutter as I drift on his filthy promise. "Yes. Please, yes."

I'm not above begging. There's no room for embarrassment with all the tension squeezing between us.

His eyes narrow further. "This won't mean anything other than fulfilling a physical need."

I dutifully nod. "Uh-huh."

But Brance isn't convinced. "Can you remain unaffected? I won't chance destroying what little common ground we've established. Ollie will always want you around. If we crash and burn at this, things will be far more complicated."

At this point, I'm breathing lust-fueled fire. "Just orgasms. Got it."

The talking abruptly cuts off when he crashes our mouths together. I moan into the kiss, arching against him. His lips drift up my cheek and temple. The move is almost tender.

"You're such a pain in my ass," he growls close to my ear.

I shift against him, rubbing along the hard ridge prodding at me. The empty space inside of me weeps. I curl my fingers on the shelf, but metal doesn't satisfy me. A chunk of finely toned Brance would do nicely. I want to grip his sculpted ass and soothe any pain he might be feeling.

He towers over my feminine frame, bending lower to box me in. "You know exactly how to play me."

"Oh?" Do I? I'm having a tough time weeding through the sloppy state my brain is in. A pitiful whine wheezes up my throat, giving me away. I shake my head slowly. Falling under his seductive spell seems like a bad choice.

Brance swipes his tongue along my bottom lip, sucking gently. He teases me with a nibble on my pout. "I'm treating myself to another taste. But this time, you'll come in my mouth." His hand snakes up my inner thigh, and I spread for him.

I bow backward, thumping my skull against the wall. The dull thud barely registers. "Please, Brance."

"Greedy girl," he growls into my neck. The vibration against my skin gives me chills.

One moment, my panties are snug and clinging to me. In the next, the lacy material is discarded in a pile of shreds. Brance lowers to his knees in front of me. He bunches the material of my skirt up around my waist. The stretchy fabric molds there, granting him a front row view to the most private parts of me.

Brance hitches one of my legs over his shoulder. In this position, I'm open to him for the taking. He blows out a slow breath against my exposed center. I shiver from the tease to that overly responsive area.

With the first swipe, I almost skyrocket out of my flip-flops. Brance chuckles against my slit.

"So sensitive." He bands an arm around my lower back, fingers digging into my hip. I'm effectively trapped between the shelf and him. There's no place I'd rather be.

His tongue is a sensual glide from my center to my clit. Holy whoa, I've missed this. But I don't remember anything ever feeling this exquisite. He breaks away, a mere sliver of space. The mewl that spills from me sounds desperate.

Brance peers up from his crouched position on the floor. "No crying, okay?"

I huff. "That was a first time thing."

His grip on me tightens. "It's a damn mood killer."

The need to laugh barrels into me. "And what do you call this?"

"A necessary discussion."

"Trust me, there's no threat of tears. If I happen to shed a few, it'll be from sheer joy." I scratch along his scalp, gripping fistfuls of that silky hair. I try to tug him into position, but he doesn't budge.

He squints at me, scrounging for bullshit.

I motion around my temple. "Up top isn't running the show. The goal is to only feel ecstasy. That's where you come in handy." I'll say anything to get his mouth back on me.

A rumble rises from Brance's chest. "Fuck yeah."

He dives in and begins his assault. The attack is a brutal lashing that frays my control. I'm slipping off the edge already. Sparks shoot from my lower belly, spreading from head to toe. I'm going to come embarrassingly fast. That'll stroke Brance's ego. He'll take that as a compliment, and I have no problem giving it. This man deserves a standing ovation for these skills. A spike of arousal hits me just considering what Brance can do with his dick. Hell, I'm likely to spontaneously climax from the sight alone.

Thoughts of what he's packing down below evaporate when his speed kicks up another notch. Brance's tongue is a tornado swirling around my clit. Faster and harder until my mind is spinning. My tether to the ground is unraveling at a rapid rate. The grip on his hair isn't enough. I reach for his shoulders and hold on. He hits a particularly sensitive spot, and I let my jaw go slack.

"Oh, oh, yes. There, more. P-please don't stop." My babbling is just a murmur, but Brance groans and delves in deeper.

When he plunges a finger into me, I detonate instantly. A wash of color blasts behind my clenched eyelids. I chase the rainbow, soaring on its vibrant hues.

Holy fucking shit. How do I recover from this?

Brance brings me down gently, alternating between soft laps and delicate kisses. Meanwhile, I'm a trembling puddle in his capable grip. This guy is the master of oral sex.

As the pleasure ebbs from my veins, I glance down at him. He's still perched on his soles below me. I attempt to brace for his reaction, but my muscles won't cooperate. My shield is down, and I'm an easy target.

He lifts himself off the floor in one effortless move. His gaze never leaves mine. Brance is watching me, a sexy smirk lifting his glistening lips. Good Lord, he's coated in me. Why's that so hot?

I clear the dust from my throat. "If that's how you celebrate, sign me up for all the parties."

His husky chuckle sends aftershocks through my core. "Consider yourself lucky."

"Oh, I do. Trust me on that."

He licks me off his mouth. "You're too fucking sweet."

"Really?" I almost ask him to kiss me. "Hit the spot?"

Blue fire crackles at me. "Hardly. That wasn't nearly enough."

"It wasn't?" My voice is more hoarse than I like.

"Not even close."

I curl my fingers into a fist. "Can I, uh, return the favor?"

Brance lowers his brow. "No."

The breath stalls in my lungs. "What? Why?"

"Fuck getting just a taste. I want the five-course meal. I want you naked and spread out, no damn clothes in my way." He tugs on my tee.

"O-okay?"

"I won't be your pity fuck," he growls.

The idea is laughable. "If anyone's being pitied, it'll be me."

He snorts. "Pity is the furthest thing I feel for you."

"Good, we're still even."

Brance dips his chin. "You using me to forget?"

I huff. "That's not possible. Are you doing this out of guilt?"

"As fucking if."

"Sounds settled to me."

"The sooner you're naked beneath me, the better."

"When?" I slide one finger over another, hoping for right this second.

"Now."

A chorus of applause erupts inside my chest. I wrack my brain for possible options. "There's a recliner in the storage room."

Brance grunts. "We'll need a bed. Where do you live?"

I point toward the street. "About ten minutes away."

His grin speaks of secrets between the sheets. "Take me to your house. We're gonna test your mattress springs."

I wink at him, but say nothing. It'll be a fun surprise for him to discover the memory foam.

Braelyn's blinker is a glowing beacon in the pitch-black nothingness. There are no street lamps lining this road. A sense of our location finally kicks in when she hits the brakes. I've been dutifully following her for miles, and we're finally getting somewhere. The lack of control was allowing reality to settle, but the slightest spark reignites my hunger.

I slow down as Braelyn turns her car into the driveway. The garage door lifts, and she pulls inside. Exterior lights flicker on, illuminating her house. I park along the curb in front of her mailbox. Maintaining some semblance of distance seems necessary in this moment. Getting too close or comfortable is a hell no. I cut the engine and sink into my leather seat. A final blast of cool air streams from the vent. It doesn't alleviate the fire in my blood.

My body is still humming, the possibilities spinning on an erotic loop. Even with time to get my shit sorted, I'm sporting a semi. Braelyn's effect on me is too intense. There're countless feet of space between us, but I can feel her against me. That level of chemistry is an intoxicating trip. I curse a blue streak into my palms. Enough fucking stalling.

I grab a foil packet from the center console, snatching a second one just in case. Nothing is safe when living with a nosey kid. He sniffs out anything of interest with the nose of a bloodhound. I shove out of my car and stride toward her.

The groan of the garage closing breaks into the otherwise quiet night. Braelyn is waiting for me on the cobbled path, gaze averted and feet shuffling. My heavy steps boom across the concrete. She takes notice, lifting her eyes to meet mine. Her slight figure appears angelic under the lamp's gleaming brightness. There's fiery turbulence in her green pools, too much left unspoken. But the heat wafting off her is undeniable. Without a word, Braelyn turns and strolls to her front door.

I'm being selfish. Making the decision to fuck Braelyn is reckless. I've plowed forward without taking her feelings into consideration. But she assured me this was okay. Her argument was convincing. She made a solid case for why this is a fantastic idea. And here I stand.

Why the fuck am I trying to find reasons opposing this? I need to drop the whiny bitch act.

But Braelyn isn't some random woman I met in a bar. This choice involves more than the two of us. I need to be absolutely certain that these lines remain drawn. That's important to me, for my son's sake. The guarantee of her word takes far higher priority than a quick fuck.

I pause on her porch, one step away from crossing the threshold. "Can you keep this," I motion between us, "separate from your relationship with Ollie?"

Braelyn's expression cools slightly. "We've already addressed this."

I return her annoyance. "I'm aware. But it's not too late for us to stop."

"I have zero expectations beyond tonight."

Can she actually be so chill about this? I haven't given her nearly enough credit. "My intentions were decent. But I can't deny my desire for you. Tell me you want this."

"I do. Pretty sure we've already crossed that line."

"Sex is a totally different ballgame."

"Ah, we're rounding bases."

I shrug. "It's kinda my thing."

She pops out a hip and crosses her arms. "You're used to this arrangement, I get it. I'm not kidding myself into believing this is special."

I smirk. Snarky Braelyn is much easier to handle. "Baseball. I used to play."

The tension in her shoulders melts. "Oh."

"Yeah. Thanks for attacking my character."

"Don't pretend to be offended. I'm sure you have a reputation to uphold."

The pressurized balloon in my gut deflates. I'm the foolish one in this scenario. "I've been known to swing for the fences."

Braelyn blinks at me. I laugh at her blank stare.

"Getting a home run," I supply.

She tilts her head. "I like this playful side of you. Dare I say, you're a bit charming."

The cheesy comment doesn't bother me. I'm over the stupidity hump. Not much can deter me at this point. The prospect of fucking her is enough to keep me immune to typical annoyances. But if I'm being honest, letting her smooth some sharp edges doesn't seem terribly unreasonable. I could probably benefit from reining in the shit.

She twirls her keys around a finger. "Ready?"

I nod and she unlocks the deadbolt. With the weight lifted off my chest, I follow her inside.

I kick off my shoes and tuck them along the entryway wall. There's a small closet propped open. I shuck out of my jacket and hang it up. A quick glance around shows me an open floor plan. The space is modest and neat. But fuck the interior decorating.

Braelyn moves down the hall. "Do you want something to drink?"

I'm hot on her heels, hypnotized by the gentle sway of her hips. "I have a nightcap planned."

She peeks back at me and bites her lip. "Straight to it?"

"Why wait?" Lord knows I've done enough pussy-footing for the both of us.

She reaches an open doorway and trails inside. The room is dark but smells of lavender and sugar. My mouth is already watering for another taste. But that can come after. The tent in my pants is far more demanding.

Braelyn flips a switch and the area is bathed in low light. My gaze latches on the massive bed in front of us. Fucking score. We can sprawl out and still have room to roll around.

The clink of my belt buckle echoes across the silent space. Braelyn watches as I loosen the leather from around my waist. I drop my pants, letting the soft material pool around my ankles. I step forward, and she meets me halfway.

Braelyn grips the tails of my shirt. "Can I?"

I quirk a brow. "Sure."

Buttons scatter in every direction, pinging off the walls and floor.

Her palms drift up my chest and around my shoulders. She pushes the soft material off me with one fluid sweep. Her hands fall to the hem of my undershirt, dipping beneath. I flex when she touches the bare skin of my torso. Braelyn's eyes lift to mine while she drags the white cotton up my abs. I stand perfectly still, more than willing to have her disrobe me. When she lifts the tee around my neck, I obediently raise my arms.

A hitch snags her inhale. Braelyn carefully traces the letters scrawling across my left pec. Oliver James is spelled out in his barely legible chicken scratch. Nothing is more permanent than a child. The tattoo is one of the best decisions I've made. Stopping in Thicket earlier is quickly climbing that list.

I reach behind Braelyn, lowering the zipper of her skirt. She shifts, and the faded denim slips down her legs. Thanks to my earlier destruction, her panties are nowhere in sight. Next comes her tank top. With a whoosh, it joins the growing pile around our feet. Her chest rises and falls with rapid breaths. I stare at the lace covering her tits.

Braelyn unclasps her bra and the obstructing garment loosens. Nerves make her fingers tremble when she lowers the straps. She doesn't shy away, letting it slide off her body. Her teardrop tits make me harder than marble. With a couple steps backward, Braelyn reveals all of herself to me.

Good Christ, she's magnificent. Blessedly naked and on display for me. Every inch of her is smooth and flawless. Desire burns in her eyes, matching the arousal clouding mine. I only see her. All slight curves and tan skin and temptation personified. This woman is mine for the having. I squeeze the base of my cock through the thin barrier of my briefs.

"Get on the bed," I order.

Braelyn doesn't hesitate, lifting herself up and scooting into the center. Her blonde hair spills over the navy sheets. She scissors her legs, settling on spreading them open. This girl.

I tug at the waistband of my shorts, stripping down with her gaze securely fastened on my dick. Braelyn's jaw unhinges on a gasp. The smirk I give her is a thousand dirty promises. I'm big and damn proud of it. She fists the blanket in a tight grip, restless movements shifting her limbs. I give a few cursory strokes just to watch her squirm.

"Don't make me wait, Brance. Please."

When the plea drops off her lips, a surge of need propels me forward. I grab a condom from my discarded pants. With calculated precision, I rip open the foil and roll the rubber down my shaft. I climb onto the mattress and move between her parted thighs. Leaning on an elbow, I lower myself until we're aligned together. My cock nudges her entrance. Braelyn loops her arms around me. She's about to let me conquer the deepest parts of her body. I line up with her center and push inside.

Her hips lift and tilt, welcoming me further. I sink to the hilt. We share a groan.

Braelyn's nails dig into my back. "B-Brance, holy shit. You fit just right."

I brush my mouth against hers. "So fucking good."

She glides her tongue along mine, and I angle us closer. Her core clenches, reminding me to move. I begin a steady rhythm, sliding in and dragging out. Braelyn tolerates this for several rounds, but soon rocks into me.

Her ankles cross against my ass, those movements picking up in pace. "Faster. I need more of you."

"Yeah?" I grind down, locking us closer. She's so damn tight. I pinch her nipple, and she bows into my touch.

"Yes, that. Oh, oh, more."

I punch my hips harder, thrusting in and out on a smooth cycle. My mouth latches onto her nipple, drawing the peak in between my teeth. Braelyn scratches along my scalp, and I growl against her supple flesh. Blood rushes south when I begin pounding into her.

Braelyn bucks into me, meeting my strokes with her own. "Break me. I wanna soar. Make me fly, Brance."

She's incredible, and I want to feel everything. The instinct to rip off this condom propels through me. Fucking her raw would be out of this damn universe. I'd bust in a second. It'd no doubt be the greatest climax of my life.

That's a risk I'll never take, but she's the first to actually tempt me.

"You're so hot."

"Mm-hmm," I bury my face between her tits. "You're so sexy."

I ghost my lips up the column of her throat. Braelyn arches her neck, granting me greater access. I gently bite along her jaw. An animalistic rumble rises off my chest. I lick a path to her ear, sucking the lobe into my mouth.

"You're delicious." I pump my hips faster, pushing her harder against me.

"Y-you feel so amazing. I never want you to stop."

"Jesus, Brae. Gonna make me come if you keep talking like that."

"I want it. Please. Give it to me."

Braelyn is vocal in the sack, and that turns me on more than I realized.

"What do you need?" I drag my fingers up and down her ribs, following the trail of subtle dips. Her skin is satiny soft.

She grips my wrist and shoves my hand down between us. I find her clit and get to work. When I hit the spot, Braelyn trembles.

She swivels into me. "Yes, there. Just keep going."

And I do. Harder and faster, plunging in and out. A pure shot of pleasure rushes into my veins. The grip on my control is fraying. Braelyn tightens around me, a noose strangling the breath from my lungs. All I feel is her squeezing and yanking me under. The sensation heightens and black spots dot my vision. This is it. What a fucking way to meet the end.

The cusp of release gathers in my balls. I circle her clit with rapid spirals until she's spasming around me.

"Holy shit, I-I'm there." Her muscles tense, triggering my own climax. We tumble over the edge with a mutual groan. I capture her next moan with my mouth. The waves crash, and I keep going. When I'm spent, my body collapses onto hers. I swallow her panting breaths, sharing every drop of my ecstasy.

Braelyn relaxes, and I break away from her lips. The smile she's wearing screams louder than anything else. I already know once won't be enough. The question forms without a doubt.

"Are we going extra innings?"

"You got more in the tank?"

"For you? Absolutely."

She slaps my ass. "Batter up."

chapter twenty-one

BRAELYN

FRAGMENTS

THE EARLY EVENING SUN POURS THROUGH THE FRONT WINDOWS. My stocking station is in direct impact of the scorching rays. As if I wasn't warm enough already. The temperature skyrocketed when a certain someone strolled through Thicket's door. This should have been taken into consideration when I assigned tasks.

Brance and his sinful smirk were too distracting. When he flashed those dimples at me, I had to wipe drool off my chin. It was a triumphant accomplishment that I was able to string a few sentences together.

I fan my clammy face. I'm tempted to crank the air conditioning. Would that be too obvious? Do I actually care?

I've been organizing a display of party supplies and swag for what seems like an hour. This would usually take ten minutes. A plastic tumbler spackled with glitter slips from my grip. I snatch it up with a huff. Where's a cold shower when I need one?

I feel Brance's overwhelming presence behind me. It's impossible not to. He's careful not to touch me. The sparks zipping through me scream that he might as well be. His broad chest is an inch away from my back when he boxes me in.

"Where does this belong?" His raspy whisper strokes my balmy skin.

I glance over to the toy corner. Ollie is preoccupied with piles of blocks, his back toward us. I grant myself permission to sag against Brance's solid form. I look down at what he's holding out in front of me. A laugh bubbles from my throat. The latest racy romance from my favorite author greets me. I blush, biting my lip. The scantily clad couple on the cover resembles us a few nights ago.

I blindly gesture to the designated row. "I keep a few books in stock over there."

"Do you like this sort of literature?"

"Mm-hmm."

"Should I read you an excerpt?"

I choke on my shock. At my silence, he flips through the pages. I slam the book closed. The idea of him narrating an erotic passage is too much.

"You're being bold." I wave a frantic hand at his son not too far from us.

"I'm not touching you."

"Trust me, that's not necessary in this case."

His nose dusts my ear. I hear his deep inhale. "I can smell how much you want me."

I press my thighs together. "What?"

"Yeah, I bet you're wet for me."

"Stop, please. Maybe later." My squeak is all breathy.

Brance chuckles. The filthy sound turns my nipples into hard peaks. My empty core clenches on nothing but air. Damn him.

He dips closer to my ear. "Yeah, we'll see."

Brance shifts backward, putting some much needed space between us. The tension oozes from my straining muscles. I appreciate the eye candy, but my body could use a reprieve.

"You don't have to stay." I've been repeating a version of that sentence countless times since he arrived.

Brance shrugs. "This is where Ollie wants to be."

I peer over at him. "And you?"

"I'm managing." He nods at the novel still in his hand.

"Feel free to pass the time reading. Just do it silently."

"That's not nearly as exciting." Brance wags his brows. "For either of us."

"You can shelf that in aisle three with the others."

He snorts. "No, no. This is coming home with me. Especially after how you reacted just now. I want to know what gets your engine revving. Maybe I'll learn some new tricks."

This man is trying to make me climax on command. He might succeed before this conversation is over. "You don't need any help in that department."

"I haven't used my best moves yet."

Good Lord. How can it get better? I blink at him. "This will take much longer if you don't quit messing with me. I'm not making any progress on all these discard piles."

Brance narrows his gaze. "Are you trying to get rid of me?"

The answer is no. But that white tee barely conceals the ridges lining his torso. And his ass in those faded jeans is getting me steamy in all the right places. With his son around, getting turned on is highly inappropriate. Would it be so wrong if I took a quick squeeze? Maybe lower his—

He clears his throat. I jerk my gaze off his zipper.

"You can stay."

"That's what I thought."

My stomach dips when he winks at me. Who knew there was swoon hiding behind all those hurtful insults and callous sneers. I think he's warming up to me. That could be very dangerous. I shove the crazy far out of my thoughts.

"I'm starting to feel guilty. You two always come here. The balance seems off."

Brance shrugs. "Because you're always working."

"That's hilarious. Take a peek in the mirror, Mister Partner."

"I make time for what's important."

I slap a palm to my cocked hip. "I'm a small business owner. This place doesn't run without me."

His eyes flare, eating up my defensive stance. "Retract the claws, Brae. We know, hence our regular presence."

I avert my gaze, appropriately reprimanded. "Okay. Sorry."

"For the record, I give Ollie the choice of going anywhere. Thicket is all he wants."

I glance at him from the corner of my eye. "Does that bother you?"

Brance is smiling. "Not as much lately. I'm reaping some benefits of his infatuation."

My cheeks flame hotter than a brick oven. "Took you long enough."

"Same to you, taffy girl."

I wrinkle my nose. "None of that."

"Sugar?" His grin is teasing.

I offer one in return. "Stick with Brae."

"That suits you, among other things."

"Such as?"

"Definitely not suitable for prying ears." He lifts his chin to where Ollie sits, twisting toward us with a beaming smile. We exchange a finger wave. Little eavesdropper.

My sigh is a hot fudge sundae with sprinkles on

top—paradise for the taste buds. "He's such a sweetheart. I'm very glad he found my store."

"The feeling is definitely mutual."

"You're my best customers."

Brance grunts and crosses his arms. "But that's superficial. It'd be nice to see you outside of these walls more often."

A swarm of bees high on honey buzz in my belly. "Would you like that?"

Why am I digging?

He squints at me. "Ollie sure would."

I accept that with a nod. "I'm actually training someone to fill in part time. Kallie is a college student off for the summer. She's looking for a few hours here and there. I can give that easy enough."

"It'll free you up for *other things.*" His emphasis on the last two words makes me shiver.

"That's the plan."

His stare is soul-deep. "What're your hobbies?"

"You're looking at it." I spread my arms out and spin in a slow circle.

He stays silent, those blue depths far too imploring.

I knot my fingers together. "What?"

"I want to know about you. There's more to your life than this shop."

With his curiosity, cleaning is officially forgotten. I'm off track and might as well share one of my passions. The old whiskey barrel sits to my right. I scoop up a handful of colorful pieces, letting them filter out between my fingers. "These are Captured Fragments. I make them."

Brance moves closer, peering inside. "What are they?"

I repeat my funneling process. "Recycled parts of random objects. Most of the items are broken beyond repair and people donate them to me. It feels really good finding purpose for something thrown away. I smash these seemingly insignificant items apart, smooth out the rough edges, and create a unique shape."

Holding up an orange cube, I let the light reflect off the shiny sides. "Alone, they're just a single sliver of glass." I reach in and snag a few more. "But together, they make something special."

I tilt my palm and catch the sun. A rainbow appears on the ground by our feet.

He smirks. "Again with the rainbows."

"I like natural beauty." I lift a shoulder.

"Me too." He rips his gaze off my face, reaching for a fragment. The piece rolls around in his hand. "They're like worry stones."

"Many use them for that."

"That'd be good for my office. There's a lot of shit going down on a constant basis."

I put several dozen pieces in a bag and pass them over. "On the house."

He crinkles the paper sack. "You're too sweet."

Embers glow in my lower belly. "That's what you said the other night."

Brance scratches his chin. "Nothing but the truth. Tell me more about you."

I glance at the ceiling, searching for anything of interest. "I dunno. Trying to think of stuff is making my life seem really bland."

"Where are you from?"

"Iowa."

His brow furrows. "I haven't spent much time there."

"You're not missing much. At least where I grew up. My hometown is tiny. You can drive along Main Street without blinking."

He laughs. "Not a lifer?"

"Not even close. I left with zero intention of going back."

"Same here. I'm from a suburb of Chicago. Like the city fine enough. There're just too many bad memories."

"We have that in common." I'm constantly plagued with them.

"Family?"

"Still living in same house. They'll never leave. How about your parents?"

His lips purse and I'm sure he's about to shut me down. But Brance is full of surprises today. "My dad is retired in Florida. He travels a lot. Hopefully he'll make it up here to visit Ollie before summer ends." Something dark passes over his features. I barely hold back a shudder. His nostrils flare, and he looks ready to spit nails. "My mother is on the east coast, terrorizing her current husband."

I wait for more, not wanting to pry. He moves his jaw back and forth, chewing on something big. In the end, he swallows it down without sharing.

I'm about to resume the organization mission when forty pounds of little boy plows into my leg. I topple sideways, bracing for the unforgiving ground. A strong arm loops around my waist and keeps me upright. Brance tugs me into his body while Ollie wraps around my leg. We're all in a cuddle huddle. For a brief moment, I wish this wouldn't end. But that's crazy ridiculous.

Brance is the first to pull away, keeping his hands on my shoulders. I offer a smile and mouth a silent bit of gratitude. Ollie clings tight to my thigh without showing any signs of letting go. I laugh and comb through his hair.

"Hey, sweetie."

He looks up, resting his chin on my hip. "Hi."

Brance pats Ollie's back. "Having fun?"

His son shoots him a wide smile. "Uh-huh. The best. Thanks for bringing me."

"As if I had a choice." There's laughter in Brance's tone, but I detect a slight edge.

I quirk a brow at him, and he nods to the romance novel perched on my register. The grin stretching my lips explains plans for next time we're alone. A low noise escapes Brance's throat.

Ollie's gaze bounces between us. "Whatcha talking about?"

I draw my lips between my teeth, hoping Brance will take this one.

"You, of course. It's always you, Ollie." He swipes a thumb down his son's cheek. A tiny piece of me melts beyond recognition. This man is ruining me.

Ollie makes a running lap around us. "I want ice cream."

"We need dinner first," Brance reminds him.

The Tasmanian tornado comes to a halt. His pout could put child actors out of business. "But I'm not hungry."

I tap my lips. "How about we clean up and go to Dapper? We'll share a bunch of stuff."

I almost expect Brance to lunge at the chance to correct me about who knows what. But he remains silent. His eyes bore into me, and I'm helpless to look away.

Ollie giggles. "I'm gonna pick up my puzzles. Have fun with your staring contest. I hope you win, Miss Braelyn."

I blink my gaze off Brance, focusing on his son's retreating form. He's so damn perceptive. Can we really keep this a secret?

Brance tugs on my belt loop. "Quick. Give me something good to tide us over. This might be a long-ass meal."

I bounce up on my toes, reaching his ear. "I read dirty romance novels."

He scoffs. "You already gave that up."

I *tsk*. "I never officially admitted it. You know what they say about assuming."

Brance buries his nose in my neck. "I wouldn't mind making an ass out of you and me together."

I stretch, giving him more room to explore. "You're bad."

"Oh, you have no idea."

"I might have a hint."

He bumps his hips into mine, giving me a feel of exactly what he's suggesting. "You're asking for trouble."

"Read chapter seventeen in that book," I purr. "It's a really good scene."

Brance leans back, his jaw slack. "Yeah?"

"Hell yeah. There's some great unconventional position inspiration."

His lips press against my temple. "In that case, you better get the recliner ready for later."

THE MEMORY OF BENDING BRAELYN OVER HER STORAGE CRATE flashes before my eyes. The high from yesterday hasn't worn off yet. That doesn't mean I won't try to sneak a quickie later. It's been two weeks of fucking her at every stolen opportunity. She's extremely flexible and down for anything, in all ways that matter. Each hidden location has given us inspiration for trying something new. The sex is damn hot, and it still feels like we're only scratching the surface.

We've managed to keep our hookups a secret. But this could set off waves and rock our arrangement.

I reach for the tickets and fan them out. There's three, same as when I checked five minutes ago. The debate builds strength, two sides rioting and demanding to be heard. My mind is ripping in half. Is this crossing a line? Those boundaries I've been so damn adamant to keep.

This won't be pushing too far. It's just one game. Ollie will be with us. There's no potential of this being a date.

Man the fuck up, I scold myself. *She's just a chick.*

One my son happens to love. A lot. Braelyn will agree to anything for him.

That indisputable fact slams down a gavel. Decision made, I grab my phone and tap out a text.

Me: Hey. What're the chances you'd like to see the Blues play tonight?

I hit send before finding ten reasons not to. The ball is safely lobbed into her field. I glare at my cell until the screen fades to black. Fuck. But what was I expecting? That she's waiting to hear from me, desperate and ready at all times? Even I'm not that arrogant.

Ollie darts down the stairs and runs toward me. "Did you ask her?"

I point at my phone. "Just sent a message."

He plops onto the chair beside me, resting his chin on an open palm. We take turns staring at the dark screen. This isn't constructive for either of us.

"Do you want a snack?" I move to the fridge.

"Cheese wheel, please."

I pull open the deli drawer. "Coming right up."

"Miss Braelyn will say yes."

I'm not sure if he's talking to me or himself. I choose to let it slide, handing him the wax covered circle. Ollie tugs at the tabs, revealing the white Swiss inside. Half the chunk is gone with one bite. He happily munches away, humming the theme song to his favorite cartoon. The strain collecting at the base of my neck ebbs slightly. Crisis averted.

"Shu mwe cull herm?"

Ollie resembles a chipmunk storing food for winter. I barely make out his garbled words. With a tense chuckle, I shake my head.

"No, buddy. We'll wait for her to answer. Be patient."

I almost laugh at my own suggestion. That request is along the lines of asking him to hold off on watching the new episode of Paw Patrol. He gobbles down the remaining cheese, his throat bobbing in an effort to swallow it all.

"But she's not working. It's Sunday. Why is she taking so long?"

"Ollie, it's been five minutes."

His lower lip sticks out. "That's a long time, Daddy."

He's bouncing in place, unable to sit still. My gut clenches while weighing the possibility of her turning us down. We didn't plan far enough ahead. She probably won't be interested or has other stuff to do. I look at my son who's vibrating with excitement. He'll be fucking crushed if she doesn't join us. And if I'm being honest, he won't be the only one.

My phone vibrates on the counter and I snatch it up.

Braelyn: Baseball? With you?

The need to correct her flexes my fingers. I type in a blur, resting my hip against the table.

Me: And Ollie. We have tickets for the game later.
Braelyn: That could be fun. What time?
Me: Game starts at seven. We usually get there an hour early.
Braelyn: Okay. Is parking expensive?
Me: Are you good with trains?
Braelyn: Yes. No traumatic history there.
Me: Meet us at the Light Rail station off 73rd and Oakville. Let's plan on five-thirty. Want me to send a pin drop?
Braelyn: Ah, smart. That's okay, I found it. See you soon.

"What's she saying? She's coming, right?" Ollie is leaning over so far, he might fall out of the chair.

His lips twist in that adorable way I love. "You're happy."

I straighten off the counter ledge. "Of course I am. We're gonna watch the Blues play."

He shakes his head. "But we do that a lot. This is different."

I turn away before he can dissect my expression further. The kid sees far too much. All I need is for him to start hounding me about marrying Braelyn again. He's dropped the subject more recently.

"Let's get ready to go, buddy. Is your jersey clean?" I call to him over my shoulder.

His footsteps follow close behind me. "I dunno."

I smirk. Searching for his shirt will keep him preoccupied. "Well, get looking."

"Kay, Daddy. I'll find it." A light huff precedes him taking off toward the laundry room.

I climb the stairs for a quick shower, trying to ignore the pep in my step. I'll never admit the effect that woman has on me. This shit will be taken to my grave.

Between chasing Ollie all about and inconvenient thoughts of Braelyn, three hours fly by in an arch of rainbow colors. We're decked out in our gear and ready to roll. Whenever she's involved, it's a snap to get my son in the car and going. We're on the road in record time, practicing our hoots and hollers for rooting on our team. I might need to keep her around for reinforcement purposes. But that would add more complications than I can count. I don't allow that idea to take root while steering my car around the final curve. The crowded parking lot appears in front of us.

Ollie begins kicking his feet wildly, the passenger seat jerking from the force. "We're almost there. I'm so excited. Do you think Miss Braelyn is already here, Daddy?"

Anticipation for a Blues game has never been higher.

I smile up at the rearview mirror. "Maybe, buddy. We'll see."

After finding one of the last available spots, we get out and walk to the pay station. I spot Braelyn almost immediately. She stands out in the swarm of people milling about. A bright blue hat hides half her face, but I'd recognize that ass anywhere. Especially in white cutoff shorts. Twin braids dangle over her shoulders, a red tank covers her tits and torso. She's wearing the perfect outfit for a ballgame.

I have to force my feet to keep moving without stopping to gawk. Ollie tugs on my hand, dragging me faster.

"Miss Braelyn!" His loud squeal carries above the rowdy groups of people between us.

She turns toward us with a wide grin. My son ditches me in a flash and latches himself around her bare legs. Braelyn hugs him in return, bending low to whisper something in his ear. A piercing bolt strikes my gut. For a split second, I'm jealous of their open affection. Would it be so bad to crash my lips down on hers? Yes, it sure as hell would be.

Braelyn waves at me. "Hey, Brance. Thanks for the invite."

"It was Ollie's idea." That's not true, but I'm good with giving him credit.

She ruffles his hair. "You're sweet to think of me, kiddo."

"Always." His smile is megawatt.

With a sigh, I leave them to catch up on the last twenty-four hours. I pay our round-trip fares and motion to the platform.

"All set. Let's go."

Braelyn digs out her wallet. "How much do I—"

I hold up a palm. "I took care of it."

"You're treating me?"

"Don't read into it. By showing up, you've made Ollie's day."

She leans close, pretending to dust lint off my shoulder. "We'll see if I can make your night later."

And just like that, I'm harder than stone. Dammit.

"Wicked woman," I growl.

Her grin is all knowing. "You're welcome."

She reaches for Ollie's hand and they skip into the nearest rail car. The entire ride, he chats her ear off. He talks nonstop about baseball and all the batting average stats in his memory. Braelyn keeps her attention locked on him, but sneaks glances at me every so often. Those quick peeks are a jolt straight to my cock. I adjust in the plastic seat, spreading my legs apart to hide any evidence. A sense of ease settles around me while Ollie's excited voice rambles on and on. It should be relaxing. But I can't help feeling as though we're on the tracks leading to epic disaster.

When we arrive, the stadium is bustling with pre-game activity. People clad in red, white, and blue gather in every available pocket of space. The smell of hot dogs and victory cling in the early evening air. My blood pumps faster being here. I'll always miss the thrill and hype of playing.

We make an initial lap around the outer edge, checking out our options. Ollie settles on cheese curds to start. I give him some cash, and he hops in line.

Braelyn digs in her purse and pulls out a pouch of Big League Chew. I feel my eyes bulge.

"No way. I haven't had that stuff in years."

Her grin speaks of secrets. "I actually carry it in stock at Thicket during baseball season. There isn't a more appropriate occasion to have some than now."

I blink at her, trying to process this curveball. "You're pretty fucking epic, Braelyn. Bonus points for the throwback."

She holds the package open for me. "Want some?"

Like a moth, I swoop into Braelyn's flame. It's not bubblegum I'm after. I tug on the hem of her tiny shorts. "I like your outfit."

She glances down at what she's wearing. "Yeah? I wasn't sure about the dress code standard."

"You nailed it. You've been breaking necks since we walked in."

Braelyn tucks her chin. "I mostly care about snapping yours."

I release a rumble into her ear. "You make that sound sexy."

"You're sexy period."

I skim my fingers over the strip of exposed skin between her waistband and shirt. "I better make sure Jordan is up for watching Ollie after this."

"Please do." Her voice is a low rasp that wraps around every part of my body. When she tips against me, it's a fight to keep my hands off her.

Ollie finishes ordering and grabs his food. He saves us from being arrested for indecent exposure. Braelyn leaps sideways, separating us by a few feet. I chuckle and stuff my fists deep into my pockets. My son seems none the wiser and eats his second cheesy snack of the day.

Between bites, Ollie glances at Braelyn's outfit. "Why aren't you wearing a Blues shirt?"

She shrugs. "I don't have any official memorabilia. I've never been to a game before."

His mouth pops open. I pat him on the back, encouraging him to keep walking. Braelyn gets a wink from me. "During the seventh inning, we'll get you some swag."

Ollie claps. "Or you can win something from the cannon."

I nod slowly. "You can definitely take that chance."

She giggles. "I'm good with buying something. Then I'll have it for next time."

My chest tightens, but I don't comment. What's there to say with my son around? Promises with Braelyn are fleeting.

We continue wandering until everyone has something. After stopping for popcorn and peanuts, I guide us to the front row near the team's dugout.

"Is this where we're sitting?" There's a tinge of wonder in Braelyn's voice.

I shake my head. "Nah. We hang out here during pitching and batting practice. The players are pretty good about giving the kids a ball once they're done warming up. Ollie loves this stuff."

As if proving my point, he's hanging over the railing and waving to the coach. A few guys jog over to slap his little palm. Ollie eats up the attention, giving them all an award-winning smile.

Braelyn watches closely, taking everything in. "So, you used to play?"

I suck in a deep breath and look up to the cloudless sky. "I did. Second base shortstop to be exact."

"Yeah? In high school?"

I scrub over the stubble lining my jaw. "Uh-huh. I was pretty decent. Made varsity as a sophomore. Scouts were already sniffing around my games. The coaches were grooming me to go pro. I ate up the attention like pudding snacks."

Braelyn glances over. "What happened?"

"My mother."

I feel her stiffen beside me. This is the point where I always veer off-topic. But there's something different about tonight. Fuck it.

"My mother tolerated the sport for long enough. She wouldn't have her only son wasting his life being an athlete. I needed to become some prestigious business owner or a crooked politician to appease her. That wasn't the life I wanted." I widen my stance and get lost in the diamond pattern crossing the outfield.

I lift the hat off my head, only to tug it right back down. I lower the brim to shield my eyes. "It was more than her habit of being pretentious, of course. She knew how much I loved playing, saw it as a way to hurt me. Taking baseball away was a direct hit. My coach tried to reason with her. He was willing to sponsor me and take care of the paperwork. But nothing would sway her decision. She wasn't having this sort of groveling at her doorstep any longer. She made it clear that any opposition would end in a bloody battle. It wasn't worth his effort, or mine. My mother wouldn't stop, and I knew that well enough. I didn't let her see how much that crushed me. I wouldn't give her the satisfaction."

The popcorn in my stomach curdles into sour acid. I swallow the thick bile down, coughing over the darkness in my past. The only strength through this disgusting pit was the woman next to me. By some unspoken reason, I knew she understood.

"She never laid a hand on me." I spit the words out. "Her form of abuse was emotional. She used my love against me. A total mindfuck for a child. No mother should threaten to take her affection away. My father was helpless against her. She was the mom, and our system grants them full custody far too easily. He tried to fight her in court but lost over and again. She thought it was hilarious that I was stuck with her. Just one more way to torture me. I tried to leave a handful of times, but the police always brought me back. She was vindictive and spiteful. I don't wish her hate on my worst enemies, even Veronica."

Braelyn shivers beside me, and I loop an arm around her shoulders. "I'm fine. Stronger because of it. She was my sole motivation behind becoming a lawyer. I wanted to fight for those who couldn't on their own. She might have given birth to me, claimed the title of mother, but I never called her Mommy. I have to thank her for the valuable lessons. I'll let Ollie play whatever sports he's interested in. He can study any major. I already have a hard time telling him no. But that doesn't seem like a problem." One of the finest points of that fact is currently snuggling against my chest.

"You're an amazing father." Braelyn grips my forearm, and I tighten my hold on her.

I stare at her fingers linked around me, choosing not to focus on the pounding in my chest. "That means a lot. Thank you."

She cuddles closer. "Thank you."

I bend backwards until her face is visible. "For what?"

"Trusting me."

"Bottling it up doesn't help anyone. You make it easier to share."

Her forehead bunches. "I do?"

"Of course. You've been through far worse."

She looks down at her tennis shoes. "It's all relative."

"Whatever makes you feel better."

Before I can open my big mouth any wider, Ollie bounds up to us. He looks at Braelyn curled around me, smiling in that secretive way. I drop my arms, and she slinks out of reach.

"I was keeping Braelyn warm."

It's a balmy eighty degrees out here.

Ollie's grin spreads. "That was nice of you. But the game is gonna start. We should find our seats."

I point across the field. "We're in the home-run porch. Ollie's dream is to catch a ball. So far, we've struck out."

He shakes his mitt. "It's gonna happen today. I can feel it."

Braelyn squeezes the leather glove. "Definitely. This is your lucky game."

Ollie bounces in place, gobbling up the possibility. It's bound to happen sooner or later with the amount of games we attend. Maybe she's right about tonight.

As we're nearing our row, Braelyn glances around. She hitches a thumb toward the sign. "I'm going to the bathroom before the excitement starts."

Ollie stands quietly beside me while we wait near the aisle. I grab a handful of peanuts and start cracking the shells.

"Daddy?"

"Yeah, buddy?"

"Do you love Miss Braelyn yet?"

I grunt. "No, Ollie. We're just friends."

He peeks up at me, shuffling his feet. "Are you sure? She smiles at you a lot. Just like you smile at her."

"Positive. We're just happy to be around you." I ruffle his hair, but it doesn't have the usual effect. Ollie's features remain flat.

In the next beat, his eyes take on their familiar sparkle. "You should hold her hand. I'll take the seat on the end so you can be together."

My little matchmaker is back in action. Guns blazing at rapid fire.

I look in the direction Braelyn went but don't see her. "No, buddy. You can sit between us. Otherwise it would feel funny."

He stomps his foot, and I laugh. Ollie sees something over my head, his gaze expanding with something I'm terrified to discover.

This time, his smile is victorious. "Well, what if you two get on the big camera screen? Will you kiss her?"

The evening plays out before my eyes, and I groan. Inviting Braelyn to this game suddenly seems like a horrible idea. Or the best one yet.

With a bit of coaxing, or bribing, Ollie agrees to sit between us. Until the sixth inning. I didn't think much of it until that cheesy ass music started up. A knot the size of Lake

Superior twists my stomach. This type of fanfare gives major league sports a bad name.

Spread across numerous jumbo screens are unsuspecting couples, or two random people of the opposite sex trying to enjoy a simple non-date. From the corner of my eye, I catch Braelyn laughing and pointing. She's enjoying the show, of course. I want to chuck a ball at the video camera hovering nearby. With each passing duo, the bricks in my gut crumble. The chances are damn unlikely they'll plaster us up there.

But, as my shitty luck would have it, Braelyn's gorgeous face and my scowling mug flash on screen. I watch her eyes bulge, a flush already racing up that slender neck. Asshole I might be, but leaving her hanging isn't my style.

So, I do the reasonable thing. I lean over and kiss her.

chapter twenty-three

BRAELYN

CASTLES

Brance buries his face in my neck, nipping at the sensitive skin. I arch up and silently beg for more. He gives it, thrusting inside of me faster and harder. Good Lord, this man was made for sex.

He licks a trail down my throat while picking up his pace between my legs. The dual sensation is almost enough. I tighten my arms around him, nails digging deeper into his back. An upward arch of my spine. Oh, oh, yes. Brance does some magical grind with his pelvis. I crash our hips together and he hits my clit just right. Holy wow, my—

Incessant buzzing yanks me from the X-rated dream I was having. Dammit, things were just getting really good. The fantasy is officially popped with my loud groan, followed closely by a stretch to make any cat jealous. It's my one day to sleep in. Who the hell is calling so early?

I reach for my phone, prepared to give the recipient a tongue-lashing. I falter when catching sight of the screen.

There's a slew of messages waiting from Brance. Even in my state of dismay, I snicker at his nickname.

B-Ran: Good morning, Brae. Plans today?
B-Ran: Ollie says hello. (image attached)

The picture gives me pause. I rub the crust from my eyes and take a better look. That kid is so cute. Smiling wide for the camera, dimples on full display. I resume scrolling.

B-Ran: Still sleeping?
B-Ran: (image attached)

When I open the picture, all the fizzling heat in my lower belly launches to piping hot and ready for action. I zoom in on Brance's handsome face. He's not smiling, but the cocky tilt to his lips is even better. His jaw is dusted with weekend stubble, just the right amount to leave evidence on my inner thighs and neck. Or breasts. I squeeze my legs together and check the time. Maybe I can self-love before coffee. With this new spank-bank material, my orgasm is already halfway there. It'd probably only take a few swipes. I scan the remaining messages with a quick glance.

B-Ran: Nothing? Would below the belt work?
B-Ran: Tough crowd.
B-Ran: Ollie is getting restless.
B-Ran: Wake up, babe. Please?

Babe? Please? What alternative universe did I wake up in? We've been sleeping together for weeks, but I wasn't aware that granted me an upgraded nickname.

Plans of getting myself off are forgotten with a simple word. This is a game changer. Or I'm digging far deeper than he intended. Probably the latter. It's just a pet name, the most causal one at that. But Brance using it feels very different.

My cell vibrates in my hand, and I almost drop it.

B-Ran: I tried the simple way.

I furrow my brow. What does he mean by that? I jump ten feet straight in the air when my doorbell rings. The loud knock calls out immediately after. My lungs seize, and I cough out a breath. He wouldn't just randomly show up. I glance back at my cell. This morning's events have proven his recent unpredictability. Shit.

With the speed only several mugs of caffeine induce, I get my ass moving. I toss on a shirt and stumble into some shorts. There's no time for a mirror check so I pat my hair down into some semblance of tame. I dart down the hall, tripping over who-knows-what in my haste to investigate his level of crazy.

I swing the door open to find Sadie standing on my porch. She has a hand raised, preparing to offer another knock. The disappointment clouding over me must show on my face.

Sadie purses her lips. "Nice to see you too, Brae."

"Good morning." The belated greeting doesn't appease her.

"It's almost ten o'clock. What have you been doing?"

I peek at my empty wrist, clearly missing the presence of a watch. "Uh, sleeping? It's Sunday."

"So? Get out and enjoy the sunshine."

"Okay, thanks for the advice. What's up?" I lean against the frame, crossing my arms.

Sadie is smiling now. "I'm the reinforcements."

I blink at her. Without coffee, my circuits aren't quite connecting. "Wait. Brance sent you?"

"Don't forget Ollie and Jordan."

"O-okay. Why?"

She quirks a brow. "Aren't you gonna invite me inside?"

I sweep toward the hallway. "As if you need to be asked."

"Here." She hands me a plastic bag while passing by. "I took the liberty of buying you a new suit."

I peek inside, finding a crisscross of strings and some scraps of fabric. "Uh, what?"

Sadie parks a palm on her hip. "We're going to Lake Vask."

"Swimming?"

She waves off my question. "Sunbathing. Day-drinking. Whatever."

I take another careful look in the bag. "And you expect me to wear this?"

She's nodding too fast. "Trust me. This is the latest trend."

"Showing up to the beach naked?" My voice is a pitchy squeak.

Sadie claps. "Yeah, you're finally understanding. Brance will love it."

Thirty minutes later, I'm showered and shaved. My lady bits are tucked and stuffed into this microscopic bikini. I toss my hair up in a messy bun and throw on a coverup. My friend frowns at me, shooting a glare at the sheer dress.

"That defeats the purpose." She wrinkles her nose, the slinky material apparently offending her.

I roll my eyes. "The summer heat is getting to you. There's no way I'm leaving this house wearing next to nothing."

Sadie huffs. "It's not that bad."

"Let's see yours." I lift a brow in challenge.

She averts her gaze. "I have nothing to prove."

"Uh-huh, that's what I thought."

She grabs her purse and heads toward the door. "Let's go. The guys are waiting. You can drive."

"Because there's another option," I grumble.

I open the garage and unlock my car. Sadie drops into the passenger seat. She flips the visor down and checks out her reflection, flawless as always. I slip behind the wheel with a sigh.

"Whenever you're ready to hand over the keys, I'll be here."

I smile at her. "Thanks. The thought isn't as traumatizing lately."

Sadie's face lights up. "Really? Wow, that man has magical powers."

I reverse out of the driveway with a laugh. "All he needs is another ego boost."

"I bet. You're stroking that bad boy several times a week."

A puff of air escapes my lips. "You're so bad."

"Likewise," she replies.

I curl my fingers around the leather grip. "I've been feeling better lately, Dee."

She rubs my shoulder. "It shows, girlfriend. Why do you think I bought that suit? Strut your hot ass."

"I wouldn't go that far."

"That's why you have me around. I sure will, for your benefit."

"Such a great friend." I wink at her.

"In all seriousness, I'm happy for you. No matter the cause or reason, seeing you smile is damn refreshing."

"It really is."

I turn onto the main road that leads down to the beach. The lots look full, so I park along the curb. A little walking will do us good. Sadie climbs out and steps toward the meter.

"It's the weekend. Don't waste your quarters."

She points at me. "Good call. I'll save my change for the vending machine."

"We could've stopped for snacks."

"And delay this adventure even longer? Brance wouldn't appreciate that."

I groan, peeking down at my outfit. "I cannot believe you talked me into this."

She makes a disbelieving noise in her throat. "Brae, you look smokin' hot. Brance will find some tiki hut for you two. It's gonna be a wild ride. You better spill all the deets. You owe me, sistah."

I gape at her. But there's no denying the rush of heat spreading through my veins. "There will be none of that. We're in a public place."

"Oh, come on—you're creative. Don't pretend."

I bow my head, hiding the fire traveling up my cheeks. "Whatever."

"Take off that shapeless sack and show him what you've got."

"He already knows," I whisper.

Sadie tips her head back, cackling way too loud. "That's my best friend. You're gonna get laid."

I almost slap a palm over her mouth. "Will you keep your voice down?"

"Why hide the truth?"

"Jeez, no pressure."

She bumps her hip into me. "Okay, fine. This is a fun family outing. No need to panic."

"Friendly," I correct. "We're just friends."

"With hella good benefits." Her grin stretches wide.

"You're one to talk. How's Jordan?"

Sadie's attention snaps forward. "Oh, look! They're here."

Brance, Ollie, and Jordan are huddled in a small circle. She conveniently avoids my question by racing off toward the group of guys. I follow behind at a leisurely pace. There's zero need to hurry in any part of me. I have every intention of relaxing my scantily clad butt.

My flip-flops fill with warm sand as I narrow the distance. The sun is high in the cloudless sky, bathing us in glorious vitamin D. Ollie splashes into the water, leaving Brance standing off to the side alone. My heart gallops at the sight of him in those sinfully low swim trunks.

As if he senses me approach, he twists around and traps me with his piercing gaze. His eyes trace across every part of me. Regardless of the summer humidity, I break out in goosebumps. I've never felt so exposed. But that's not unpleasant under his focus. In two strides, Brance closes the remaining distance between us.

"Well, look at you."

I bite my lip. "Hey yourself. Sorry about not returning your texts."

His lifts a broad shoulder. "No worries. You're here now."

I flutter my lashes. "Miss me?"

Brance grunts. "Maybe."

A zing of something sharp shoots through my chest. "Oh?"

He wipes over his mouth, hiding a grin. "Don't make it weird."

I bite my tongue and try keeping the giddy butterflies in check. "M'kay."

"Whatcha hiding under here?" He pulls at the collar of my dress.

"This ridiculous bikini Sadie bought for me. It belongs on a porno shoot."

He bends lower toward my boobs. "I'd love to see it."

I shove him off. "I'm sure you would."

Jordan wanders over and claps Brance on the back. "Ready?"

I look between them. "Going somewhere?"

"We're gonna play volleyball. Wanna watch?" Brance wags his brows.

I suck in a sharp breath, imagining him diving all over the court. My ovaries couldn't handle it. "Uh, what about Ollie?"

He seeks his son out in the lake. "He can join us."

"No, he's having too much fun. I'll hang back and keep him company."

He bops me on the nose. "Good call."

In a move far too calculated, Brance whips off his white tee and tosses it at me. I swallow the lust billowing up my throat. Brance has the furthest thing from a stereotypical dad-bod. With chiseled abs and defined muscles, he puts others to shame. For me, he's a total standout. I'll never tire of staring. Hopefully he doesn't mind. Based off his wicked smirk, this man appreciates my gawking.

Good grief, he's sexy. I'm certain a collective sigh rings out from every woman lining this strip of beach. My seat is front row, and hot damn, I'm enjoying the show. Should I clap? He gently drags a finger down my arm. "See you in a bit, babe."

With that parting shot, he struts off in all his cocky glory.

"Miss Braelyn!" Ollie races up to my side. "You're finally here! Now we can build a sandcastle."

His words sound lost in a tunnel, barely a low whistle. I'm still tracking Brance's retreating form, a golden beacon glowing in the sun. He's too damn hot.

"Miss Braelyn?" Ollie taps my arm.

I blink out of my Brance-haze. My eyes flicker to the sweet boy in front of me. I comb through his wet hair. "Sorry about that, buddy. I'd love to help you. We'll make the big-gest castle ever."

He hauls over a heaping bucket full of toys. We find the optimal area and get to work. Time passes in a sweaty blur. Ollie's exuberance keeps me digging long after my biceps feel like pudding.

With the use of several molds and tools, we have quite

an impressive fortress. The castle is taller than my knees and covers several feet of beach. I dust off my hands, stepping back to admire our project.

"This is quite a fancy castle. I'd totally live here if it wasn't made of sand."

Ollie plops down and points to one of the corners. "This is my room." He carves a square in the front, making a window. "And you can stay here." He drags a finger to the indent next to his.

I tap my chin. "What about your dad? Where will he sleep?"

"Right there." His thumb jabs at the space allotted for me.

I want to pout about being displaced so easily. "But that's my room."

"So? You can share."

I make it a point to scan the expanse of our sand creation. There's plenty of other options, make-believe or not. I wrack my brain for a viable reason why this living situation wouldn't work. A different solution is on the tip of my tongue.

Ollie bulldozes through my silence. "Daddy always says it's nice to share. I'm sure he won't mind."

Brance chooses this exact moment to appear. He sits down next to Ollie, inspecting our castle turned family home. He glances at his son. "What do I tell you?"

"We should always share. That's why you and Miss Braelyn are in the same room." Ollie motions to our assigned plot.

"Is that so?" Brance's searing stare is fixed on me. Those ocean blue waves are liable to pull me under at any second. The afternoon sun is suddenly too hot. Maybe I need some shade.

Ollie isn't aware of the combustible chemistry moments away from boiling over. Or he's choosing to ignore it.

"Uh-huh. We'll have so much fun. Miss Braelyn can come to our house for dinner. She'll sleep over and stay so we can eat breakfast together in the morning."

I'm certain a concave dent is marring my forehead. This kid has it all sorted out. "Um, well, I already have my own place. That's where all my stuff is."

Ollie looks to his dad for backup. Brance scratches the nape of his neck. I scrub my clammy palms on a nearby towel. Who's going to crack? My money is on me.

Brance clears his throat. "How about we start with just dinner?"

I let my mouth hang open. This must be a straight violation against our code of conduct. I'm frozen in contemplation, my gaze jumping from Ollie to Brance.

"Can you eat at our house, Miss Braelyn?" Ollie's little hands are clasped together.

My heart squeezes painfully. "Sure," I wheeze.

Ollie bounces to his feet. "Great! My daddy will cook something super-yummy."

My eyes fling up to meet Brance's waiting stare. "You're gonna make dinner?"

His lips kick up in a half-smile. "Should I be offended by your tone?"

I rein in my shock and smooth the tension from my features. "Um, no?"

"Who'd you think prepares the meals at our house?"

"Mary?" I bury my toes in the sand, wishing they were my head.

Brance snorts out an exhale. "Thanks for that. But due to mommy dearest being the worst, I was self-sufficient at age eight. I have an extensive collection of recipes. Which is helpful since Ollie gets bored easily."

My brain is trying to pick apart this new revelation. What a strange day this is turning out to be. I rub my throbbing temples. "Well, okay. I guess that sounds good. Are you thinking sometime this week?"

"Why not tonight?"

I think my jaw is still slack and gaping open. The surprise didn't have a chance to ebb yet. "W-what?"

Brance strokes his stubbled chin. "I can whip something up quick. No hassle or fuss. I'll think of something easy and delicious."

Ollie whispers something in his father's ear. Brance nods while looking at me. "I bet she'll love that," he murmurs.

Ollie is smiling wider than I've ever seen. "Come over at six, 'kay?"

Considering we've been at the beach for hours, that might be right around the corner. But what difference does it make? The odds of me not showing up are super slim. Stalling will get me nowhere fast. My stomach grumbles, giving away how I really feel on the matter. I laugh and pat my belly.

The Stone men wear matching expressions of impatience. There's no hint of humor in their taut postures. Ollie appears ready to leap at me, being held off by a fraying string. Brance's frown grows more intense. I swallow another giggle and put them out of their misery.

"I'll show up hungry."

SET AN OVERFLOWING CASSEROLE DISH ON THE MIDDLE RACK. A small pan of extra tater tots goes in next. I close the oven with a quick lift of my wrist. After setting the timer, I turn to my son. He's humming a happy tune while coloring. His legs swing back and forth from his spot at the high-top counter. I move closer to get a better look. My stomach tightens almost painfully. A vibrant rainbow decorates his page.

Ollie looks up, his baby blues glittering. "Is Miss Braelyn coming soon?"

The question distracts me from the subject of his artwork. I check the clock on the stove. "About fifteen more minutes."

His face screws up a bit, wheels turning quickly. I'm sure he's trying to calculate that length of time in his terms. "Can I go play in my room until she gets here?"

"Of course, buddy."

He hops off the stool, pushing his picture toward me. "I

made this for Miss Braelyn. Maybe she'll stick it on her fridge. Or hang it up at Thicket."

"I'm sure she'll love it, little man." And I know she will. That woman has the softest spot set aside for my son. If he wasn't mine, I'd be jealous of the smothering attention she dishes out to him.

"I'm really excited for dinner. Are you, daddy?" He blinks those wide eyes at me.

There's only one answer to give without crushing his dreams. "Of course, Ollie. I love eating with you."

"And Miss Braelyn," he adds.

I don't bother confirming or denying that. Am I encouraging him by agreeing to have her over for dinner? Maybe. Was it a terrible decision to indulge his meal idea? Probably. Will this make things more complicated? Absolutely. Did that stop me? Not at all.

With a parting grin, Ollie dashes out of the kitchen. I grab plates and silverware, three of each. The odd number doesn't register as a snag in my routine. If I allow myself to be honest, the sight of an extra place setting feeds that starving piece of my heart. Braelyn is doing one hell of a job restoring strength in the most desolate parts of that beating organ. And I've decided to stop fighting against what feels good.

A tentative knock breaks into the soft music I have going. I stride to the entryway and swing the door open. Braelyn is waiting there, a pillar of bright light against the darkening sky. Everything else fades into a blur. She's all I see, a vision meant to carry me through the hardest of times. This woman manages to strike deeper with every glimpse.

"Hi, you." Her easy smile threatens to steal my breath.

I force my features to remain stoic. "Hey, Brae."

She holds up a package of Ollie's favorite grape flavor. "I brought juice boxes. And the adult version for us." She turns the box in her left hand, exposing the wine label.

A chuckle barks out of me. "You're too damn thoughtful."

Braelyn shrugs. "Couldn't show up with nothing."

I take the beverages off her hands. "Thanks for this. Ollie will appreciate the extra treat. Especially from you."

She chomps on her bottom lip, still hovering in the doorway. "I'm a bit early."

"Couldn't wait any longer?"

The grin I get in return is a reward for my cock. That sweet mouth will be wrapped around me later.

"Something like that," she murmurs.

I pivot to let her by. Braelyn steps inside, her gaze dissecting every nook and cranny. Her eyes sweep across the walls and vaulted ceilings. I notice the moment she catches sight of the floor-to-ceiling windows in front of the dining table. She peeks in the living room next to us, pausing on a few framed candid shots of Ollie. I can't stop the feeling that my life is on display. But I don't mind her taking a better look, peeling back my layers. Seems fitting since I've had the chance to view most of hers.

Braelyn is in my space, the sanctuary very few have the privilege of seeing. I wonder what she thinks. Does she feel the current changing? Women aren't invited over here, as in ever. With the exception of Mary and a few random babysitters, our home is male dominated.

Until now.

I watch her study my house, willing those mossy pools to land on me again. I almost crave her rapt focus. When Braelyn lifts those soulful depths to me, another piece slides into place. She's wearing a different outfit, and her hair is down in loose waves. It's probably best that she ditched the skimpy bikini. I got the chance to peel those strings off her earlier. If I knew those scraps of fabric were still hidden underneath, getting through dinner would be even harder. The massive pun is absolutely intended. The semi tightening my jeans agrees.

Braelyn spins in a slow circle, taking another look around. She takes an audible sniff of the air. "It smells delicious. Whatcha making?"

"That's a surprise."

She walks toward the kitchen. The boxes in my grip get tossed to the side. I cinch my arms around her waist from behind and press us together. Her ass cradles my hardening dick.

"Maybe I'll eat you first," I growl in her ear.

"Didn't you get enough on the lake?"

"Not nearly."

She leans into me, her temple brushing my mouth. "Who's gonna watch Ollie?"

Sadie and Jordan agreed to take Ollie for ice cream earlier. That gave me another stolen slice of time with this woman. We rented a paddleboat and found a hidden alcove. She wasn't lying about the swimsuit Sadie bought her. If she ever wore that when I wasn't around, we'd have a serious problem.

"He's upstairs building a Lego fortress. That usually keeps him occupied for hours."

Braelyn purrs. "Do you have a large pantry?"

"I sure do." I bump her forward in the right direction.

But, of course, nothing is that simple.

As if sensing her presence, my son comes bounding down the steps. He flies full speed at Braelyn's legs. The collision is harsh and probably would've knocked her over if I hadn't been here.

I bite back a groan, stepping away from the comfort of her body. The image of her spread thighs vanishes in a flash. "Great timing, Ollie. Dinner should be ready."

"It's gonna be so good. I can't wait for you to try my daddy's specialty. Are you excited, Miss Braelyn?" My son babbles all that on a single breath.

Her nod is eager. "Oh, yes. I can't wait to find out what he made for us."

"Let's go sit down." He steals Braelyn's hand and drags her toward the table.

I grab the discarded drinks and follow them into the kitchen. "Ollie, guess what?"

He whips around to face me. Like a sniper, his gaze zeroes in on what I'm holding. "Juice boxes? No way!"

"Braelyn brought them for you."

Ollie beams at her. "How'd you know those are my favorite?"

That earns him a smile in return. "Lucky guess."

"Daddy, can I have one with dinner? Or maybe two?"

I chuckle and rip off the plastic wrapping. "Start with one. We'll see about more."

He takes the pouch from me. "Can Miss Braelyn have one?"

She giggles. "Those are especially for you, sweetie."

I wink at her. "We have our own juice."

He shrugs. "More for me."

"Ollie, can you finish setting the plates?" I point to the short stack on my way to the oven.

He races to finish the task within ten seconds. The faint noise of wood scraping against tile accompanies his efforts. With potholders handy, I place the steaming food on the table. Braelyn finds a corkscrew and opens the wine. The makings of a well-oiled machine are underway.

Ollie abandons his usual seat next to me, dashing to the chair on the opposite end. "Miss Braelyn?"

His voice is way too innocent. I brace myself for whatever scheme he's whipping up. He jabs a finger at the empty spot beside me. The chair has been pushed very close to mine, as in almost touching. That's not suspicious.

"You can sit by my daddy." His hands are folded in that

innocent way he tries to pull off. I know better. This is a battle I'll never win.

I pat the seat. "I'll try to give you space."

My son squeaks, the tone one of outrage. "What? No. Sit on his lap."

"Oliver James," I warn.

He presses his lips together, having the decency to look guilty. "Sorry. Just thought it'd be easier for talking."

I snort and roll my eyes. "Yeah, sure. Eat your dinner."

"It's all right. I don't mind close quarters. Is footsie allowed?" Braelyn laughs while wedging herself in. "There's not a lot of legroom."

Ollie tilts his head at us. "What's that mean?"

"Never mind," I mutter. Braelyn gets a squeeze to her knee for that.

She yelps and shoves my fingers away. "Oh my goodness, this looks fantastic. Tater tot hotdish?"

I nod and serve her a double portion. "Yep. It's a staple around our house. I'd tell you it's a family recipe, but that'd be a lie. My mother never cooked a day in her life. I highly doubt my grandmother did either."

Braelyn smacks her lips. "This was one of my favorite meals growing up. My day was made when a restaurant had it on the menu. What a great surprise."

She takes a big bite, moaning around her fork. The sound is filthy and shoots a potent dose of arousal into my veins.

"Really?" I make a point of staring at the bulge in my pants.

Her face turns the same shade as our cherry red napkins. "I can't help it. This is really good."

"You better repeat that while I'm buried deep later," I murmur into her ear.

There's a hitch in her breath, but she recovers quickly enough. Braelyn's toes climb up my shin. "Even louder."

I choke on a ball of lust. "Dirty girl."

"Just wait," she whispers.

"Is it working?" Ollie's question is equivalent to a bucket of cold water.

I wrench my gaze off the temptation next to me. "What's that, buddy?"

"Are you two getting married? Then Miss Braelyn can live with us?"

Braelyn gulps audibly. I steeple two fingers in front of my mouth. Ollie watches us for any sudden movements, like a sprint to the chapel.

"Ollie," I start.

His shoulders slump. "Okay, I know. Forget I asked."

A seed of guilt sprouts and grows roots in my stomach. "How about cookies for dessert?"

That perks up his posture. "Yes! Chocolate chip?"

I scoff. "Of course. Is there another kind?"

"Nope." He adds extra pop to the word.

Braelyn giggles. "You two are adorable. I could listen to this all night."

Ollie rests his elbows on the table. "Really? Wanna stay longer?"

She taps her lips. "Maybe. What will we do?"

"We can play cards. Or a board game. I have Candy Land." His voice raises higher with each suggestion.

"That could be fun," Braelyn muses.

I find myself digging the hole a bit deeper. "How about a movie? Ollie can choose."

He pumps a fist in the air. Braelyn winks at me. I've made the right call.

Ollie scoots off his chair, dashing toward the television. "There's a new cartoon we can rent. It's about puppies and horses and zoo animals. Right, Daddy? We saw a commercial yesterday."

"Slow down, buddy. Braelyn hasn't agreed yet."

She nudges me. "As if I'll say no." She dips her chin and tilts closer. "To either of you."

The desire to kiss her slams into me. I barely find the control to restrain myself. Would it be so bad? I stare into her eyes, the bright green swirling with tender passion. Instead of demolishing that boundary, I slide my palm along hers. I link our fingers together and give a gentle squeeze.

"Should we make popcorn?"

Her laugh is silent, just a soft bounce of her upper half. She's captivating.

"Yes." With one syllable, she solves a slew of problems.

"Do you like butter and salt?"

"Mm-hmm, I'm always on board for flavorful goodness."

I press my lips to the crown of her head. "I'll keep that in mind."

The three of us pile on the couch. Ollie doesn't fight us on being plopped in the middle. He snuggles between us with a huge smile. I could get used to this. The thought is dangerous and should have me running for the mountains. My ass remains firmly planted on the couch.

I pass the popcorn bowl to Braelyn, the move natural and effortless. Nothing about this situation should be comfortable. But I can't dredge up the effort to pretend otherwise. Regret hasn't sunk in yet. I'll worry about clearing up our disintegrating lines tomorrow.

chapter twenty-five

BRAELYN

STARS

THE FINAL SCENE OF THE MOVIE FADES TO BLACK. MY INNER child claps with glee. It's been years since I've watched a cartoon. And I couldn't have asked for better company.

When the credits begin rolling, I attempt to shift my arm. Shooting pain stabs into my muscle. A wild fire spreads from that inch of movement, and I swallow a moan. Dammit, that hurts.

Ollie is snoring on my shoulder. I don't have the heart to move him, but my limb is dead asleep. Something has to give.

I look up and find Brance's gaze locked on me. My belly flip-flops at the desire I find reflecting in his blue pools. With a nod at his son, I send a telepathic message for rescue. He smirks, dimples denting his scruffy cheeks. That earns him a scowl.

I burrow deeper into the couch. It's apparent my knight isn't in the saving mood. I let my lashes flutter shut. A muttered curse from my right follows shortly after. I peek one eyelid open and watch him spit out a few more expletives.

"What?" My voice is barely a whisper.

Brance stares at us silently for a few more beats. His gaze travels slowly, as if committing this moment to memory. Those blue depths are alight with something I can't decipher. A real smile curves his lips, followed by a heavy sigh. He stands and scoops Ollie up with practiced efficiency.

Once the weight has been removed from me, sharp tingles attack my left side with gusto. I'm quick to rub feeling into my arm. When the burning sensation subsides, I flop against the cushions with a whoosh. Having that kiddo sleep on me was totally worth it. I'd take that type of numbness any day.

Brance is back a minute later, hovering in front of me. "Need a lift?"

"Where to?" I walk my toes up his denim-clad leg.

My skirt shifts when I scoot closer to the edge. Brance takes advantage, shoving the material up higher. My pink panties are on full display. His finger gently traces the lace trim. My core coils from the hunger in his expression.

"My bed. Now." The grisly tone seems edgy, impatient. Opposite of his touch against my center.

I peer up through hooded lashes. "We're gonna test your springs?"

"There's a first for everything, babe."

"Yes." I grant permission, but we know it's not needed.

These late-night hookups are our dirty secret. I'm not the least bit ashamed to admit how much that turns me on.

Brance hauls me into him with a growl. I arch my spine and purr. He hoists me up with zero effort, cupping my ass in his big palms. I cross my ankles against his lower back. With a spin on his heel, Brance strides across the hardwood floor. I grip the muscular rocks of his shoulders and hold on for the ride.

It feels like we're flying. I'm pretty sure he's clearing

three stairs at a time. The same urgency courses through my veins. His grasp on me is firm. I'm not going anywhere. A door swings open, and we're cloaked in darkness. Brance pauses for half a second to flip a switch. He turns and deposits me on the mattress with a light toss.

I crawl backward until my head bumps against a pillow. He reaches behind him and strips off his shirt with one smooth move. I'm antsy, rubbing my thighs together before spreading them apart. Brance undoes his jeans and shoves them down. He stands before me in a black pair of briefs, tenting in the front with his desire.

For me.

I prop myself up and lick my lips. With a curl to my fingers, I beckon him to me.

Brance strokes himself through his shorts. Such a damn tease. "Take off anything you don't want ripped into shreds."

A shiver skates over me with his filthy promise. I slowly remove my tank, throwing the cotton top at his bare chest. Brance catches it and brings the material to his nose. His gaze burns a hundred degrees hotter. I'm sure scorching heat shimmers in mine. The flouncy fabric of my skirt slinks down my legs. With a flick, my bra is tossed on the floor. I leave my panties firmly in place.

Brance's eyes flare with blue flames. He bends forward and reaches for me. The flimsy elastic is no match for his brute strength, snapping with one jerk. The torn satin gets balled in a fist and tossed aside. I drift a palm across my naked breasts and bare torso. My touch wanders lower and a loud rumble rises from Brance.

He makes a circular motion with his finger. "On your elbows and knees."

I follow his command instantly, flipping onto my stomach. The bed dips with his weight as he settles behind me. He grips my hips and angles me higher. I proudly stick my ass out, which earns me a light slap. My legs tremble as I wait. Brance swipes along my core, finding me slippery and wanting.

"Always wet for me. Such a needy girl."

I'm nodding fast. "I'm ready for you."

I feel his cock at my entrance, barely a whisper. My hips automatically wiggle back. I push further into him, seeking more.

Brance runs a hand over my lower back and ass. "You're eager."

I bow into his touch. "Yes, please."

He groans. "Love you begging for my cock."

"Make me feel good."

"Don't I always?"

I open my mouth with another plea. Brance lines up and slams into me. A burst of color blooms in my vision. I claw at the sheets and tumble under his spell.

Holy shit.

Brance's hips grind against me, forcing us closer. There's not a sliver of space separating our bodies. I swallow the saliva pooling in my mouth. He drags out and pushes in, paradise spreading through my center. I'm soaking in rainbows and sunshine on a tropical beach. It's like our first round each time. I'll never tire of this euphoric sensation. That's a scary thought. But not one that fits in this moment.

His forceful thrusts shove me forward. The unforgiving grip on my sides yanks me right back. This tug of war makes me dizzy, my mind spinning in useless loops. I clench around him for more. Brance moves faster, his strokes punishing.

"You like this?" His panting breath accompanies the slapping of skin.

"Love it," I moan. "Harder, please."

His fingers trail along my waist and lower belly. He finds my clit, strumming with rapid circles. My inner muscles quiver while molten lava spreads through me. I curl my toes into the blanket, reaching for leverage.

"A-almost there," I wheeze.

Rather than propel me over the edge, Brance pulls out. The loss of him is an instant blow to my impending orgasm. I whine low and glance over my shoulder. His focus is locked between my legs. Brance bites his lip, spreading my cheeks with a thumb on each side. His touch skims from ass to cleft. The slow slide makes me squirm.

He lets loose a long groan. "You're so fucking sexy."

"Stop teasing me." I squirm in his hold.

I get a spank to my thigh for that.

"Roll over. I wanna watch you come."

Before he can blink, I flip and stretch myself wide. Brance fills me to the hilt with a single drive. He drops on top of me, balancing his weight on a bent forearm. Our mouths fuse together, tongues meeting in the middle. I inhale his want, giving him my desire in return. When he stabs deep, I gasp into our kiss.

He breaks away from my lips with a snarl. Lust colors his naughty smirk. I scratch along the flexing muscles in his back. Our bodies pound together in a fevered pitch.

Brance licks a path down my tilted jaw. I arch into him, my soft breasts pressing into his hard pecs. Brance buries his face into the dip between my shoulder and neck. I hear him breathe me in, trembling when he nips along my ticklish flesh.

He rolls his hips, crashing into mine. We're a fluid wave gaining momentum. "Is this what you want?"

I press my lips to his throat. "Yes. So much."

Brance draws my earlobe between his teeth. "More?"

"Is that even a question?" My wispy tone dances across his cheek.

He punches into me with a new level of vigor. I raise

my pelvis and meet his rough jabs. His movements become sloppy, bucking into me with jerky glides. I can tell he's straddling the line with me. I dig my heels into his ass, slamming us harder together. He tweaks my nipple, pinching the stiff peak. That bite of pain is enough to hurdle me into oblivion.

"O-oh, t-there! M-more," I squeal.

After one final push, Brance's body tenses and spills into mine. The room fills with our shared pleasure. I shatter into a million sparkling pieces. Shooting into the sky among the stars.

He twitches with the last of his release, collapsing onto the bed beside me.

"Best yet," he murmurs to the ceiling.

A soft smile lifts my lips. "I agree."

"Damn glad you came over."

"Mm-hmm, this is another spot to check off our list."

Brance chuckles. "Seems odd considering it's my house."

There's not much I can say to that. I burrow into the pillow with a heavy exhale. He crosses his arms behind his head, settling in for the night. A soothing silence envelops us. With every touch, he erases more empty space. These days, the hole in my chest is nothing more than a shallow divot.

When the floating sensation subsides, I sigh and struggle to sit up. I shuffle to the end of the mattress. My bare feet hit the cold floor, and a chilling spike snakes through me. I bend over, gathering my discarded clothes. Brance is quiet behind me, which I've come to expect. A quick peek over my shoulder tells me he's drifting off. I tug on my shirt, turning away from his shuttered stare. The bed dips with his shifting movement. I glance at him again, finding him leaning forward.

Brance reaches for me, but stops before touching my skin. "Brae—"

I shrug off the placating tone of his voice. "Don't worry, I know the score. This doesn't mean anything."

Protecting my heart is becoming a greater challenge lately. I seal my lips and gulp the romantic notions down like a bitter pill. Those words have no meaning in this space.

His grunt is a dull echo. "What if you, uh, don't leave."

The uncertainty wafting off him has me twisting around. Brance's eyes are boring into me. His expression is stern and serious.

"What?" I need him to repeat that.

"Maybe you stay with me tonight."

I gape at him. "I don't get it."

Brance frowns. "Did I stutter?"

My jaw is still popped open. "Let me get this straight. You," I point at him, "want me to sleep here."

He nods. I blink at him with a blank expression.

"In this bed? With you?"

Brance scrubs over his mouth. "Why is that so crazy? It's just an idea. I hate that you run out immediately after we finish. No matter where we are."

I quirk an eyebrow. "Does it make you feel cheap?"

That earns me a laugh. "Yeah, something like that. Are you just using me, Braelyn?"

I wrinkle my nose. "Are you?"

He strokes a thumb down my arm. "I'm the one asking you to stick around."

"What about Ollie?"

Brance seems to ponder that. He waves it away a second later. "Adults can have slumber parties."

I chew on my bottom lip. I'd hate for Ollie to find me here. The assumptions he'd make wouldn't be stellar. In his opinion, we'd be one step closer to being a happy family. I shake that possibility off my mind. What'd be worse is having a panic attack in the middle of the night.

I give Brance a truth. "I don't sleep well."

He glances at the darkened window. "Me neither."

"Even more reason for me to leave," I murmur.

"How bad is it?" His question is a whisper.

I swallow thickly. "The nightmares are brutal. I usually wake up screaming."

"When did you have the last one?"

I scratch my temple, having to think about it. "Two months ago, maybe?"

Brance locks me in a gaze I can't escape. "Let's try it. If something happens or you're not comfortable, feel free to leave."

My resolve crumbles into a pile of dust. I'll worry about what this means tomorrow. Consequences be damned. "Okay."

His features brighten. "Yeah?"

I giggle. "Your reaction alone is solidifying my decision."

"C'mere, babe." He opens his arms. "Let me hold you."

Brance lifts the covers, and we snuggle underneath. I slide toward him, resting my head on his chest. That shallow divot shrinks a tad more. I let his steady heartbeat settle my lingering doubt. Not five minutes later, my lids are getting heavy.

In his protective embrace, I fall into a peaceful sleep.

chapter twenty-six

BRANCE

REMIX

I FINISH ADJUSTING MY TIE IN THE HALLWAY MIRROR. AFTER smoothing the silk flat against my shirt, I stride into the kitchen. The sun is barely over the horizon, and my routine is already off-kilter. But that doesn't bother me the way it usually does. Probably due to waking up with Braelyn's ass snuggling my morning wood. She blinked her lazy eyelids open long enough to straddle my lap for a quick fuck. That woman could give any rodeo queen a run for her bonus check. Two orgasms later, Braelyn toppled into the mound of pillows with a blissed-out sigh. She was snoring before I made it into the shower.

With the flip of a switch, the coffee begins brewing. The strong aroma of dark roast wafts from the steaming machine. My mouth waters at the scent, energizing me with one inhale. The smell is slightly less effective than Braelyn's pussy. Lucky for me, I got a double dose.

I open the cabinet for a mug. There's five to choose from.

My collection is not very extensive. I've never needed more than one at a time. Braelyn lives alone and has a least twenty filling several shelves. She's always prepared. Even when I least expect her to be.

Maybe I should take two down. Braelyn is bound to want a cup. It'd be nice to have one set out for her.

The realization stops me short. Where did that shit come from? I'm planning ahead for her? It's enough I let her share my bed. I should draw the line there. Encouraging her to stick around longer after waking up is asking for trouble. I bow my head and force out a slow exhale.

This needs to end. But does it really? My hand pauses in midair, hovering at the halfway point. In the end, I take the mug out and place it next to mine. Something deeply broken and sharp settles inside of me. I rub at the odd sensation in my torso. What's the big fucking deal? I'm already trudging into uncharted territory. Might as well push a bit further.

Asking Braelyn to stay was instinct, a reflex I couldn't control. It seemed like the only option. I'd held my breath, waiting for regret to rain down on me. But there were no gloomy clouds or sinking feelings. Nothing of the sort. Only that faintly familiar clink as another piece found its place.

Because I'm greedy, or a glutton for bad decisions, I practically begged Braelyn to agree. I plowed through every reason she served. She was ready to leave and follow the rules I'd crammed down her throat. Maintaining that semblance of order no longer appeals to me. There're always stipulations. Addendums are created for a reason. And I'm damn glad.

Movement near the foyer has me lifting my gaze. Braelyn makes her way down the stairs, all sleep-rumpled and sluggish. She's wearing her clothes from yesterday. Her blonde waves are more tangled than smooth, and a natural blush colors her lightly freckled cheeks. I guarantee she still smells like me. Why is that so fuck-hot to imagine? Our sweat mixed with arousal is a potent combination. Everyone will be aware she's spoken for. Would it be too much if I demand that she doesn't wash it away?

Braelyn is unaware of my creeping, trailing her delicate fingers along the banister. Her bare feet shuffle along the floor. The wrinkled fabric of that bright skirt clings to her toned thighs.

Damn, she's beautiful.

When she turns the corner and finds me waiting, her steps falter slightly. She blinks, over and again. Her smile is floppy and uneven. "Good morning."

"Morning." I curl my hands into fists, killing the urge to hug her.

We take several moments to ogle one another. Her gaze eats me for breakfast. I feel like a piece of meat on display. For once, it doesn't annoy the shit out of me. I gorge on her tan legs for dessert. It's my favorite meal. Braelyn sways further into the room, those hips composing a hypnotic rhythm. "You're looking awful dapper for"—she glances at the clock—"seven o'clock. Do you always get up so early?"

I toy with the lapels of my jacket. "This is actually late for me. I'm typically in the office by now."

Braelyn's swollen mouth parts with a soft gasp. "What? No. Why?"

A chuckle bounces my shoulders. I point to the freshly brewed coffee set in front of an empty spot. "Poured you a cup. Sounds like you need it."

She makes grabby-hands while moving closer. I shove the chair, giving her space to sit. Her ass hits the padded seat, and she scoots in. After taking a drink, her lashes flutter shut. "Oh, yeah. That's the good stuff." She licks her lips. "Wow. This is delicious."

I enjoy a sip from my own mug. "That's becoming a common saying for you."

"Keeping track?"

I tap the middle of my forehead. "Hard not to. Makes great material for when I'm alone."

Her slim brows inch upward. "Thought I was the only one fantasizing."

Blood rushes south, straining the material of my pants. Filthy footage of Braelyn masturbating goes straight into my spank bank. "That'd be a negative."

She peers at me over the rim of her mug, giving me another exaggerated moan.

My grip tightens on the cup's handle. "Glad to be providing stimulation for your taste buds."

Braelyn chokes on a large gulp and sticks her tongue out. "Ah, that's hot."

"Yeah, just like that."

She huffs at me, laughter in her eyes. "You're in an awful great mood."

I stretch my arms out. "Why wouldn't I be? Got my dick wet before sunrise. Hot shower. Strong coffee. Gorgeous scenery. Can't beat that."

She lowers her chin, but I catch the blush. "I'd almost call you a romantic."

I wink at her. "And you'd be dead wrong."

"Worth a shot."

"How'd you sleep?" I pull her seat closer, linking our fingers together.

She covers her yawn with the other hand. "Really well, actually."

"Are you surprised?"

"Honestly? Yes."

I furrow my brow. "Why?"

Braelyn stares into her mug. "Even without the terrors, I'm lucky to get a few hours a night. My mind won't shut off. But here? No problem."

I dust my lips over her temple. "You're welcome."

She leans into my touch. "Ah, taking credit. Nice work."

"Didn't I tell you about the endorphin release? Easy solution."

"Mm-hmm," she hums. "Might have to make it a habit."

I allow the idea to simmer, almost expecting a sour bite to sink in. But again, nothing rises to the surface. Fuck, I'm knee deep in this shit.

Braelyn giggles. "Don't bust a brain cell. It was just an offhand comment. Maybe you need more caffeine."

"I'm not gun shy." I point to the semi testing my zipper's strength. "Feel free to take advantage whenever the need arises."

"Tell me something I don't know," she says.

"Well," I divert. "I slept really well."

"Congratulations?"

I chuckle. "Such a smartass. That's rare for me. Seems we have another thing in common."

She tilts a hand back and forth. "Fantastic sex leads to sound sleep. Who knew?"

"There's probably a few studies already proving the theory."

"Doesn't mean further examination is off the table."

"Want a repeat?"

She raises a brow at my suit. I snort and shake my head.

"Dirty girl. I mean dinner. But there's a condition."

"I'm listening."

I turn more toward her, our knees nudging together. "Can I ask a favor?"

She sets her mug down and nods. "Sure."

"Feel free to tell me no."

Mossy green eyes open wide. "Please don't suggest a threesome."

I frown. The thought of sharing her turns my stomach. "Hell no. Who do you think I am?"

"It was a legit guess."

My scowl deepens. "For future reference, I'm not into that sort of shit. You're plenty."

I want to erase the last two words the instant they escape. Dammit. What the fuck is my issue?

Braelyn lets my slip tumble down her back. "'Kay, good to know. Spit out the real thing."

The knot in my chest releases. "Can you watch Ollie tonight? Mary has an appointment, and I have a late meeting. I shouldn't be home later than seven."

She nods. "Conveniently enough, Kallie is closing Thicket this evening. I'm free after four."

"You can be here at five?"

"Yeah, sure."

I squeeze her hand that's still locked in mine. "That's great. Saves me trouble."

Her smile is too sweet. "Happy to be helpful."

"Speaking of," I dip closer, "thanks for lending a hand earlier."

She hums. "I provided more than that."

"If I didn't have clients lined up and stacks of files to review, we'd be back upstairs."

"Promises, promises."

I growl in her ear. "Don't tempt me."

Braelyn suddenly break away from me. "That reminds me I have something to ask you. All the sex and orgasms were clouding my memory. I forgot until you got all alpha again."

"Okay?"

"Why were you cursing a blue streak after the movie last night?"

I glance down, collecting the scatters of truth. "You two looked like a dream I never wanted to have."

She tips her head sideways. "What?"

"You and Ollie on the couch. Cuddled up like that. Hit

me in a spot I didn't know was there. Just weird, I guess. Never mind."

Braelyn's mouth curves into a secretive smile. "That was a very sweet moment for me. I would have stayed in that uncomfortable position all night if it meant Ollie was sleeping soundly."

"That's part of the issue," I mutter.

Her lips twist to the side. "Of course it is."

I almost laugh at her flip in expression. "We don't need to spend a ton of time delving into my fucked-up frame of mind. It was a moment of weakness."

"Have you ever been in love?" Her question comes out of left field, smacking me in the face. I let my expression grow taut. "That's outrageous. I have a child. I love him irrevocably. To assume otherwise is asinine."

"That's not what I meant," she whispers.

"Other than my son? Nope."

"I'm talking the passionate, Eros kind."

I scoff. "Absolutely not. Why?"

She studies me far too closely. Her gaze flickers away a moment later. "Just curious."

"Problem?"

"No." The word is so soft my ears strain to hear it.

"Why bring up the concept of love only to drop it immediately after?" Now that we're on the subject, maybe a few boundaries can be reinstated.

Her mossy eyes aren't sparkling when she peers up at me. "I didn't mean anything by it. Just popped into my brain."

Guess we'll have to discuss our situation tonight.

I drop her hand, checking the time on my watch. "On that note, I gotta go."

Braelyn startles, looking over her shoulder. "What? Where's Ollie?"

"Still sleeping. Mary is in the office, doing who knows what."

"O-okay." She looks a little lost.

I press my lips to the crown of her head. "If you're concerned about exposing our cover, I'd get gone. Little man will wake up sooner rather than later."

She leaps to her feet, almost knocking the chair over. "Yeah, good idea."

That gets a loud laugh out of me. "I didn't mean right this second."

She twists her fingers together. "It's fine. I should be going anyway. Thicket won't open itself."

"Well, if that's the case." I sweep an arm toward the entryway. "I'll walk you out."

Braelyn is quiet, to the point of concern. Maybe I should prod deeper. But that might make it worse. We slip on our shoes and step into the garage. I press the opener, the gears grinding as it lifts. We stand next to each other without saying a word. The silence stretches, making the air dense and hard to swallow.

I loop an arm around her. "You okay?"

She seems to snap herself out of something. I haven't witnessed this type of reaction from her in weeks. "Uh-huh, yeah. It's nothing, I'm fine. Sorry for being weird."

"No worries, babe. We're all good. This is still working for you, right?" I motion between us.

"Of course. I'm not acting odd because of you. Promise. Just a funk." She taps her temple. "This baby never shuts down, remember?"

I pull her into my chest. "Except with lots of sex."

"Right." She giggles, and the tension seeps out of me.

"'Til tonight then?"

Braelyn nods, those green pools vibrant once again. "Looking forward to it."

chapter twenty-seven

BRAELYN

SPITE

KNOCK ON THE DOOR, MY PALMS STILL SWEATY FROM THE DRIVE. My fingers shake, and I curl them into a fist. For whatever reason, my nerves are shot. I've tried to calm the chaos that's building in my belly. There's no explanation for the unsteady pulse thrumming through me. My day was uneventful, which suited me fine. Other than my strange reaction with Brance this morning, nothing has been out of the ordinary.

As I wait on the stoop, a chill sweeps over me. A quick glance at the sky confirms thunderous clouds descending at a rapid rate. I can't help feeling there's more than one storm rolling in. But that's just my weird mood whispering poison.

Mary swings the door open, a wide smile stretching her weathered features. "Braelyn, welcome."

I offer a small wave. "Hello, Mary."

"Come in, please." She moves over and makes a path, gesturing toward the hallway. "Have a seat at the table."

After slipping off my shoes, I shuffle into the kitchen. My

eyes land on the massive windows along the far wall. A few hints of sunshine are fighting to peek through the torrential gloom. Rain is imminent.

"Sit, sit." Mary bustles in behind me, humming a cheery tune. Her giddy demeanor lifts my mopey spirits.

One of the spots is clearly occupied, an open magazine and glass of iced tea waiting. I make my way to the opposite chair. Mary remains standing, wringing her hands together. I'm sure she's ready to leave.

"Shame about the weather. You'll have to stay inside with Ollie. He was looking forward to showing you his sandbox."

I grin up at her. "Next time."

Her sharp gaze locks onto mine. "Certainly."

"Is there anything I need to know?"

She waves me off. "Ollie is easy to please, as you know. Just hang out and play with him. He'll love every moment."

That loosens the remaining knots tightening my chest. "I'm looking forward to that. How about dinner?"

Mary begins gathering her stuff off the table. "Brance should be home by then. But you can check the fridge. Feel free to help yourself to anything."

I drum my fingers on the wood. "Great. Simple enough."

She pats my shoulder. "Thanks for doing this. You're becoming quite the staple around here."

"It's nothing serious. I'm not trying to invade your space or anything."

She laughs. "Please do, dear. These boys need you. Far more than you think."

I gulp audibly. "Um, all right."

"But remember, you're not just getting involved with Brance. There's Ollie to consider. He cares a great deal for you."

I'm unsure if she's talking about Brance or Ollie. It doesn't matter. "We're just…friends?"

Her lips purse. "That sleep together?"

I choke on the suffocating air in my lungs. Mary quirks a penciled eyebrow. I'm sure my face is the color of a stop sign. Maybe that'll halt this conversation. If only I could run and hide without being suspicious.

"Well, um, I guess?" My voice is a meek whisper. Mary resembles my overly religious grandmother in this instance. Am I being scolded?

She clucks her tongue. "Ollie isn't blind, Braelyn. He's very aware of what's happening between you two. That child is so desperate for a mother. Well, that's not true. He's not looking for just anyone. Ollie is hoping you'll be filling that role. Very soon."

I blink the moisture from my vision. Oh, that sweet boy. "He's mentioned things along those lines. I try not to feed his comments."

"But your actions aren't discouraging him."

I tug at the collar of my shirt. Is it hot in here? The pressure suffocates me. "I never meant to complicate things."

"I believe you, dear. Unfortunately, it's far too late."

I avert my stare. "So, what now?"

"You have to make a choice, dear. I'd recommend making it soon."

Mary's words go along with my spiral earlier. How long does Brance plan for this to go on for? What are we doing? Just messing around? My heart is starting to nurture some pretty serious feelings for that man. Try as I might, remaining unaffected isn't possible. I figure that concept was created for robots. Or Brance.

At my silence, she prods further. "Ah, what's the saying? Shit or get off the pot?"

My shoulders shake with a laugh. "Really?"

She sends me a knowing look. "Don't judge this old bird by her fading feathers. I can keep up with the times."

I don't doubt her for a moment. "You're quite surprising, Mary. I appreciate that."

"Well, thank you." She glances at the clock. "I must run. Just think it over, yeah?"

"I will." I nod and stand from the table.

"Thanks again, Braelyn. Ollie is waiting for you upstairs. I held off calling him down so we could chat." She winks. Sneaky old lady.

Mary collects her bag, strides to the door, and leaves my sight less than a minute later. She can hustle when necessary.

Thoroughly reprimanded, I trudge up the steps. I barely make it to the landing when Ollie zooms into the hallway.

"Miss Braelyn! You're here."

He rushes at me, and I crouch down. I wrap my arms around him, hugging him close. This is just what I needed.

"Can we play now?"

"Of course, sweetie. What should we do?"

Ollie taps his lips, a recent habit. Pretty sure he picked that up from me. "How about Legos? Or Uno?"

"Why not both?"

He bounces on his toes. "Yes! This will be a great night."

My stomach grumbles. "What time do you usually eat?"

"Around seven. My daddy makes me dinner."

"Okay, we'll wait for him."

Ollie turns around and races into his room. I giggle, following his trail of dust. He's already sprawled on the floor when I walk in.

"I'm building a huge fire engine. Will you help me?" He waves a colorful pamphlet at me.

"Of course, sweetie. I've never made one before." I ease myself down next to him.

"Me either. It's taking me a long time."

I study the progress he's made so far. It looks like the base frame, maybe a space for wheels. The basics might be complete. It's hard to tell with these small blocks.

Reaching for a few loose pieces, I try to find where they belong on the vehicle. "Let's see how far we get."

The instructions turn out to be very self-explanatory. We set up an efficient system and get most of the truck complete. The tips of my fingers are sore, but the sense of accomplishment takes the pain away. Ollie's grin is the greatest gift.

"Wow, we almost finished the whole thing." He stares at the object with wonder reflecting in his eyes. "Thanks, Miss Braelyn."

I ruffle his hair. "Thank you for showing me how to play."

He snickers. "That's silly. It's super easy to fit Legos together."

"Is it? I couldn't tell." I smile at him. "You made it so fun."

"Now what?"

I seek out a clock. It's a quarter past seven. "Well, it's time to eat."

"Yeah, my tummy is talking."

That gets a laugh from me. "That means you're running on empty. Better fill you up with some good stuff. Should we check in with your dad?"

Ollie bobs his head. "M'kay."

I reach for my phone and type out a message.

Me: Will you be home soon? Ollie is getting hungry.

"What do you usually eat on Monday evenings?"

He lifts a slim shoulder. "Whatever. How about grilled cheese?

I nod. "Okay. Hopefully we hear from him."

Twenty minutes later, and there's still no response from Brance. Ollie whimpers about his stomach growling. Mine echoes his pangs. I make the executive decision to whip up some sandwiches. Brance can yell at me later.

Me: Making dinner. Should I save you some?

I giggle while imagining him eating a gooey grilled cheese. That'd make up for his delay. His meeting must have run late. We head downstairs, and I settle Ollie at the counter. He doesn't want to be more than two feet away from me. This kiddo loves attention. And he's so darn polite. His father could learn a few things about that.

After finding all the needed supplies, I whip up two sandwiches. Ollie holds up the plates so I can drop one on each.

"Squares or triangles?" I poise the knife over his bread.

His button nose wrinkles. "Huh?"

"Do you want me to cut your sandwich in triangles or squares?" I trace the potential lines, showing him what each option is.

"What do you like?"

"I'm a triangle gal." I slice mine diagonally.

Ollie's claps and points at his. "Me too. I want mine to match."

I make it happen with one swipe. He attempts to whistle. The breathy sound is adorable.

"And watch." I lift both halves and slowly pull them apart. "Look at all the melty goodness in between."

Ollie parrots my move with seasoned efficiency. Quick learner. He collects all the cheese around a finger and gives me a proud smile.

"Thanks, Miss Braelyn."

"For what, sweetie?"

"Cooking. Playing. Hanging out. Taking care of me." He ticks them off on his little hand.

"It's my pleasure, Ollie. I'm having a blast. Too bad your dad isn't here."

He shrugs. "That's okay. I don't mind."

That reminds me to check the time. Brance is almost an hour late. A prickle of concern climbs up my neck, making me shiver. I swallow a bite of my dinner and shove the worry away. But that doesn't stop me from sending another text.

Me: Hey, me again. Are you all good? Starting to wonder where you are. :)

I add the smiley face for my own sake. There's no reason to freak out. And I'm not. Brance is just working late. I'm sure this happens often. I look at Ollie for confirmation. He smiles wide. I blow out the weight on my chest.

He rests a chin on an open palm. "Should we play Uno?"

"That sounds great." I inject extra pizzazz into my tone.

After cleaning up, we settle around the coffee table in the den. Ollie shuffles the cards and deals out seven in two piles. I grab a stack and fan them out in my grip. We drag through three rounds in thirty minutes. Just when he'd be down to one, I'd slap down a draw card. Our back and forth is fairly comedic. Turns out Ollie is quite skilled. He uses strategies I didn't think of.

After completing his latest victory dance, Ollie flops down beside me. "Should we play again?"

It's getting late. The sun has almost set. "When's bedtime?"

Ollie's expression deflates. "Eight thirty."

"You little turkey. That was ten minutes ago." I tickle his sides.

He giggles and collapses onto the carpet. "I was having so much fun."

"We'll do this again soon. Don't fret." Speaking of, my

cell has remained silent. The blank screen mocks me. I do my best to keep my wits intact and not overreact.

Ollie hops up and bounds up the stairs. "I'll put on my jammies. Then I'll brush my teeth. We can read books after, 'kay?"

His voice follows him down the hall. I stretch along the floor with a groan. If only I had his level of energy. My body is draining more by the minute. I shuffle along at a snail's pace, shackles strapped around my ankles. The possibilities are beginning to swirl like poison in my veins. My cell trembles when I tap out yet another text.

Me: Getting Ollie ready for bed. I hope to hear from you soon.

How hard is it to send a quick message back? Dammit, Brance.

My mind is elsewhere while waiting for my phone to buzz. I'm using all my willpower to remain planted in this rocking chair. What I really want to do is call Brance and demand that he answer me. This is an entirely new level of asshole for him. I've read Ollie seven books by the time his eyelids droop closed. I'm tempted to shake him awake. The impending doom is much heavier when faced alone.

For my sanity, I keep Brance in the loop. Maybe he'll finally respond.

Me: Ollie is sleeping. Please tell me you're okay.

But nothing pings in return.

The first hour bled into two, followed by three and now four. Soon, it's after eleven o'clock. I've worn a path in the hardwood floor from pacing. This can't be happening. I've texted him at least twenty times. The two voicemails I left are bordering on hysterical. I'm sure he'll get a real kick out of hearing me wail.

I resume my pacing. A tropical storm of repressed nightmares swoops down on me. Ripping my hair out at the roots. I'd moved past the traumatic memories. There hasn't been an episode for months. I'd kept a straight face for Ollie, but he's tucked away and safe. All there's left to do is crumble inside. The edges of my vision are officially blurring with murky darkness. The horrible possibilities start pinging inside my brain. My thoughts turn black. I can't stop the images from washing over me.

There's his car and an accident. But instead of Devon, Brance is dead inside. Toxic visions replace the positivity I've been working so hard keeping in the forefront. Lethal vines wrap around my legs and snake upward, tightening their hold.

Why is he ignoring my calls?

What if there was an accident?

Is he hurt?

Would someone contact us?

What if he's dead?

How will I find out?

The pictures flash in front of me on a panic-inducing loop. I can't handle going through this again. It's brutal and eats at my soul. The wounds rip open with a scream. The only thing keeping me above ground is Ollie sleeping upstairs. He's relying on me. This can't happen now.

When I hear the garage crank open, my knees buckle. I grip the counter and manage to stay upright.

The door swings open, and Brance appears in the foyer. His smile falls when he catches my expression. "Brae? What's wrong?"

I can't speak. I'm shaking my head, tears gathering in my eyes. My vision tunnels, narrowing further with each gasped breath. He's okay. Thank the Lord.

Brance rushes toward me, gripping my shoulders. "Is it Ollie?"

"No," I croak. "He's sleeping."

His exhale is harsh. "Don't fucking scare me like that. What the hell is wrong with you? Why're you crying?"

The whooshing in my ears subsides. I gulp down some much needed oxygen. "I haven't heard from you all damn day, Brance."

"My phone died."

The limp explanation skewers my panic, allowing a spark to flicker. "You didn't think to charge it?"

"I was in the middle of dinner with a client. What's the big deal?"

His defensive tone rattles me. "Are you kidding me? I've been worrying myself sick. You're a father. Shouldn't you check in for Ollie's sake?"

"Don't you dare attack my parenting."

"That's not what I'm doing. Shit. Sorry. This is just... I don't know. I need some air."

I start to turn away and he grabs my arm. "We're not done discussing this."

"Why wouldn't you let me know about being late? We waited up for you. Ollie wanted to say goodnight."

Brance glares at me, blue flames threatening to incinerate my heart. "Low fucking blow, Braelyn. Excuse me for assuming he was in capable hands and my tardiness wouldn't be noticed. I figured you'd be too busy having fun."

I let my jaw hang loose. "Tardy? This was way beyond a few minutes, even an hour or two."

He growls, loud and low. "So fucking what? I don't answer to you, Braelyn. Don't jump down my damn throat. Everyone is fine. You need to relax."

A loud crash booms inside of me. His temper feeds my fading panic, giving the shadows strength and power. Everything is certainly not okay. Dammit, I can't go back there. A shaky hand covers my gaping mouth. No. No, no, no. I won't go down this road. Not again. There's no surviving that type of loss twice.

"But it's not." I refuse to look at him.

He smacks his chest. "Alive and well, right here. Calm down."

I swallow the glass shards in my mouth. "I can't risk it."

Brance snorts. "Oh, give me a break. Being with me is a risk?"

I'm nodding fast, almost manic. "Yes. I couldn't handle losing you."

"There's nothing to lose."

"To me there is."

He rolls his eyes. "Sounds like a you-problem. The reward isn't worth this apparent risk?"

I blink more moisture from my lashes. "You don't get it. Can you at least attempt to understand how I'm feeling?"

"No, Braelyn. I can't. We're not the same person. You're dealing with some shit I cannot see. It sounds like exaggerated bullshit."

My entire body wracks with a broken sob. "You're being cruel."

"That's just me, babe. Thought you'd gotten used to it."

"No, not like this."

I'd almost forgotten how terrible it felt to have his anger targeted at me. My shields are lowered, his blows striking in the weakest areas. I'm too exposed. He couldn't care less.

He tosses his hands in the air. "Where the hell is this coming from?"

My stomach is caving in, everything inside of me tumbling into a black hole. "I assumed the worst, Brance. I'm not a normal worry-wart. I've been through hell trying to get over the accident. You and Ollie are the main reasons I can smile again. But when you didn't answer or show up? The hole in my chest immediately burst open. I'm not healed. This proves I never will be."

His gaze is a laser searing through what's left of my soul. "You better not abandon my child over some stupid bullshit. You've made a lot of promises."

The thought alone is a punch to my belly. "I'd never leave Ollie."

"But me? You don't give a shit about me." His sneer is coated in contempt, but I'm not backing down.

I take a turn in the chest pounding, thumping my own. "Do you see me standing here? I'm going nuclear over you. Get that through your thick skull."

Brance scrubs a palm over his face. "But I'm fine. All in one piece. You can stop the downward spiral."

My laugh is bitter. "It doesn't work that way up here." I grind the heel of my palm into my temple. "All I see is you dead on the side of the road. I-I just can't handle that."

"Go take a walk, and we'll fix this when you're calm."

"No. There's no solving this."

He's in front of me, yet miles away. "Don't be dramatic. This was a minor hiccup."

I look to the ceiling and beg for patience. This man is more stubborn than a jackass. "For you, Brance. To me, this was a major collision."

"What are you suggesting? We call the whole thing off?"

"Yes, exactly. I'm permanently scarred. This was a mistake. I don't belong with anyone. I can't go through that again."

"You're a fucking coward."

I can see Brance in the courtroom, mowing down vulnerable witnesses and bending their will. I'd never wish this type of rant on anyone.

"Oh, that's rich coming from you. All you do is hide behind an asshole mask. But you're more scared than me."

He swings his arms out wide. "What the fuck do you think I'm doing right now? Fighting over some crazy shit. I've been trying to put myself out there for you. This is the fucking thanks I get."

"You're so arrogant. It's not all about you. When you realize that, things will go much smoother."

"Guess you won't be around to find out."

"Must you be so cold? We shared something special. At least for me."

"You fucking started this. Not sure what else you expect."

He's a master at avoiding, deflecting anything worth feeling. I shouldn't be surprised by this reaction. Yet, his words are a lash from an iron whip.

"Real feelings are forming for me, Brance. It's better to stop things now before this gets more complicated."

His smirk is nasty. I brace myself for the words swirling over his tongue.

"You almost had me fooled. But I guess this was meant to end in disaster. That's almost too bad. I was enjoying you."

I sniff, regretting so much of this already. It's only temporary. The numb is taking effect. Soon, I won't feel anything but the cold comfort of my mistakes.

"Bran—"

He waves me off. "Just go, Braelyn. I can't stand to look at you anymore."

With that final blow, the walls tumble down. With tears streaking my vision, I grab my purse and run for the door. With the twisted knob in my hand, I give one last peek over my shoulder.

"For what it's worth, I care about you."

"That's your own damn fault."

chapter twenty-eight

BRANCE
BULLY

I RIFLE THROUGH THE STACKS OF DOCUMENTS STREWN ACROSS MY desk. The vice around my ribs cranks tighter. My irritation spikes. Why is there so much shit scattered everywhere? With a flexed arm, I sweep all of the contents onto the floor. My monitor lands with a crack, the keyboard bouncing off its screen. Sticky notes and pens launch across the room. Papers and folders rain down on me in a sloppy blizzard.

Fuck this shit.

"Kathy!" I bellow through the closed door.

There's no instant response. I count to five. A snarl curls my lip. The sleek shine of my desk mocks me, reflecting light and memories of her. I smash a fist against the gleaming wood top.

"Kathy!" My bark has more bite this time.

A slow creak alerts me to her presence. She peeks inside, not crossing the threshold. "Yes, sir?"

"What took so long? Get in here." I'm two seconds away from snapping my fingers.

Kathy's steps are dipped in molasses. A growl threatens to claw up my throat. She's shaking worse than an autumn leaf. It's hot as a furnace in here so the temperature isn't to blame. Damn, she better not be getting sick. That would be a cherry on top of this shit sundae.

Her eyes bulge when catching sight of the disaster my office has become. "Uh, sir?"

"What?" My voice snaps through the silence between us.

"Is, ah, everything all right?"

I whip a hand across the shit decorating my floor. "Doesn't it look okay to you?"

She gulps audibility. "Um, no."

I steeple two fingers in front of my sneer. "Why wouldn't it be?"

Kathy is wringing her hands together so hard that the skin is turning white. "I'm not aware, sir."

"Then why ask the damn question?"

She clenches her eyes shut. "Is t-there something you needed?"

My sigh is loud, unnecessarily so. But I seem to be on a D roll. "Where's the Hueltsen file?"

She points a trembling finger toward a heap of garbage in front of her. "There, sir."

I glare at the offending mixture of contracts, client briefings, depositions, and other court proceedings. Some help she is. There're at least twenty different cases thrown together. It's obviously down there somewhere. Now I have to sift through this trash.

With a flick of my wrist, I dismiss Kathy. She hovers in my peripheral. I lift my narrowed eyes to her pale face.

"Do you have more stellar wisdom to enlighten me with?"

She shakes her head. "No, not really. But I hope whatever happened to make you upset gets better."

I groan into my fist. "I don't pay you for emotional support, Kathy."

She shuffles backward toward the door. "I didn't mean to overstep, sir. My apologies."

I wave her off. "Get back to work."

Kathy nods and scurries from the room. I push away from my desk and stand. The chaos I created isn't going to clean itself. I scoop it all into a cluster and start sorting.

I'm shoving contents into the final folder when my phone rings. With a grunt, I reach up and grab the receiver. "Stone."

A familiar tsk greets me. "Is that how you answer at work?"

"Hello, Mary. What a pleasant surprise." My tone suggests anything but.

"Yeah, I'm sure. Listen, we need to talk."

I snort. "Oh, really? I wouldn't have guessed based off the fact you called me."

"Don't be a smartass. I'm serious." The steel in her voice has me sitting up straighter.

"What's going on?"

Mary clears her throat. "Ollie is pretty down, Brance."

"Okay?" I drag the word out until it's stretched five seconds.

"He's not himself, you know? I can't get him to smile. He's not interested in going to the park or swimming in the lake. I'm at a loss."

A hot iron stake drives into my chest. "Where are you?"

"Maple Street." She doesn't need to say more.

I drag rough fingers through my hair. "Why did you feel the need to contact me at this specific moment?"

"Ollie doesn't want to leave."

"Great. Feel free to let him stay until that place is out of his system. Is that all?"

I can practically hear Mary's composure thin. "Pull your big head out of your stubborn ass. Your child is sad."

"And that's very upsetting for me. I'm unclear what you're expecting me to do about it while at work."

"Listen to me." She says this in the same manner one would scold a disobedient toddler.

A rumble fit for a lion rises from my gut. What is it with women lately? They're all grating on my nonexistent tolerance.

"I am," I spit.

She makes an approving sound. "Good. Cut him some slack. You're not the only wounded party in this breakup."

"We didn't break up."

"No?"

"No. There was nothing to split. It was fun. Now it's not. We just ended our part of this… agreement."

Mary crows down the line. "That's a good one. Very clean cut transaction. But Ollie gets stuck in the middle."

"I specifically told her to maintain the relationship with him."

"She's trying. He wants more. The transition is tough on him."

I choke down a curse. Ollie and his tender heart. "Most life lessons are. Hell, I'm still getting my ass handed to me on a regular basis. Shit doesn't seem to get easier."

That couldn't be more true after this recent experience with Braelyn. I never went through a custody battle. Veronica's one gift to me was leaving in peace. But this feels an awful lot like what I would have dealt with. Maybe worse because I actually give a shit about—

Nope, not going there. Thinking about Braelyn is worse than jamming toothpicks under my fingernails. That woman stole any decency from me. Not that there was much to begin with. She's the exact reason why I never form relationships.

Mary murmurs something to someone else. I assume it's Ollie. She comes back on the line with a resigned sigh. "What do you recommend I try next?"

I inhale a deep breath through flared nostrils. "Take him away from that awful store. Being there so much isn't good for him. Especially after recent events. Why doesn't he want to go somewhere else?"

"You know the answer. Thicket is his favorite."

Pressure builds in my already flexing muscles. "I'm well aware and trying to be supportive. But refusing to leave isn't an effective solution. He's doing this on purpose."

"Oliver is a child. Of course he's pushing for his way. He takes after someone else in that respect."

"Yeah, great. Is my daily dose of guilt over?"

Mary doesn't relent. "You were on a good path. Things were going very well. Then what?"

I exhale a heavy breath, a bull backed into a corner. "We've already discussed this."

"Be sympathetic. Try imagining his feelings in all this. The thing he seeks most was almost in his grasp."

My skull squeezes in a vice grip. I'd almost let myself believe in that possibility. I rub at the ache in my chest. "Okay, I surrender. Please stop this. Let Ollie buy extra candy. Give him a lifetime supply of movie passes. Take him to the water slides."

"He doesn't want any of that," Mary states.

"What then?"

She pauses for several moments. "He's asking if Braelyn can come over for dinner."

My snort is a straight shot of disbelief. There's no way Mary missed it. "That's not happening. Ever again."

"Brance—"

I swipe through the air. "Save it. That woman isn't welcome under my roof, around our family table. I tried and my efforts were wasted."

"Braelyn was scared. She's been traumatized. Her reaction was extreme, yes. But it's one more thing to practice."

"Are you taking her side?"

"Of course not—"

I grind my molars. "Sure about that?"

She huffs. "Brance, stop cutting me off. You're being unreasonable."

"Am I? Doesn't seem that way to me."

"Take a moment and look around you."

She can't see me, but for whatever reason I find my eyes sweeping around the office. This space was one of my sacred domains. That's not the case anymore. All I see is Braelyn perched across from me, smiling bright and filling my empty heart with bullshit.

It's been several days since Braelyn stomped out of my house. Any edges she managed to smooth are more jagged than ever. Lord help anyone who stands in my trail. With her absence, they'll bear the brunt of my anger. I almost lost my shit on Kathy. Mary is pushing the last of my buttons. I'm ashamed to admit my patience with Ollie has been lacking. I have a lot to make up for.

Maybe we'll go to a Blues game this weekend. But the thought stops me short. Even that experience is tainted.

Mary's voice breaks through my revere. "What did you find?"

"Nothing," I tell her honestly.

"Exactly. Fix it. And this time, make her stick."

I roll my eyes to the ceiling. "This has been quite invigorating, but I need to go."

Mary hums. "Sure, dear. Maybe you'll finish up early today."

"Doubt it," I grumble.

"Just try," she murmurs.

I sag into my chair, the will to argue draining from me. "Great chat, Mary. Thanks."

"You're very welcome. Have a lovely afternoon."

I lock my fingers behind my neck. "Tell Ollie I say hello."

"And to Braelyn as well?"

The fight roars back to life. "You better be joking with that shit."

Her laugh is sharp. "Had to try. Bye, Brance."

I slam the receiver down. The plastic cracks in my grip. A knock on my door immediately follows. I bite back a slew of expletives.

"Come in," I snap.

Don's wrinkly mug appears around the corner frame. "Kathy told me you're off the phone. Do you have a minute?"

As if I can say no to one of the founding fathers. "Sure. Take a seat."

He ambles over and parks himself in one of the leather chairs. "How's the week going?"

I make a show of checking my jam-packed calendar. "Just fine."

Don leans forward. "No issues I should be aware of?"

I cross my arms. "Seems like you know something I don't."

He shrugs. "Not necessarily. How's morale lately?"

"Good. Did something happen? Is there a problem?"

"No. You've just been… off."

I feel the muscle in my jaw jump. "Oh?"

Don holds up a palm. "Now don't get defensive. It's just an observation."

"From?"

"A few around the office."

I furrow my brow. "In regards to what?"

"You just seem out of sorts. Issues at home?"

His assumption ratchets the tension is my shoulders. "Nah. No trouble there."

"Is there too much pressure being partner? I thought you were ready—"

"I am," I interrupt. "I love my job."

He chuckles. "Maybe you should start acting like it."

I curl my fingers into a fist under my desk. "With all due respect, I've never stepped out of line in all the years I've been working here."

His beady eyes narrow on mine. "That can change very quickly."

I blow out the fire in my veins. "I'm good, sir. Just a bad few days. We all have them."

"Get your damn head in the game. I don't need clients or employees complaining."

A wrecking ball barrels into me. I force my features to remain neutral. "Have they?"

Don flings a meaty hand at me. "Only rumors. Nothing worth reporting."

Why the fuck is he interrupting my day for this hearsay drivel? Three fucking strikes and I'm burning out. This day just needs to end. I tug at the collar of my shirt. If I didn't have a meeting in an hour, the top button would be popped.

I swallow the sand in my throat. "I'll make sure it doesn't turn into an actual issue."

He nods. "Good. I'd hate to rescind your promotion. We know you're a bit of a wild card, but the risk was easy. These recent developments have us worried. We don't need bad press."

I rip through the company catalogue, searching for the asshole who reported me. The easy assumption would be Kathy. But if I go, so does she. That'd be a real stupid choice.

My gaze locks on his. "I won't let you down, sir."

Don strokes his chin. "You need a vacation?"

One swift jerk of my head. "Nah, I'm good."

"Maybe it's not an option."

I ease back in my chair. "You forcing me out?"

"Are you giving me a reason to force you out?"

My seams fray and I push. "Maybe."

He snorts. "Cut the cocky shit, Brance. Get it together, or we'll be discussing your position here."

I glare at him, knowing the threat is thin. He can't fire me without a fight. I'd take half the clients with me. But I still relent with a grunt.

"Fine. I'll curb the attitude."

He knocks on my desk. "That's all I'm asking."

I nod. "Don't worry, sir. I'll get it handled."

Don stands, straightening his suit. "Tell that little boy of yours hello for me."

"Will do." I offer him a hand to shake. He takes it, applying more pressure than necessary. I quirk a brow. Really, old man? Get back to the golf course.

After he leaves and I'm left in silence, reality seeps in. It's a damn bitter pill. Everything is fucking unraveling. I need to get a grip and shove through this dip.

Of the three, that last conversion stuns me most. I'm a fucking professional. I didn't work this damn hard to piss it all away over a woman. This job allows me to provide for my son. Nothing has the power to fuck with that.

Mary's concern clangs in my ear. Ollie is top priority. I'll start by patching up the recent dents this lapse in judgement are causing. He'll forgive me. And one day he might understand. The thought of him turning into a scorned asshole leaves me chilled. I'll do my best to avoid that.

I crack my knuckles and settle in. This might be a long-ass day after all. I'll clean up my act and forget about Braelyn. Two insignificant problems with one large boulder.

chapter twenty-nine

BRAELYN

FLICKER

My house is too quiet, but that's nothing new. A few blissful months couldn't change what always lurks just under the surface. Reality is a cruel bitch. I couldn't escape for long. And here I am. Right back where I started.

But I'm going to be fine. Better than that.

I allow my eyelids to slide shut. The comforting words form on my lips. *I'm strong enough. Today is better than yesterday. Nothing will break me again.* I've been repeating these since stumbling out of Brance's house a week ago. So far, it's been vital for keeping my head above water. I'm not drowning today.

Loneliness echoes off the floors, a taunting sound I can't hide from. I hate it. The hollow feeling festers, bubbling inside of me with no outlet. I'm one step away from getting a dog or cat. Something to take the isolation away. Companionship would be a bonus.

The lack of sleep isn't helping. All I see is Brance. In my

own damn house. He's haunting me. The thought is laughable considering the visions are erotic. He's banging me into the wall. So hard that the picture frames crash with our thrusts. He's carrying me up the stairs and into my shower. The mirrors steam up with our pleasure. He's spreading me out on the kitchen table, feasting on me for hours. Who needs food when we have each other?

Okay, enough. I need to get out of here.

I toss my purse over a shoulder and dash outside. Keys in hand, I slip behind the wheel of my car. With a quick twist the engine is purring. I grab the stretched leather in front of me. A circuit misfires in my brain. Where the hell am I going?

The idea of visiting Devon waffles through the cobwebs. The last thing I need is more silence. And talking to him about Brance doesn't seem right. I'm not sure he'd appreciate what my mind has been picturing. I settle on driving until something strikes.

Down the winding roads I go. Light filters between the overhead trees, showing me the way. I follow with an easy smile—my first natural one in days. In the end, I turn my car onto Vicksburg Road and drive toward the cliffs. The steep views from Cliffton Heights have always been my favorite. They're the best for rainbow sightings. Catching the rain on my face. Listening to nature surround me with music. Feeling the wind twist my hair. All the organic beauty often overlooked.

My fingers skip across the overgrown grass. The lush meadow swallows me as I wade deeper. On the tips of my toes, I can see the edge. That unsteady pulse slows inside of me. This place is reliable, carrying the burden for a while. I'll gladly forget my troubles and get lost among the wildflowers.

I find my patch of worn turf and plop down. The slight breeze tickles my cheeks. I breathe in the fresh air and tip backwards. The warm ground welcomes me with an open embrace. My arms spread wide, giving a hug in return. The sunshine instantly thaws the frost that's been building inside of me.

The bright rays break through the murky haze I'm caught in. But I can't quite reach for the other side. I shield my eyes and let the bridge narrow this gap. A vibrant rainbow arches across the baby blue sky. There're a few white fluffy clouds floating by, but otherwise it's a clear backdrop. A flock of boisterous birds chirp a summer song. The lazy lapping of waves against the shore lull me. But swirls of restless energy remain. A thick sigh wheezes from my tired lungs. Even this slice of paradise can't lift the gloom.

Brance Stone is a menace. There, I said it. Again. I can't seem to avoid him. Who does that man think he is? He's bad for me, but that doesn't stop my body from wanting more. After ripping apart my heart, that man won't quit. But I'll take the blame for that. I tumbled and fell when all signs pointed to danger.

I still have Ollie. But in a one-dimensional capacity. Without Brance, things will be very different. Guarded. Stagnant. There won't be dinners or slumber parties or hope for more.

A shadow blocks the sun, stealing the warmth.

"How'd I know you'd be here?"

I peel an eyelid open to find Sadie bending over me. "Hey, Dee."

"Hi, yourself. Getting lost in your bubble?"

She's well aware of my attachment to this spot. It's been my solace ever since that rainbow called to me three years ago.

I pet the warm earth beside me. "The lookout has saved me a time or two. Figured I could use some familiar comfort."

"So, what's with the catnap?"

"Trying to relax."

Sadie settles next to me, stretching her legs out. "Rough shape?"

I lift a shoulder. "Better than expected."

"Nightmares?"

"No."

"Panic attacks."

"Nope."

"Just down?"

A jerky nod from me. "It's been a bit bumpy. Nothing I can't handle." I'm glossing over the truth, of course.

"I suppose that explains the staycation." She motions around us.

"It's nice to get outta my house. Too eerie." I shiver regardless of the humidity clinging to me.

Sadie shuffles closer. "You should have called. I'm always up for hanging out."

I offer a limp grin. "Thanks, Dee. But you can't come to my rescue every day. I love it here. It's peaceful and makes me happy."

She's quiet for a moment. "Have you seen Ollie lately?"

A familiar pinch cinches my chest. "Yeah, he was in yesterday."

"How's he doing?"

I lick my dry lips. "He seems to be plugging along. There was definitely a lack of pep in his step. He keeps asking if I'll be coming back to his house." My sniff is quiet. "That breaks my heart a little more each time."

Sadie rubs my arm. "Damn, that's rough. I'm sorry, friend."

"It'll be okay. We'll figure it out. I'm glad he still wants to visit after what happened."

She huffs. "You couldn't keep that kid away. He adores you. Pretty sure you've got a friend for life with that little boy."

I smile at her. "I can handle that."

"Speaking of favorite customers," her voice trails off slightly.

I know what's coming before she can ask. "Mary is always the one to bring him in."

"Damn."

"Meh, it's better that way. There's enough awkward tension without Brance stomping close by. I'm not sure how to act with Ollie. Everything is screwed up. Things should go back to basic, right? He's just an adorable kiddo who loves candy and is a regular at my store."

Her lips go flat. "He's far more than that to you."

I press my cheek into the grass. "I don't wanna make things worse for him."

"Cutting off your love will. Business as usual, Brae. Until further notice."

I roll onto my side. "That's my plan. It really sucks, but definitely could be worse."

"Amen, sister. Save your day."

I gather all the courage brewing in my belly. After a deep inhale, I let it all out. "How is he?"

Sadie rocks a palm back and forth. "I only have backwash knowledge. Prying isn't really my style."

I scoff and roll my eyes. "Since when?"

She nudges me. "You're a different story. Always will be."

This girl keeps me thriving. "Thanks, friend."

"Welcome." A sassy wink follows.

I pull up a clump of weeds. "Okay. Tell me about Brance, Dee. It was hard enough to ask the first time."

Sadie wrinkles her nose. "Jordan says he's being a tyrant. Fairly intolerable at work. Barking orders and expecting perfection. Apparently, one of the big bosses had words with him. That was a bucket of cold water and snapped him outta the fury. Since then, he's mostly keeping to himself."

She grips my wrist. "But who knows how much of that is fabricated."

My stomach sinks into a black pit. "That's sad."

"Is it? Brance is an asshole on a good day. I don't see much of a difference. But Jordan seems pretty concerned."

I frown at her. "How do you mean?"

"They've been friends for years. I guess this is a new low for Brance. Pretty hard to imagine him being worse." She cringes.

"It is," I murmur. The hole in my chest cracks wider.

Sadie averts her eyes, focusing on a pile of rocks. "Do you want to text him?"

I snatch one off the top and bobble it between my fingers. "Every other minute."

"Why don't you?"

"What's the point?"

She shrugs. "You can patch things up."

My laugh is bitter. "That's not an option."

Sadie hums and peeks over at me. "Are you a quitter?"

I narrow my gaze. "Hardly."

She rolls her shoulders. "Then fight for the good. He was bordering on tender and almost sweet, right?"

"He had his moments," I mutter.

"Mm-hmm." She bobs her chin. "Don't forget about that. You got a sugary piece of him no one else ever did."

"He was so mean, Dee. I mean, shit. I get he was mad, but this was something else entirely. If I'm being reasonable—"

"Which you tend to be."

I frown at her interruption. She winces and mouths an apology.

"There's fault on my part. I did overreact. The toppling spiral was beyond reason. I should have been calmer. But it doesn't matter."

Sadie creases her forehead. "What? Why?"

I trace a heart in the dirt only to erase it. "Because we were just a fling. It's over. We move on."

"Uh, says who?"

"Brance. Me. Our ties are severed."

"Really?" Sadie mumbles the word with a pound of disbelief.

I tilt my head toward her. "Why do you say that? Are you hiding something?"

"Not necessarily."

"Spit it out, Dee."

She reaches for my hand. "Okay, ready?"

I huff at this production. "Obviously."

"He's the one for you, Brae. No offense to Devon. I liked the dude well enough. But he never made you sparkle and shine. One look from Brance and you freaking glow. Like neon at a blacklight party." She shimmies a bit for added effect.

As if on command, heat rises in my face. There's fire in my blood just thinking about how he makes me soar. But that's past tense now. I barely hold back my groan. "That was never what we were about."

She flicks my elbow. "Don't give me that, Brae."

I rub at the sore spot. "It's the truth."

"According to?"

"Our laws and regulations."

Her flat expression speaks volumes. "Life doesn't come with a manual, girlfriend."

"If anyone has proof of that, it's me." The blush dims, fading from my features.

Sadie holds up a hand. "I know, I know. But why go into something with such limitations? Breaking rules is part of the fun."

I jab a finger at myself. "I will not be the one to fix this. At least not alone. I don't believe he cares enough to try."

She snorts. "Oh, my beautiful friend. How wrong you are."

I raise a snarky brow. "We might have to agree to disagree."

"Just don't slam the door on him yet."

"Fine," I relent. "I won't sign up for that dating app quite yet."

"So spicy. I'm glad you haven't lost the spark."

I tap my lips. "Speaking of all things rosy, how's it going with Jordan?"

Sadie flutters her lashes. "He's fantastic. We're two seconds away from being in love. I think it's gonna happen."

"Yeah? That's super-duper, Dee. You deserve a good guy."

"And he certainly is one. He makes me want to have all the babies. Whenever he watches Ollie, my ovaries sing a seductive tune. It's the greatest aphrodisiac of all time."

I giggle, picturing her swooning all over that man. "You're too cute."

"Just you wait. There's more where that's coming from. We've recently teamed up for a new project."

"Oh?"

"Yep." She checks her imaginary watch. "Jordan is actually rolling out phase one tomorrow."

I squint at her. "What, dare I ask, does that involve?"

"Getting you and Brance together, duh. As in permanently. Wasn't that clear?" She bops me on the nose.

A laugh shakes my entire frame. This girl is a nut. "Good luck with that, Dee."

She brushes off her palms. "Oh, we won't need it. There's an expert matchmaker on our side. He's very dedicated to the cause."

At hearing that, my pitiful heart puffs out a cloud of hope. I almost believe it could happen. And just maybe it will.

chapter thirty

BRANCE

STAKES

I STRIDE TOWARD THE DEN WITHOUT ANOTHER WORD. THE COUCH is calling my name. I drop onto the middle cushion and settle in deep. There's nothing like falling into a familiar space after a stressful afternoon. I slouch lower, resting against the fluffy pillows. I close my eyes and attempt to calm the tornado tearing through me.

All is well until Ollie and Jordan follow suit, one on each side of me. I hoist my legs onto the coffee table with a grunt. I'm surrounded. Again. They played this same setup on the deck. Then I was boxed in by them while trying to relax on a kitchen stool. They didn't ease up while I prepared dinner. And their seating arrangement during the meal was worse. I need some damn space.

They're trying to drive me insane. This recent move proves their motives.

"Seriously?" My low grumble bangs around the otherwise silent room. I glare at them, no longer giving a shit about hurt feelings. They've effectively ground my patience into dust.

"What's the matter, Daddy?" Ollie's voice is so innocent. I almost believe he's clueless, except for the sneaky grin lifting his cheeks.

"You two keep following me around. What's your problem?" The question is directed at Jordan. My son is clever, but he's not at the level of orchestrating a plan of this magnitude.

"Not sure what you mean. We're just enjoying a quiet evening. Do you have an issue? That pulsing vein in your temple is kinda scary." He taps the side of my head.

I dodge away from his touch. "Are you fu-lipping joking?"

Ollie gasps. "Daddy! You almost swore. That's naughty."

I scrub my pounding forehead. "Yeah, sorry. I'm a tad on edge."

Jordan claps me on the shoulder. "Know what the best cure is?"

"Knock it off. Not around my son." I grind on my molars.

"He'll find out eventually," Jordan replies.

I glare at him. "He's five. It better be at least fifteen years."

That earns me a bark of loud laughter. "Because you waited until twenty. Hilarious."

I elbow my friend in the ribs. Hard. "We're done discussing this. I thought we were gonna watch a movie."

"But we can't talk with the television on." Ollie pouts.

I wiggle his bottom lip. "That's the entire point."

"We haven't discussed all the perks yet. Just hear us out." Jordan wags his brow.

"I don't think there is anything left to say. I've heard your arguments for Braelyn's case. You just finished yapping about her when I left the kitchen. That was five minutes ago." I hitch a thumb behind me in an effort to eliminate any confusion.

Jordan chuckles. "That was only the introduction. I can skip ahead to the good stuff if you're getting antsy."

"You're wasting valuable breath."

He studies the ceiling with far too much focus. His calculating stare slowly sinks to mine. "Am I? Are we? Think about it."

"You're being a dou-weirdo."

Jordan snorts. "Nice save. Not."

"I think you've been hanging around my child too much."

He frowns. "Not as much lately. Your dates with a certain someone came to a premature halt. But that's only temporary. We'll be back on track soon enough."

Ollie is watching us with wide eyes. I give him a strained smile and turn back to my so-called friend.

"Please don't drag my son into this evil genius plot to get me hitched. He's been through enough."

Jordan smirks. "Who do you think planned all of this?"

I grunt and cross my arms. "You."

He makes the sound of a buzzer. "Wrong. Ollie isn't surrendering."

My son nods along. "No white flag for me, Daddy. I'm stepping up my game."

Where is he getting this shit? "Oh, really? How do you plan on doing that?"

"I tried being sad. That didn't work. I'm going to be bossy now. You need to see Miss Braelyn again."

I gape at my son. "Oliver James, that tone won't get you far."

He hunches his shoulders. "But Daddy, you aren't listening."

I've heard numerous different versions of that line over the last week. My resolve is an iron gate. There's no breaking me down. My fiery stare bores into my friend's profile. The fucker won't look at me. "See what you're teaching him?"

He peeks over, raising his hands. "Don't blame me. Ollie told us his plan. We're the assistants."

"Us?" I grind the word out.

Jordan winces. "Forget I said that."

"Not a chance. Who else is involved in this scheme?"

"Sadie."

I'll never admit to the foul drop in my gut. The beating organ in my chest offers up a weak thump. It'd be stupid for me to be disappointed. Braelyn is the one who called things off. I don't expect any effort on her part. Not after the way she shredded our simple arrangement. But I find myself frowning. Nothing about this seems right.

My friend notices. "Were you hoping for someone else?"

I give a slow shake of my head. "Nah. Pretty easy to guess."

Ollie pipes up beside me. "I wish Miss Braelyn was with us."

Jordan gets a glare from me before I turn toward my son. I make sure my expression is neutral. "I know, buddy. She's probably working. I'm sure she's busy."

He makes a frustrated sound. "No, she's not. Miss Braelyn was leaving early today. Miss Kallie is there."

I can always count on him for updates. "I'm sure you'll see her soon."

His eyes glitter. "Does that mean you'll take me to Thicket tomorrow?"

"It's Saturday." I'm not sure what I hope to accomplish pointing out that indisputable fact.

Ollie claps. "Yeah, we can get extra candy because Braelyn is closed on Sunday."

I gesture to the traitor on my other side. "Ask your uncle."

They exchange a look. "I'm busy, bro. I have plans with Sadie. Not negotiable."

I don't bother masking my sneer. "How fu-reaking convenient."

My son is a curse word hunter. He doesn't miss this near slip any less than the last one. "Daddy, stop using bad language."

I groan into my fist. "Sorry, buddy."

"It's okay. I know you're sad."

"Uh, sure." That response seems easier than correcting him.

"And Daddy?" He taps my shoulder.

"Yeah, buddy?"

Ollie leans in close. "Miss Braelyn is sad. You need to fix it."

I can hear my jaw snap. "Is that so?"

"Yep. You can make it all better."

Any response I have won't be good. What a fucking circus. Jordan is the face of gloating smugness. Yeah, he's so damn proud.

An idea occurs to me. "Hey, Ollie? Would you mind getting the water bottle on my nightstand? I'm thirsty."

He blinks at me. "But that's all the way upstairs."

I nod. "Right. But you love climbing the steps. Maybe you can grab a game on the way back down."

That gets him moving. He's off the couch and dashing toward the foyer before I finish talking. I whip my attention to Jordan.

"What the fuck are you trying to accomplish?"

He combs through his hair. "I just wanna see you happy."

"What makes you think I'm not?"

"You can't bullshit me, man. This surly-ass shit you've been spewing is getting old."

I stare at a speck on the wall. "Too damn bad. That's not gonna change."

"Braelyn is one of the good ones, Stone. Done let her slip away."

I fight the urge to give him the finger. "She left me."

"You didn't give her reason to stay. She's protecting herself."

I roll my eyes. "For no reason."

"Says the asshole who's been emotionally closed off for the better part of his life."

"That's different," I mutter.

Jordan crosses an ankle over his knee. "How? You've both seen a lot of trauma, just in different forms. If anything, you could help each other. You were already well on the way. Things were going so smoothly for a change. Even you can't deny that."

And I can't. Everything had a brighter shine when Braelyn was around. Returning to the dingy dullness has sucked sweaty balls. Not that I'd know. It just sounds fucking horrendous.

I brush off his advice. "She's gone. I need to move on. In a month or two, we'll all be fine again."

He forces out a heavy exhale through flared nostrils. "That would be a huge mistake. For real, Brance. She belongs in your lives. I'm sure you've thought about it."

I hate when the fucker is right. "You don't know shit."

"You're a better person with her around."

"Fuck you, asshole."

"Thanks for proving my point."

If this is how my evening is already panning out, I should just go to bed. "How are we still friends?"

He rubs his nose with a middle finger. "Would it kill you to be open-minded? How about considerate? For everyone's sake? It's not impossible to understand where she's coming from. You know her story. Calling her that night wouldn't have been hard. Dead phone or not. Sparing a minute or two isn't asking a lot. Solve this shit and get the girl. Braelyn is the only one willing to put up with your grumpy ass. You can't give that up. A life of empty fucks is no way to live. Take it from me, man." Jordan slaps me on the back, making his words stick.

Ollie zips into the room before I can argue. He's panting from running at full speed. This kid can't stand to miss any action. He passes me the bottle I asked for. I take a drink for show. Jordan laughs and grabs the cards from Ollie's grip. He shuffles the deck.

"Should we play a game?"

My son thrusts his fist into the air. "Yes!"

"I'm not gonna like whatever you're about to suggest." I raise a brow in challenge.

Jordan smirks. "Dealer's choice. Red means you take Ollie to Thicket. Flip a black and you can merely think about it."

"I'm not agreeing to that." As fucking if.

Ollie and Jordan slap palms. "Majority wins."

It's no surprise the queen of hearts lands face up on the table. Go fucking figure. Jordan and Ollie cheer as if the Blues won the World Series. That vacation Don suggested isn't sounding too bad right about now. A secluded island by myself would really hit the spot. Most importantly, I'd be separated from these pestering Braelyn fans.

Ollie folds his little hands together. "Daddy, please?"

I'm a sucker for that plea. It's a problem I'm very aware of. "Don't I get a vote in any of this?"

"Nope." The response comes from both of them, in unison. I'm beginning to think this was rehearsed.

I pinch my eyes shut. "Fine. I'll think about it. Happy?"

Their matching grins tell me everything I need to know. I never stood a chance. But in the end, maybe I never wanted one.

chapter thirty-one

BRAELYN

TASKS

PICK UP ONE MY FAVORITE MUGS AND CRADLE IT. THE CHEERY rainbow paint resonates deeper than usual today. Especially with my pint-size helper zipping in and out of aisles. Ollie arrived an hour ago and shows no signs of leaving. The distracting presence of his father doesn't appear to be either. He's a damn beacon on my stoop. Women will be flocking in hoards any minute. I have my broom ready just in case.

It's been over a week since I laid eyes on his handsome mug. I'd be lying if I didn't admit to missing him. My legs just about gave out when he appeared on the sidewalk. But he didn't cross the threshold. For some reason that makes me more upset than anything. Why can't he come in and face me?

Damn coward, I think. But I'm mostly talking to myself.

This has been a trial of resistance. I haven't helped our lack of a friendly situation. A text wouldn't have been out of the question. It could have been related to Ollie. Some form of communication to maintain our ties. Maybe a rainbow hologram in the sky. Am I reaching? Absolutely.

I sigh and rest my elbow on the counter. Brance Stone has officially ruined me. Staring at him now confirms it. I won't be getting over his type of sexiness anytime this century. He's a forever-stamp of seductive ruin. I might as well contact the convents now.

"Miss Braelyn?"

I turn toward the soothing voice. "Yeah, sweetie?"

Ollie holds up a pair of patterned socks. "Where do these go?"

"Aisle four." I raise my hand and point to the left side.

He counts each row with a bounce of his finger. When he finds the right one, his little feet take off in a blur. Those flashing sneakers squeak across the floor. Ollie's zest is infectious. I can't stop the laugh from bubbling out.

I continue stacking the latest order of greeting cards. A smiling bear offers encouragement. Fireworks for the upcoming holiday. Some jokes about getting older. There's a steamy quote meant for a lover. The final one draws me in more than the others. I've never received one of this caliber. Not that I want to. What would I do with a sexy promise of midnight action? Nothing as of late.

My gaze naturally trails to Brance. He's still perched on the brick wall, one booted foot resting against the coarse surface. Those damn aviators hide his emotions. I bet he's brooding. His posture screams laidback, but I sense tension in his subtle shifts.

At that exact moment, Brance turns to look through the window. My lungs seize, and I fight the urge to hide. What're the chances he can really see me staring that clearly? Pretty damn good considering I keep that barely-tinted glass squeaky clean. Should I wave? Offer a come-hither smile?

Maybe I should get some stocking done in a far off corner where this won't be an issue.

As if hearing my plans to flee, Ollie dashes around the counter and screeches to a stop in front of me. His blue stare squeezes my heart. "Miss Braelyn?"

"Yeah, sweetie?"

"Why haven't you been around as much?"

"What do you mean? I'm always here." I made a promise that things wouldn't change for Ollie. I intend to keep it.

"No, not really. Miss Kallie has been working more. Why?"

I'd been calling on Kallie more often this week, but the hours off hadn't been beneficial. Quite the opposite. After several days of carrying an inconsistent schedule, I'm trying to get back on track. Having Brance randomly swoop in isn't making that easier. Mary is far more understanding.

"Well, I need a little space for myself. Do you ever get that way?"

A dent forms between his brows. "Uh, like a timeout?"

I laugh. "Kinda. But I'm choosing to go."

His jaw drops. "Why would you wanna be on timeout? They're not fun. Were you super-naughty?"

"It's different for adults. I'm sure your dad can explain." That last bit slips out before I can trap it. I'm not trying to dig myself a deeper ditch.

"He can?" Ollie's gaze swings to his father outside. "Is he on a timeout now?"

I take a moment to consider that. Brance has his head resting against the window. He's not talking to anyone. The answer seems simple. "Yeah, I think so. Do you wanna ask him?"

A tiny bubble of glee forms in my belly thinking about Ollie confronting his father. Turns out self-preservation isn't high on my priority list. Poking an agitated Brance could provide some much needed relief.

Ollie's lip twists in an adorable bow. "No, I don't wanna

bother him. My daddy needs some alone time to think about what he did."

That earns him a genuine giggle. "You're too cute, Ollie. Thanks for being here with me."

He shuffles his feet. "You've been sad again."

I attempt to broaden my smile, but it feels limp. "I'm doing okay, Ollie. Don't worry about me."

He shakes that unruly mop of hair. "No, you're not fine. I can tell, remember? Your eyes are super-sad."

I suppose he's right. If they're the windows to my soul, he's witnessing an all-out sob fest on a constant basis. I smooth my expression and try again. "It's a busy season for Thicket. There's a lot of people to help all day. I'm tired a lot, you know?"

He studies my straining features. "I guess. My daddy is extra grumpy lately. He hasn't been sleeping well. I think he's staying up too late. Maybe he should have a bedtime. His face is puffy. What does that mean?"

Oh, this kid is the ultimate mood booster. "You're very observant. I'm not sure many boys your age would catch that stuff. Maybe your dad is stressed?"

Try as I might to stop it, the hopeful part inside of me springs awake. Brance might be feeling the effects of our demise. Perhaps Sadie wasn't telling a tall tale after all. But I'm not going to feed that sappy spot. At least not yet.

Ollie is nodding fast. "Uh-huh, yeah. He needs to smile again. I haven't heard him laugh in a really long time. He's been getting mad at Uncle Jordy. We're just trying to help."

My gaze automatically seeks out Brance. He hasn't moved, still slumped against the building. "That's too bad. It will get better soon. I'm sure he's also busy at work. That can take a toll on people."

He gives a sharp shake of his head. His neck is getting a heck of a workout today. "No, my daddy misses you."

I choke on the shop's sugary scented air. "I'm not so sure about that, sweetie."

Ollie's pointed stare hasn't left my face. "And you miss him."

There's another half-truth waiting on my tongue. But the runaround of diverting is exhausting. My bones are weary enough. "You're right. I do."

He gasps, his mouth popping wide open. He spins in fast circles while clapping. "I knew it, I knew it."

I grin at his exuberance. There's no doubt he's been in on Sadie's not-so-secretive mission. "You did? How?"

"Because I'm a smarty-pants. That's what my daddy told me."

"You're very wise, kiddo."

Ollie reaches for my hand, jostling me with a few strong tugs. "I'm so happy you miss each other. Can I tell him?"

I crouch down so we're eye-level. "How about we show him?"

He shimmies in place. "With what?"

I reach under the counter for the captured fragment hidden there. When I made this piece the other day, Brance was on my mind. Sadie's words have been whispering in my ear. Ollie's frequent visits have been keeping me steady. But I want more. This morning is the last bit of proof, not that I needed more.

"Here, sweetie. Bring this to your dad, okay?" I'm not sure what I hope to accomplish by giving this to Brance. Maybe it's a peace offering. Or a way to mend our broken fence.

Ollie looks down at the aqua piece of glass. The mixture of blue and green makes a beautiful blend. He holds it up to the light. A beam of brightness casts across the floor.

"Wow," he whispers. "It's so pretty."

"I hope your dad thinks so too."

"He will." There's zero nonsense in his tone.

I nibble on my bottom lip, not feeling so sure. "M'kay. Let's bundle it up and see what he says."

Ollie slides the fragment into the little drawstring pouch I'm holding open. I watch him skip toward the door. Am I being foolish? Brance probably won't give a rip about what I'm offering. But if he does, everything will change. That possibility stirs up a swarm of sugar-high butterflies in my stomach.

Brance has always been unpredictable. That's one of the things I love about him. The L-word hitches my breath. It's flickered in and out of my thoughts more often than not. There's no denying my feelings. I cross one finger over the other. Here's to hoping love wins.

Ollie wore me down. I've been standing outside of Thicket for over an hour. The weather is warm without being oppressive. It's not a hardship to be holed up under the sun. There're pink and white striped awnings to shade me if need be. This is clearly the spot for chilling while my son enjoys his favorite store. Not sure why I didn't consider this an option prior to now.

Except it's probably due to the fact I've been a stubborn asshole. Big fucking surprise. I didn't need Jordan's insight to realize the errors of my ways. But this is who I am. Braelyn can accept this from me or look elsewhere.

That last line is a certifiable reason for slamming on the pause button. What the fuck am I thinking? Maybe the fresh air is getting to me. Actually, it's more likely the significant lack of sleep. That shit can cause hallucinations. Maybe that explains Braelyn floating in and out of my subconscious. I need to try harder at repressing that shit.

Maybe I should have gone for a walk. Or grabbed a beer at the bar across the road. But leaving didn't feel right. Neither did going inside. I agreed to bring Ollie, but there was no discussion of my involvement beyond that point.

I'm minding my own damn beeswax next to the awful lollipop sign. The blinking neon lights are mocking me. I can almost hear a scolding tone through the electric hum. I'm keeping busy by counting the hundredth car to drive along Maple Street. The next one cruises along with loud-ass music blaring through the speakers. Real awesome, dude.

Ollie bursts through the door with a clang of wind chimes and that awful bell. His smile is brighter than the mid-morning sunshine.

"All done, buddy?" I stop myself from asking if he wants to stay longer. Again with this wild desire to stick around.

"Nope. I have something for you. Here." His little hand thrusts forward. He peels open his fingers, exposing a little pouch.

I study it with a wary eye. "What's that?"

Ollie lifts his arm higher, shaking the so-called gift a bit. "Miss Braelyn made it for you."

A lift a skeptical brow. "Oh, did she?"

"You have to open it. Like right now."

He drops the leather package on my palm. The item is small. I picture a wad of used gum or belly button lint or a stink bomb. Anything could be hiding in here. I cautiously untie the strings and peek inside. Light catches on the edge of colorful glass. My mind whirls as the contents become abundantly clear.

She was right about these things seeming insignificant upon first glance. I would have continued thinking that until this piece landed in my grasp. It's us. This small piece of glass is a combination of Braelyn and me. Damn, I love her.

I love her. That fact is more solid than the concrete beneath my shoes. Those three words have never passed my lips. No woman has received them from me, not even my mother. But Braelyn will.

Green and blue reflections catch my focus. I stare down at the aqua fragment in my palm. The truth is a lead weight sinking to my very core. This was my fault. I've been a coward. I let her leave. I didn't fight for us. But I will now if it's not too late.

Ollie pulls at my shirt. "Miss Braelyn is still sad. You need to make her happy, Daddy."

"You're right, buddy. I do." This piece of glass gives me faith that we're not beyond repair. I can fix us.

He claps and bounces on his toes. "Yes! She's gonna be so excited."

Ollie's confidence is infectious. The need to see her barrels into me with the strength of a sonic boom. My pulse rockets with newfound energy. The window behind me rattles with the force. Those three words need to be said, and so much more.

I'm going to need additional backup. And that fucker owes me.

After taping out a quick text, I gesture to the entrance. "Lead the way, little man."

That's all he needs. Ollie takes off at the speed of light. He's opening the door before I've straightened off the wall. I barely catch the frame as its closing. After whipping off my shades, I step inside.

Braelyn is standing directly in front of me. The counter is behind her. It appears she's using the surface to keep her upright. Her beauty sears into me, burning into my memory. How did I ever let her out of my sight?

I can tell she's unsure. Her fingers fidget and knot together. She's biting that plump bottom lip. I'm going to kiss her worry away. Permanently.

Ollie darts across the room, turning down a far aisle. If

he's giving us space on purpose, I'll reward him with an extra juice box at dinner. I don't waste time moving slow either. My stride to Braelyn is fast and long. We're separated by a mere few feet before either of us can blink.

Is it fucking weird that my stomach is in knots? Too damn bad if it is. One more pansy-ass thing to add to the list I no longer give a shit about.

"Hey," I whisper.

"Hi, you." There's a rasp to Braelyn's voice that touches the soft spot in my chest.

"I got your gift. Thanks for this." I rub the glass between my fingers.

She glances up from under shuttered lids. It's my job to take that doubt away. "Do you like it?"

"More than you know."

The catch of her inhale draws my attention to her mouth. "Really?"

I tuck a few stray strands of hair behind her ear. "I never told you how special these pieces are. Especially this one."

She lifts a slim shoulder, leaning into my touch. "I found those glass parts and thought of you. The colors make sense for… us."

"They do. I got your meaning right away."

Braelyn swipes across her forehead. "Phew. I was concerned it was way out there."

A few beats of silence pass. The pause is thick with everything hanging between us. I breathe deep and dive in. "I'm so damn sorry, babe. Mostly for the shitty way I treated you last Monday. But there's plenty else for me to apologize for. I've been fucking rotten since we met. Over and again, I shot you down. I never gave us a real chance past some superficial bullshit. Not sure how you put up with me."

She sucks on the inside of her cheek. "The amazing sex didn't hurt."

My tension deflates, and I release a heavy exhale. I grab her hand, sliding our palms together. "There's that smartass wit I love."

Her gaze flings to mine on the last word. "W-what?"

I brush a thumb down the side of her face. "Isn't it obvious?"

"No, not to me."

"I'm fucking crazy about you, Brae. The last week has been hell. Worse than any shit I've ever experienced, which is really telling."

Braelyn gulps, the action making her slender throat bob. "I d-don't know what to say. I wasn't expecting all this. I figured you'd stay outside and never wanna see me again."

I squeeze her fingers that are still in my grip. "But I walked through that door to be with you. Ask me why, Brae."

She sniffs, peering up through wet lashes. "Why're you in here?"

My blue depths blend with her mossy green pools. "Because I love you. And not for Ollie, although you fit with him crazy well. But for me. Be in this for me, for both of us."

"I love you, Brance. So much. And Ollie. I can't believe this is real." Braelyn's eyes slide shut, a single tear trickling out. I brush it away, and she nuzzles into my palm. I dip closer, giving her a gentle kiss. She whimpers into the soft caress.

"How've you been?" I trace her nose with mine.

Braelyn sighs. "Better now. It wasn't so great without you. After Devon and the accident, I'm always waiting for the worst."

"Betrayal feels that way," I murmur.

"He didn't—"

I press my lips against hers. "I'm not saying he did, but it's all the same in the end. The pain leaves its mark. Just depends what we do with that. Not sure that shit ever goes away. The sting is less intense, but the impact remains."

She cuddles into me. "You make it hurt a little less."

"That's how I feel about you." I bury my face in the crook of her neck. Damn, I missed her sweet scent. Jordan better be on call for watching Ollie. Plans are stacking up in my brain.

"So, we're doing this? For real?" Skepticism bleeds through her voice.

I pull away enough to see the indent creasing her forehead. "You don't believe me?"

Braelyn averts her gaze. I grip her chin and lift until she looks at me.

"I know we have more shit to solve. That'll all come out soon enough. You're my sunlight and rainbows after a lifetime of storms. Don't leave me in the dark."

She nods. "There's no doubting you. I've been caught in a daze, and you're waking me up. I'm still a bit sleepy. Hell, I was one step away from getting a cat or a dog."

That gets a bark of laughter from me. "Really?"

"It was too quiet at my house. I don't like the silence. Living alone has never been my favorite. But these last few days were terrible." She trembles in my hold.

Rusty gears spring into action. The seed of thought sprouts and grows. I study her beautiful features. This is absolutely the right call.

"Might be nice to have a pet," I start. "Ollie asks for one every other minute."

"Oh, he'd love that. You'd make his year."

"I think he'd like to pick one out with you. It could be ours, at our house."

The lines between her brows deepen. "Okay, that'd be nice. But that doesn't solve the dilemma at my place. I guess we could—"

"Move in with us, babe."

Braelyn's jaw goes slack. Shaking fingers lift to cover her gaping mouth. "You're serious."

"Never been more serious. I guarantee Ollie will agree with me."

A smile splits her lips. "You love me." It's not a question.

"I do."

"And you want me to move in?"

A curt nod. "Yes."

She raises a sassy brow.

I grunt. "Please, babe."

"That has a nice ring to it."

I hold up a palm. "Now, now. I never said anything about a ring."

Braelyn giggles. "I don't need any of that. I'm happy just having you by my side. Paradise is life with you and Ollie in it."

This woman and her words. She gets to me.

"No worries there. You, Braelyn Miller, are the lucky owner of this bitter, cynical heart. I hope you enjoy it." I pat the area on my pec.

Her hand settles over mine. "I will cherish it with every breath."

"That's all I ask. I didn't plan on falling in love. You know, the romantic kind."

Braelyn's grin stretches wider. "Then why did you?"

"Couldn't help it if I tried."

She purrs against my jaw. "We're gonna owe Ollie and our friends big time."

I shake my head. "I never had a horse in this race."

"The stakes were too high?"

I sweep that off. "Nah, I just didn't wanna bet against us."

Her gaze sparkles brighter than the fragment in my pocket. "Yeah?"

"Of course, babe. We're stronger together than we'd ever be apart." I kiss her again. We haven't done that nearly enough. "I'm going to take you on a proper date."

Braelyn wiggles against me, eliminating the sliver of space between us. "Will there be dessert?"

I ghost my mouth over her lips. "Is that even a valid question?"

"You already know how to make me break. Let's see if you can put me back together."

I palm her ass and press us together. "Want me to smooth the hurt? Mend the cracked edges?"

"Mm-hmm, I think you already have. But we can test that theory. Maybe later we can put your tie collection to use."

My cock gets hard just thinking about her squirming against those silky bonds. She gasps when noticing my reaction.

Ollie chooses that exact moment to collide into our duo. But there's no denying him. He's proven the power of this trio. This is our new normal. I'm more than ready for it.

"Did you guys make up yet?"

I wink at Braelyn. "Yeah, buddy. We sure did."

His grin is full of mischief. "Took you long enough."

"Well, you weren't quite persuasive enough. I had to beg Braelyn to give me another chance." I can't go giving him all the credit. I'll never live it down.

He gawks at us. Little fists notch on his hips. "Do you need another timeout, Daddy?"

I give him a blank stare. "For what?"

Braelyn sucks air through her teeth. "No, Ollie. Your dad said sorry. And I apologized too. No more timeouts."

He yips. "Forever?"

"Let's not get ahead of ourselves," I tell him. Braelyn winces and mouths something about making it up to me. That'll do just fine.

Ollie shrugs. A second later, his face lights up. "Daddy?"

"Yeah, buddy?"

"Can I sleep at Uncle Jordy's house tonight?"

Ollie blinks at us. Braelyn laughs. I smirk at my son. "I already have it taken care of."

Ollie wiggles in his seat while I finish adjusting the straps. This kid needs to stop growing. It seems like yesterday he was facing backwards in the carrier. I've learned my lesson about the value of time. A few hours can change so much, as in a life's worth of poorly executed decisions.

I started this day with a massive chip on my shoulder. Selfish motivation was in the driver's seat. I set out to prove everyone wrong, including that damn soft spot that refused to shut up. Turns out I should have been listening all along. I rub a thumb over the smooth glass in my pocket. Lucky for my stubborn ass, Braelyn is crafty enough for the two of us.

That woman has every reason to be guarded and jaded. But she's not. Her inner strength persevered in spite of the shit hand she was dealt. Braelyn has given me the ass-kicking I needed to be a better man. And I'm far overdue on proving myself.

"Daddy?" The little voice interrupts my rapid planning.

"What's up, buddy?"

"Why'd we leave Thicket? I was having fun."

I smirk at my son in the rearview mirror. Ollie was having a blast singing and dancing around Braelyn's legs. A tune that sounded an awful lot like The Wedding March had been humming off his lips. I'm certain he's already planning the big event. A slight pause gives me a moment to digest that. There's a tingling sensation spreading through my chest. The space reserved for Braelyn blooms and swells. The thought isn't unpleasant or terrifying. Hell, maybe my kid is onto something.

First step is getting Braelyn into my bed on a nightly basis. Waking up to her gorgeous face is how I want to begin each morning from now on. We'll see what happens from there. I gave her the key. She's opening the damn floodgates.

A chuckle escapes me. "We can't stay at Thicket forever, Ollie. I think you love that store more than anywhere else." Although, it's the woman behind the counter he really cares about. Leaving her behind will no longer be an issue. "Braelyn has to close the place up. She's gonna meet us at the park."

He stretches to glance out the window. "Which one are we going to?"

"You'll see. Uncle Jordan is meeting us there."

"But where?" His huff borders on the type of annoyance I'm very familiar with.

"How does batting practice sound?"

Ollie's pinched lips burst into a wide grin. "We're going to Otter's Grove? Yay!"

His legs flail all about. I imagine him tearing it up around the bases. He's going to kill it in Little League. All the more reason to smack some balls around.

Jordan is leaning against the chain link when we pull into

the lot. His smile is cocky and too knowing. I'm sure he had this all figured out with Ollie and Sadie. I can't even be mad about them going behind my back.

He straightens and waves at us. "Hey, guys. All went better than expected, huh? I figured Ollie was just restocking his taffy supply."

The teammates exchange a wink. Real covert. Great sneaking skills, right there.

"Uh-huh. My daddy swooped in and saved the princess. Miss Braelyn is happy again." My son has quite the active imagination.

Jordan gives him a high-five. "I'm sure you slayed the dragon, little man."

Ollie nods. "Yep, it was really big and scary. I had to use my super-sharp sword." He stabs the air with this newfound weapon.

"I knew you could do it," Jordan roots.

That gets him a snort from me. "Listen, Nancy Drew. You've been real helpful and all. But I have plans of my own, thanks for asking."

He bounces his brows. "Big?"

"Huge." I spread my arms wide.

He claps me on the back. "There's the man I always knew was hiding under the bullsh—crap."

Ollie points at him. "I get an extra hour before bedtime."

My friend looks at me for confirmation. I just shrug. He deserves a little runaround.

"Well, in that case, I better tire you out. Batter up, kid." He hitches a thumb at the equipment resting near the cages.

Ollie squeals and bounds over the pile. He slips a helmet on, patting his head. Safety first.

Jordan glances over my shoulder. "Ah, good timing. Your lady-love has arrived."

I turn and follow his line of sight, the beginning of a

smile curving my lips. Braelyn parks next to my car and steps out. The heat in my chest expands beyond means. Her steps are slow, as if she's dragging this out on purpose. I don't mind the show one fucking bit.

Blonde hair spills over her shoulders and arms in loose waves. The skirt of her dress billows in the slight breeze. The short hem kisses her upper thighs. I wonder what color her panties are. Maybe she'll flash them at me on our way to the restaurant.

Jordan laughs beside me. "You're sunk, brother."

"Don't I know it."

Zero fucking regrets.

"Hey, Braelyn. I hear you're stuck with this ass on a more permanent basis." My friend sure knows how to talk me up. Guess it worked on the one lady who matters.

She rocks on her flip-flops. "Something like that."

"Well, congratulations. Don't let him scare you off again."

Her warm eyes lift, melting into mine. "I won't."

I stroke a finger down her arm. I'm rewarded with a sexy shiver. "Ready for date night?"

Braelyn nods. "Do you have a place in mind?"

"Sure do. Mind driving?"

I'm granted a giggle for that. "Not at all."

Jordan claps. "Well, this is a nice change of pace. We're all one big happy family."

"Not quite." I chuckle. "But getting there."

Braelyn tucks her chin, a rosy blush already rising in her cheeks.

I check my watch and smile. "We should get going, babe."

"You two enjoy yourselves." Jordan shoos us away.

"Thanks for taking care of my little man. Don't wait up." I give Jordan a salute and steer Braelyn toward the parking lot.

His laughter booms behind us. "Wouldn't dream of it."

"What're they spending the evening doing?" Braelyn asks.

"Ollie is more than ready to play Little League. Jordan has graciously volunteered to help him perfect his swing."

"You're such a good dad."

I link our fingers together. "One of my best qualities. I hope to add being a great boyfriend to that list."

She squeezes my hand. "You're well on the way."

"I'm gonna wine and dine you so hard." I dip down and nibble on her earlobe.

Braelyn grips the front of my shirt in her fist, hauling me closer. "Are you sure we need to eat first?"

"It'll be fast, promise."

"Okay." Her pout almost does me in, but this is important.

We buckle up, and I get the address keyed into the map app. The robotic voice bleeps out directions. We're only a few miles away. Plenty of road for an appetizer.

I emit a low grumble and stare at her lap. Braelyn bites her lip, making a very subtle shift to her hips. The fabric rides up, and I'm treated to a view of blue lace. My growl is a starving man staring at a feast fit for a king. Show me to the damn throne. I'm swinging for the fences.

The drive goes too quick. We arrive at the restaurant a few minutes later. Braelyn shifts her car into park and cuts the engine. The lot is dotted with other vehicles, but not many. Should be another quiet Saturday night. I can always count on The Lair to deliver.

She whistles. "This is more what I picture for you."

"What's that supposed to mean?" I look through the windshield and try to picture the place through her eyes.

Braelyn waves toward the brick building in front of us. "This bar screams upscale establishment. When you took me to Pour Spout, it threw me off. The Lair fits your swanky image."

"Should I be offended?"

She quirks a sassy as fuck brow. "That I'm calling you classy and sleek? Uh, sure?"

"Give me that smart mouth."

I lean over the console and kiss her. Our lips brush for a few moments, the fire burning hot in my blood. This is going to be the greatest test of control. Or a kinky push of limits. I'll have to see where the evening takes us.

We stroll hand in hand. I open the door for the woman on my arm. She falters when we step inside.

"Oh, yeah. This place is very attention-grabbing. I feel a little spoiled." Braelyn's eyes are wide while she absorbs the interior.

It's clear I made the right choice. "Good. Our first official date should be one to remember."

She presses into my side. "I'll never forget a single moment of it."

I guide her toward the gleaming main attraction ahead of us. A few short months ago, Jordan was hassling me about Braelyn. We were sitting on these stools, in this bar. All I had to do was believe. I refused to see what was directly in front of me. Braelyn had been there, waiting, the entire time. I'd been a blind fool.

But look at us now.

She's still looking around. "Is this one of your regular haunts?"

"It is."

"Very cozy and intimate."

"That's the idea." My gaze sweeps around the dimly lit space. I stop on an empty corner spot, shadows cloaking most of the table.

I smirk at my girl. "Wanna get a booth?"

chapter thirty-four

BRAELYN

GOALS

BRANCE'S PALM IS A SCORCHING BRAND ON MY LOWER BACK. I'D let him lead me around anywhere with this gentle nudge. A zing of electric current blazes across my hypersensitive skin while he guides me to the darkened corner. We're in a public place, yet this seems salacious. The fantasy I've had on several occasions brews in my lower belly. Maybe I'll scrounge up the courage to ask… or beg.

I sit on the bench seat and slide in. Brance is hot on my ass, slipping in beside me. A server bustles over right away and grabs our drink order. Brance murmurs something to him I can't quite hear. Not that I'm trying too hard. Having his sinfully muscular body pinned so closely to mine is the ultimate distraction. I can't concentrate long enough to appreciate the stunning room we're in.

When we're alone again, I arch a brow at my date. "Same side seating?"

"Only way to appreciate these booths."

"Oh?"

Brance's palm rests on my bare thigh, drifting up and higher. "Yeah, babe."

I spread my legs without hesitation. With one touch, I'm dragged under his seductive spell. Those talented fingers roam further, disappearing beneath my dress. I've never been more grateful for my choice in clothing. He reaches my satin covered center with no signs of slowing down. I really like the direction he's taking.

"W-what are you doing?" My tone is barely a rasp.

Brance ghosts his lips over my cheek. "I've missed you. Just a little starter while we wait for the main course. Relax, babe."

I grip the table's edge, my knuckles white. "Brance, we're gonna get caught."

"We won't if you're quiet. No one can see anything."

And he's right. My lower half is hidden from view. If someone passes by our hidden alcove, they won't realize what's happening. I clamp my jaw and pass over the reins. Brance traces the edge of my panties, slowly pushing the silk out of his way. A shot of molten arousal gets injected into my veins. A whimper begs to drip off my tongue. I squirm, slouching lower to give him easier access.

"Have you done this before?" I don't know why the answer is so important. His answer could shatter this moment or launch me into the stratosphere.

Brance's nose brushes my ear when he leans in. "Never wanted to until now. This is only for you, babe."

That's exactly what I needed to hear. I sag against the seat in a pliable puddle, ready for Brance to mold me into his making. The rest of my resistance fades when he swipes across my slit. I'm so wet, almost embarrassingly so. Telltale tingles are already creeping up my legs. The thrill of getting caught. The tender warmth in his searing gaze. His strong strokes against my clit. It's a recipe for a sharp and powerful climax.

I clamp a hand over my mouth and moan. Tremors wrack my limbs, an eruption cracking through the volcanic surface. My eyes roll back while I shudder in his grip. I do my best not to rattle the booth.

"You're so fucking sexy." His voice is a hypnotic pulse lulling me deeper into the waves of euphoria.

Whoa. My mind is swirling in a lusty fog. I'm out of breath, utterly spent from that quick release. That hit the damn spot. I wipe the dots of perspiration off my brow. "We're gonna need to come here more often."

"That is definitely what she said," he murmurs against my flushing neck.

I gather my bearings and take stock of our position. No one appears to be scandalized at first glance. Two women are turned around on their barstools. But they're not staring at me. Those hungry eyes are sweeping over my boyfriend.

A fierce wave of possession crashes over me. This man is mine. I have some claim to him. There's a faint sound of someone growling, but I'm too zoned into these hussies.

Brance follows my glare and laughs. "Easy, babe. Put the claws away."

I shake off the odd sensation. "Huh?"

"Looks like you're about to leap over the table and attack those chicks."

I blow out a puff of disbelief. "Was not."

He bends to my ear. "I love that, babe. Didn't think you could get any hotter. Fierce Braelyn gets me even harder than I already am." Brance grabs my wrist and guides me to his lap. He settles my palm over the tent popping up there. I add a little pressure, rubbing up and down.

Brance hisses. "Fuck. I can't wait to be buried inside you."

It's my turn to snuggle close. "I'm sure there's a bathroom around here."

He chuckles. "Dirty girl. I can be patient. Plus, it's about to get even better."

The server appears in front of us as if conjured up from thin air. He sets this glorious creation down in front of me. Piles of ice cream, caramel syrup, crispy pieces of churro, sprinkles, whipped cream, chocolate chips, and triangle pieces of waffle cone fill my hazy vision. My mouth waters while my body still trembles with aftershocks. Is it my birthday?

I scoot to the edge of my seat. "This looks like the greatest combination in dessert history. What is it?" The wonder in my voice echoes around the elegant bar.

"Dessert Nachos."

I lift my bulging eyes to Brance. "What kind of magical treat is that?"

"All of your favorites in one bowl."

My stomach grumbles in agreement. "Wow. I never knew these existed."

His smirk stretches into a full grin. "Glad I could be of service."

He reaches for a waffle cone chip. I tug the confection out of reach.

"What're you doing?" I raise a brow.

He chuckles. "Sharing with you. Remember that it's always polite to share, Braelyn."

I wag a finger at him. "This is all mine."

"You're gonna eat that entire mound?" His scoff says it all.

My competitive side stretches her lazy muscles. They're a tad underused as of late. But the need to prove him wrong barrels into me. "Yep, absolutely."

Brance shakes his head. "I don't believe you."

"Wanna bet?"

"What're the stakes."

I think long and hard. Am I ready? The idea doesn't trap my brain into a state of panic. There's no sign of the once familiar flashbacks. I swallow any sliver of doubt.

"If I win, you drive me home." I keep my steady gaze locked on his.

Brance is the one who looks shell-shocked. His eyes blow open wide, those pouty lips parting. "W-what?"

I prepare my first bite of dessert nachos. "Stunned silent?"

"Something like that."

I wink. "You're welcome."

"Are you sure about this? I won't hold you to it." And I know he won't.

I sweep a hand down my form. "I'm good. Calm as a chilled cucumber. I trust you, Brance."

He links our fingers together and gives me a gentle squeeze. "Thank you for that."

Brance doesn't make a move to steal more ice cream. He orders his own. We eat and chat and plan for me living with them.

Once I've finished every last morsel, he tucks me into the passenger side with a tense smile. Those dimples get me every time.

Not a single drop of fear freezes my veins when he shifts the car into drive. I relax into the plush leather with a sigh. Brance smiles at me, waiting for the word. I reach for his free hand and nod.

"Let's go home."

epilogue

BRAELYN

THICKET

I PULL INTO THE GRAVEL LOT AND FIND A SPOT IN THE BACK ROW. For whatever reason, Sadie asked me to meet her at Cliffton Heights. Her car isn't one of the few parked alongside mine. I check the time, finding that I'm a few minutes early. It's too beautiful to stay locked inside. I step out of my car and stretch. It's a glorious afternoon, the temperature mild for late summer. The midday sun kisses my cheeks. A light breeze whips through the tall grass, calling me to the meadow.

I'm sure Sadie will know where to find me.

After slipping on a pair of shades, I set off along the gravel ground. My sandals find the worn grooves in the pebbled path. I've walked this trail countless times. It'd be a safe bet that I could find my way blindfolded and spun around. The pendant from my necklace glints in the sunlight. The rectangular prism casts brilliant rainbows in front of me. The vibrant array of scattering colors infuses this moment with a new type of significance. I clutch the gift from Brance in my palm and smile.

That man knows me well.

There's a new sweetness in the air. Fresh blossoms and pollen accompany my hike. Flocks of birds chirp a welcoming tune. Goosebumps rise on my skin under the high noon's direct rays. The familiar comfort envelopes me in a soft gust of wind. I almost skip across the remaining distance.

When I near the ridge with my flat plot of turf, it's not Sadie waiting for me. Brance and Ollie stand there wearing matching smiles. My pulse does a little dance. They're so handsome. The lake sparkles behind them, adding to their already undeniable appeal. I remove my sunglasses to get a better view.

"Well, hello. I didn't expect to see my boys up here. This is a surprise." I give them a little wave while erasing the space between us.

"Hey, babe." Brance's smirk is etched with promises for later.

Ollie is practically vibrating beside him. He probably had extra sugar at lunch. "Hi, Miss Braelyn."

He gets a bop on the nose for that. I add in a cheesy grin for special effects. I've been living with them for almost two months. I feel the formality can be dropped from my name. But it's a tough habit to break.

I pop up on my toes to give Brance a kiss. Ollie gets a high-five and a hug. "I thought you were going out for quality guy time? What're you two doing here?"

Brance makes a show of looking across the field. "What do you call this? No better way to spend an afternoon. We wanted to see what all the fuss was about."

I laugh. "You could've told me. I would have gladly brought you out here."

"We figured this would work out better." Brance lifts a lazy shoulder.

Ollie nudges his leg. "Daddy?"

He shakes his head at him. "Not yet."

Ollie's hands are hidden out of sight behind his back. "But when?"

Brance puts a finger to his lips. "Really soon."

I watch their exchange. "What's going on?"

"So, this area is really beautiful." Brance's deflection is clear as the blue sky, but I let it slide.

I still quirk a skeptical brow at him. "It sure is."

"How'd you discover this spot?"

I stare off toward the ledge. "Three years ago, after the accident, I wasn't in a great place. I'd been wandering around, searching for something of meaning. Anything at all. I came across this park with these amazing cliffs. It clicked for me." I motion around us. "This is the original thicket. Did you know that?"

Brance nods. "That makes sense. "A place to get lost for a while."

"Find purpose. Center yourself."

"Find true happiness," he murmurs.

"Exactly," I whisper.

"C'mere, babe." He tugs me closer by my belt loop.

I fold into his chest without effort. "This is nice."

Brance kisses my forehead. His heart is racing a thousand miles a second. I'm about to question his rapid pulse when he takes a step back. Brance reaches for my hand, the touch gentle and delicate. A quiver trembles my muscles. There's a subtle shift weaving within the air.

"Brae, I love you."

That alone has tears pricking my eyes. The combination of everything plows into me. Being at this sacred space with my favorite people hits me deep in the feels. Brance smirks and wipes the streaks off my face.

"Keep it together, babe. I have an entire speech planned."

"Don't forget me. I have stuff to say," Ollie chimes in.

His father winks at him. "Yeah, buddy. Hold on for one more minute."

Brance lowers to one knee. With a shaking palm, I cover my gasp. I lose the fight against my tears. The rivulets are rolling down my cheeks in earnest. He tugs me closer by the arm, still holding my left hand in his. A gentle kiss is placed on my ring finger.

He clears his throat. For the first time, this man looks nervous. I'm too spellbound to focus on his shaking grip or bobbing throat. All I see is the love shining in his baby blues.

"I have a limited vocabulary when it comes to sweet stuff. I'll apologize in advance."

I laugh, but the sound is broken. I jerk my chin up and down instead of bothering with garbled words.

Brance takes a small velvet box out of his pocket. He snaps open the lid and my knees threaten to buckle. The ring has a center diamond haloed by blue and green alternating stones. It's stunning, but I can barely take my gaze off the man proposing. My vision is crazy blurry, but that doesn't matter. I've never witnessed anything clearer than this moment.

"I wanna marry you. See you wear white while walking down the aisle toward me. You'll be glowing. Taking my last name. Being mine, ours." He nods at Ollie, and I sob harder. "Say you'll marry me, Braelyn Miller. Agree to be with us forever. Will you be ours, babe?"

I'm accepting before he finishes the first sentence. I repeat the word silently after each point he makes. When he's done, I leap at him. Brance is a solid wall and catches me easily.

"Y-yes. A million yeses," I whimper in his ear.

He stands, lifting me with zero effort. Brance slips the ring on my finger. The platinum band is a perfect fit. He pulls me near, and I collapse into his waiting embrace. I'm a weeping mess and have never been happier.

Brance's strong arm cinches around my back, his fingers clutching my hip. His other arm hauls Ollie into our sides. Two little arms weaves around our legs. I reach over and draw Ollie closer. Brance and I link our fingers together against Ollie's back. The three of us are a complicated twist of limbs. Where one ends, another begins.

We fit, all swaddled together in a love huddle that can't be broken. This is the greatest moment of my life. I'm crying openly at this point. I don't bother trying to stop the outpouring of emotion. A tug at my shirt draws my attention down.

"Miss Braelyn?"

I give him a watery smile. The need to correct him feels more important now. "Sweet Ollie, you can drop the Miss. Just call me Braelyn."

He picks something up from the ground, cradling it in his little palm. "What about Mom?"

Fresh tears pool in my stinging eyes. "W-what?"

He opens his hand, revealing a silver bracelet. He lifts the piece up within reach. "Can I call you that?"

A large heart charm stands out against the chain. Engraved in the center is one word. Beyond meaningful. Extremely special. Irreplaceable. And granted to me as the greatest gift.

Mommy.

My gaze shifts between Brance and Ollie. I'm checking for confirmation or reassurance or something that hasn't quite sunk in. They're both smiling wide. My heart hiccups.

"R-really? Are you sure?" Again, I'm not sure who to address. My insides are a jumble of too many feelings.

"Uh-huh. Super-positive." Ollie passes the jewelry to Brance. He opens the clasp and loops it around my wrist.

"He picked this out all by himself." Brance spins the links until the charm is facing us.

"I love you both so much. My f-fiancé and my… my son."

Brance wraps me in a hug with Ollie in the middle. "You belong in our little family."

"I love you, Mommy and Daddy." The soft murmur soothes the few broken pieces still part of me.

My boys hold me tight while I whisper, "I love you, too."

Not that long ago, I contemplated something inconceivable on this cliff. And now, because of these two wrapped around me, I'm healed.

bonus epilogue

BRAELYN

NEXT

WAKE ON THE BRINK OF ORGASM, CERTAIN IT WAS A DREAM. BUT Brance's face is buried between my thighs. The sun is rising over the ocean behind him. A salty breeze tickles my cheeks. I could definitely get used to this.

"Good morning." His greeting puffs against the overly sensitive nerves twitching along my slit.

"Indeed." I arch and stretch wider. My muscles sing with glorious warmth.

Brance takes a languid lick. That tongue doesn't miss a spot, swiping across every private piece of me.

"W-why'd you slow down?" I wiggle in his hold, seeking more of what he's giving.

One massive palm cups my ass, lifting me to the optimal angle for his feast. I spread further until my hips threaten to snap. He has full access, permission granted to everything.

"Patience," Brance murmurs.

The sheets are fisted in my grip. "I'm s-so close. Please."

His lips brush along my throbbing core, a filthy kiss meant to keep me hovering over the brink. Brance tongues my clit, swirling faster the louder I moan. My lungs are already burning. A finger nudges my entrance. The teasing makes me whimper.

I try to press closer, but his grip is unrelenting. "More, Bran. Please. Please make me break."

"You always beg so pretty, babe. Love hearing you plead for me. I wanna shatter the windows with your screams."

While he talks, his finger is pumping into me with lazy strokes. A slow rhythm meant to drive me wild with lust.

"You're torturing me." My whine is aimed at the ceiling.

The man sprawled between my legs laughs. "My wife is so spoiled. Maybe you need to wait longer."

I clench my teeth and hiss. "No, please. I need you."

That single digit keeps sliding in and out of my clenching core. I want more—*him*—and he knows it.

"Bran." I drag the syllable out on an extended groan. "Make love to me. It's our honeymoon. You have to do what I say."

Brance inserts another finger, doubling his efforts. "My wife shall want for nothing. Relax and accept the orgasm I'm about to give you."

"But—"

My words are cut off with a silent scream as he pounces and attacks with vigor. He dives in, eating me as though this is his last meal. The tip of his tongue is flicking my clit with rapid bursts.

I thrash my head on the pillow. "Y-yes, oh my sh-sh-sha-gahhhh. There, so much there."

Brance snakes a hand up my torso, landing on a peaked nipple. The pinch is a bite on the right side of pain. My husband plays my body like the finest tuned instrument. I bow toward his touch, stumbling over the ledge. My knees lock around his ears as I buck into him. I'm cracking, splitting apart until endless desire floods in. Liquid nirvana blooms through my center, spreading beyond reach. He doesn't let up. Brance forces me higher until I'm left in a boneless heap.

I feel my chest rise and fall as the splinters gather into some semblance of sense. I'm dizzy after that, and my blink is heavy. "Wow."

"You taste sweeter in Tahiti." Brance's smirking lips are coated in me. I shiver regardless of the tropical humidity already bearing down on us. He licks the evidence away. Damn, he's sexy. And all mine. An electric aftershock ripples through my core, contemplating another round.

I skip my toes down his calf. "You're more spontaneous."

Brance nibbles a path across my inner thighs. "Have to keep our marriage spicy and exciting."

I tip my head back, a throaty laugh escaping me. "It's been two days, Bran."

"Best of my life."

I reach for him, scratching along his scruffy jaw. "So romantic. Careful or you'll make me swoon."

He nuzzles against me. "That's the idea."

The calm tide calls to us through the open bungalow doors. Coconut and pineapple linger in the air. I could lie naked in this bed for hours on end without complaint. I mean, a private exotic beach is tough to beat. Especially when it's our honeymoon.

Chilly rain showers break up the sticky heat. Rainbows frequently streak the sky. I could easily be convinced to move here. At the very least own a vacation home in this place.

"What're you thinking, Missus Stone?"

I comb through Brance's sleep tousled hair. "How much I love my husband."

"Lucky man," he purrs against my lower belly.

"And what's on your mind, Mister Stone?"

He kisses a trail between my hips. "I've determined it's too quiet."

I sway to follow his movements. "Okay? Want me to turn on some music?"

Brance nips along the tan skin of my stomach. "At home, dirty girl."

"Why are we talking about this now?" I grind into him for encouragement. "Get up here. Give me what I want."

"How about what I want?"

I scoff. "We aren't doing anal. At least not yet."

He chuckles. "Good to know it's on the list of possibilities. But I'm not talking about fucking your ass. You're ruining my plan, babe."

"Me?" I gasp.

He hums. "I was going to get you all agreeable and drowsy. Then spring this on you."

"Spit it out, husband."

A grin to rival the sun splits his handsome face. "Ollie needs a sibling. A little sister to be exact."

The air I was inhaling turns to concrete in my windpipe. I choke on a gulp of the sweet, tropical air. "W-what?"

Brance's chin is resting between my breasts. "Life is short, babe. I want more babies with you."

Emotion pricks my eyes. I'm nodding against the blur in my vision. I'm smiling so wide there's an ache in my cheeks. But nothing else reaches me while I'm drowning in pure bliss. "Okay."

"Yeah?"

"Let's make a baby."

His sky-blues sparkle. "No more rubbers."

"Or pulling out." I bite my bottom lip.

That's all it takes. When he slides into me, there's nothing between us. That barrier—thin as it was—had been the last sliver of separation keeping us apart. I'm finally getting all of him. And I want every last bit. Really bad.

I cross my ankles over his lower back. We rock together in a smooth wave. I press my mouth to his temple. "I have a feeling I'll be pregnant by next week."

A rumble rises off his chest. "Tomorrow would be better."

"Overachiever."

"Damn fucking straight, Missus Stone."

"Love you, husband."

"And I love you, wife."

That's technically the end, but are you curious about Jordan and Sadie? Well, I wrote a little bonus story for them. Brance, Braelyn, and Ollie make plenty of appearances.

Email Harloe at harloe.rae@gmail.com to receive your FREE copy of *Say You'll Be*!

acknowledgments

Well, I'm still a little shook up from this one. How about you? I'm not sure another story will ever impact me quite as deeply. But those are the best kind. Thank you very much for taking the journey with me. Fingers crossed that Brance didn't make you too mad and was able to redeem himself. Hopefully Braelyn spoke to you like she did to me. And we can all smile over the adorableness that is Oliver James. I feel like I always say this after a release, but Ask Me Why is truly my favorite.

First and foremost, I need to give a ton of gratitude to my outstanding husband. He continues to be the most patient man I know, especially when I'm nearing a deadline. If it wasn't for him, I couldn't do this author gig. I'll never be able to express how much he means to me. Above all else, he's an amazing father to our rambunctious toddler.

To all the bloggers, reviewers, and readers—THANK YOU! I'm well aware how many fantastic books are available. For you to choose mine means more than I can properly describe. Without you, the life of authors would be extremely challenging. Because you picked up a story and offered precious time to read, everything is brighter. Thank you for making a difference. Please know how much I truly appreciate it!

I have an epic group of ladies who work hard behind the scenes to keep me going. Words cannot express how much I owe to them. Talia, Jacquelyn, Kate, Sunniva, Renee, Melissa, and Lauren—I wouldn't be able to publish without you!

A huge thank you to all my wonderful author friends who

offer endless encouragement and support. I always feel the love from these ladies! Heather, Michelle, Nicole, Leigh, Annie, Tia, Suzie, Victoria, Ella, Logan, Lauren, Maria, KK, Amie, Renee, Parker, and many more—thank you for just being there when I need a solid shoulder to lean on.

A super special virtual hug to Keri, KC, Megan, Cindy, Shauna, Autumn, Crystal, Tijuana, Sarah, and Vanessa. You're all lovely and generous and fantastic peeps!

I owe so much to Candi Kane from Candi Kane PR. She's been handling my releases for almost a year and I'm not sure how I ever managed prior. Now I have the greatest marketing and promotional services around. You're such a boss and I love you. Thank you so very much for all you do!

Thank you to all the ladies of Give Me Books. I've been working with you guys for almost two years and you always provide amazing release services. Thank you, thank you, thank you!

Having genuine friends in this business is difficult to accomplish and I'm blessed to be part of several groups that keep my author heart happy. THANK YOU Book Babes Forever, Boston Babes, 60K in 30 days, Do Not Disturb Book Club, and KU Explosion.

THANK YOU to BookCoverKingdom for the GORGEOUS cover. As always, you amaze me.

Thanks to Eric Battershell, the very talented photographer who shot the perfect image of Drew. Thank you for giving me a beautiful cover photo for this story.

For my Hotties, the bestest reader group an author can ask for. I'm so thankful to each one of you for taking this journey with me. I appreciate you more than words can describe. Thank you for being dedicated to me and our bookish community. I love our special place on social media!

Harloe's Review Crew, thank you so very much for wanting to read and review my words. Somedays, I still pinch myself. I appreciate you going above and beyond to support and promote me during releases. I'm eternally thankful to all of you!

A huge thank you to Stacey from Champagne Book Designs for making the interior of Ask Me Why look its absolute greatest.

And last but certainly not least, a huge shout out to YOU for reading Ask Me Why. It's the greatest feeling in the world knowing you chose my book out of so many to read. I mean, wow. I appreciate you so much. Please know that! Just continue loving books and reading for me, okay? You've made me a very, very happy author!

One last thing? If you enjoyed Ask Me Why and want to do me a huge favor, please consider leaving a review. It really helps other readers find my books!

about the author

Harloe Rae is a *USA Today* & Amazon Top 100 bestselling author. Her passion for writing and reading has taken on a whole new meaning. Each day is an unforgettable adventure.

Harloe is a Minnesota gal with a serious addiction to romance. She's always chasing an epic happily ever after. When she's not buried in the writing cave, Harloe can be found hanging with her hubby and son. If the weather permits, she loves being lakeside or out in the country with her horses.

Harloe is the author of *Redefining Us, Forget You Not, Watch Me Follow, GENT, MISS, LASS,* and *Ask Me Why.* These titles are available on Amazon.

Find all the latest on her site www.harloe-rae.blog

Subscribe to her newsletter at bit.ly/HarloesList

Join her reader group, Harloe's Hotties, at www.facebook.com/harloehotties

Follow her on:

BookBub: bit.ly/HarloeBB

Amazon: bit.ly/HarloeOnAmazon

Goodreads: bit.ly/HarloeOnGR

Facebook Page: Facebook.com/authorharloerae

Instagram: www.instagram.com/harloerae

Book & Main: bookandmainbites.com/harloerae

GENT SNEAK PEEK

CHAPTER ONE

MA'AM

Trey

"Did you hear what I said?"

At her question, my gaze shifts to connect with the woman's stare. She's an unfamiliar face, probably lured into town by the specialty shops off Main Street. Sitting closer than socially acceptable, she's almost stuck on me. The bar is crowded tonight, though. I let the proximity slide, but her attempt at conversation is pushing it too far.

I came to Dagos for a few beers after work, not to engage in chit-chat. Usually I won't hesitate sampling fresh meat, gladly gobble up what's being offered, but not today. Try as she might, this chick is striking out with me. I have zero intentions of giving her the quick fuck she's been practically begging for since sitting down.

I clear my throat. "Ma'am, I'm not interested."

"Excuse me?" she says as her eyes widen. "Ma'am? That's what you call a grandmother. Do I look old to you?"

The dial on her annoying meter cranks up a few notches. I'm not stupid enough to fall into her trap, but still bite my tongue to keep the insults from barreling out.

I quickly scan her pinched face, covered with powdery shit likely meant to hide her age. I was trying to be polite by using a respectful term, but she's clearly not the type. I rub my forehead while blowing out a breath, frustration already building like a storm cloud.

"I mean no offense," I grind out between clenched teeth,

"but I'm spending the evening solo. Cheers." I raise my bottle in a lame-ass salute.

The yappy broad huffs and rolls her eyes. It seems she might spit more crap my way, but then her attention darts to a man across the room. She eagerly slips off the stool, nearly spilling her drink with the jerky movements. She glances back at me, shooting daggers from her eyes.

"Asshole," she shoots over her shoulder before sauntering off.

Good fucking riddance.

I lift the nearly empty beer to my lips, but a burst of laughter interrupts me.

"Wow. You sure know how to pick 'em. How are you still single with suave moves like that?"

"Not you too," I mutter without turning around, recognizing the raspy voice immediately. "Was the entire female race set on driving me fucking crazy?" My chin tilts skyward as I silently ask for patience… or a fucking break. Neither will come for me.

"Would it kill you to be nice?" Addison rests her arms against the bar next to me.

I puff air through my clenched teeth. "Most likely. And I was nice. I called her ma'am."

"You know girls hate that," she shoots back. "It's a dig more than anything and makes us feel old. Might as well call her a raging bitch or wrinkled hag."

"Those names seem more appropriate. Thanks," I chuckle but there's no humor behind it.

"Don't start, Trey. You know I'm right."

"I'm not saying shit. Just thinking I might use those instead."

"You're impossible."

"That's the point."

"What-ev-er," Addison singsongs while glancing around. "Where's Jack?"

"Still at the shop."

"Burning the midnight oil?"

"In more ways than one. Had a rough day."

She tilts her head and gives me a once-over. "You too?"

"Don't I always?"

"Meh, I suppose. You're always a grump so it's tough to tell the difference."

"And here I thought we were exchanging pleasantries."

"You and pleasant will never go together." Addison hitches a thumb over her shoulder. "Running off that lovely lady is a prime example."

I grunt and shake my head. "She deserved it for being so desperate."

She snorts and elbows me. "Why are you such a dick? All that handsome is going to such shameful waste. You need to find someone to treat right."

Peering at Addison, all toned limbs and tan skin, I consider a quick fuck after all. I grip the cool bottle, picturing her soft flesh giving in to me.

"Why haven't we ever—"

"No way. I know that look," she says. "I see you give women those bedroom eyes every Friday night only to watch them turn cold the following morning. I haven't fallen for them yet and I don't plan to start."

Just like that, our breezy banter slams to a halt. Tension strains my shoulders after being cut off. *Again.* What is it with chicks bulldozing me tonight?

Having Addison call me out does nothing to help my mood, but it's no surprise she sees straight through me. Although I've known her since kindergarten, it still pisses me off. Moments like this make living in a small-town suffocating. There's nothing and no one new around here. I know useless shit about everyone from Garden Grove, whether I want to or not.

I roll my neck and restore my typical look of indifference. "I never get any complaints. Your loss, Addy."

Addison shakes her head. "So fucking cocky. I ain't giving you any ass, but how 'bout another?" She asks and gestures to my beer.

I grumble, "That'd be great," without looking back at her.

Addison just stands there so I give in and glance over. Her arms are crossed as she raises a slim brow my way, seemingly waiting for…

"Please," I grit. The irritation from earlier whooshes in my ears and I'm ready to get gone.

Right after this drink.

She snickers and says, "That's better. We'll make a gentleman of you soon."

"Don't hold your breath, *ma'am.*"

Addison gasps and flames rise in her hazel eyes.

Before she digs into me, I add, "Chill out. I'm just fucking with you. But seriously, get back to work. I'm thirsty."

"You really are an asshole," she says while patting my cheek with more force than necessary. I'm sure she'd love to slap the shit out of me but won't risk getting in trouble for it. She shakes her head and turns away, strutting off to serve other waiting customers.

My eyes lock on her swaying hips, losing myself in the rhythm of her movement for a moment. No harm in looking, right?

Sweet-smelling perfume wafts in as the abandoned stool next to me shifts slightly.

"Is this seat taken?"

The notes are soft but rise above the booming noise in the space. The feminine lilt of her voice snakes around before I feel a twisting in my gut. I quickly shove that fluffy shit away. My jaw ticks while I ignore her heavenly scent closing in around me.

"Don't even bother," I growl loud enough for her to hear.

"Excuse me?"

Disbelief colors her voice and I can't help swiveling toward her.

Holy shit.

Bottomless blue eyes greet me, sparkling with fierce emotion. The glittering sapphires are hypnotizing, the type of pull any man would fall victim to.

Except me.

MISS: A second chance standalone romance
The boy she loved is gone. The man I've become doesn't deserve her.

Delilah Sage was the first girl I loved, my first for many things, but that's only the beginning. She was a warm embrace after especially hard nights, offering comfort where there was only pain. Delilah kept me from sinking and I promised her forever. I should have known better.

I ruined the only good in my life. Now all I have is regret, constant and relentless. My need for Delilah hasn't faded after all these years. She's the only woman who understood me. There's no moving on from that. I've accepted my fate of being alone. This is what I deserve.

Until I'm handed a second chance—whether I want it or not. A job brings me back to the small town I swore would stay in my past. The memories and mistakes are waiting to greet me. I try to keep my distance, but Delilah has always been my weakness. One look won't hurt. How quickly I forget she's impossible to resist.

After all, letting her go was never my intention.

Read FREE with Kindle Unlimited!

Redefining Us
A standalone friends to lovers, military romance.

In order to truly save him, I need to redefine us.

Xander Dixon was my best friend.
Loyal and dependable.
A brave warrior.
A permanent presence in my life until that fateful day he
boarded a plane headed overseas.

Xander's unwelcome silence haunted me for three years…
Until he suddenly resurfaces.
Blinded by misplaced fury.
Trapped in a pool of darkness.
Unable to escape the perpetual pain.

Though it would be easy to walk away, I refuse to give up on
him.
I want to know his misery and torment, so I can rescue him.
Then Xander will finally be mine.

Free with Kindle Unlimited!

Forget You Not
A standalone sweet second chance, military romance.

I didn't believe in love at first sight until Lark stood before
me.

Pretty sure I would have married her on the spot.
Too bad fate had other plans.
Duty called and I had to answer—no matter the
consequences.
There wasn't a chance for goodbye, but I'd never forget her.

Time has a way of creating change—but only on the surface.
Even after all these years, I know Lark is mine.
I belong to her just the same.
The moment I see her again, it's a done deal.
All I've got to do is convince her this is forever.
She can push but I'll only pull harder.

I'm not letting our second chance slip away.

Free with Kindle Unlimited!

Watch Me Follow
A stalker, double virgin romance.

Creep. Freak. Crazy Eyes.
I've heard it all.
Over the years, they've slammed me with every demeaning
name in the book.
Their taunts warped me like a steady stream of poison.
Anger replaced anxiety as I started believing the cruelty spat
my way.
Until she showed up and changed everything.

Lennon Bennett is pure innocence—warm sunshine
breaking apart my stormy existence.
She's everything good and maybe I can be too.
For her. With her. Because of her.
Lennon doesn't know I'm beckoned closer with each breath.
She isn't aware that I'm completely consumed with her.
It's become my sole purpose to protect her, by any means
necessary.
But if she discovers the depth of my obsession, it will be the
end of me.
So, I remain in the shadows.
Waiting. Watching. Wanting.
She'll be my first. My last. My only.

Free with Kindle Unlimited!